# Thoughts & Prayers

A novel

## LEE ANNE POST

MILFORD
HOUSE

Milford House Press

Mechanicsburg, Pennsylvania

## MILFORD HOUSE

an imprint of Sunbury Press, Inc.
Mechanicsburg, PA USA

FIRST MILFORD HOUSE PRESS EDITION: October 2021

Set in Bookman Old Style |Interior design by Chris Fenwick | Cover Art by Chris Fenwick | Edited by Chris Fenwick.

Publisher's Cataloging-in-Publication Data
Names: Post, Lee Anne, author.
Title: Thoughts & Prayers / Lee Anne Post.
Description: First trade paperback edition. | Mechanicsburg, Pennsylvania: Milford House Press, 2021.
Summary: When Lily Jeong—smothered by her parents and ignored by classmates—unwittingly aids her boyfriend in a school shooting, she struggles to hide her complicity from investigators. Forced to face the devastated survivors, she hides in plain sight as their grief turns to vengeance.
Identifiers: ISBN 978-1-62006-497-9 (softcover).
Subjects: BISAC: YOUNG ADULT FICTION / Social Themes / Violence | YOUNG ADULT FICTION / Social Themes / Death, Grief, Bereavement | FICTION / Thrillers / Domestic

*Continue the Enlightenment!*

*To all survivors.*

**Beowolf #neveragain@RockwellHighNews**
The worst part about the shooting is that I've lost everyone.
None of my friends are the same people they were before,
and they never will be. I lost myself too.

# CHAPTER ONE

## Lily

She slipped through the empty halls, invisible and silent except for her heart, which clattered like a tin can against the school's metal lockers. *This is wrong. This is sinful. You will burn in the holy fires of hell for this.* But it also hammered for him. His feathery voice in her ear. His fingertips on her wrist. The thread of his pulse on her skin. The only boy who ever paid attention to her. He was her salvation.

They would burn together.

Down the stairwell, through the east corridor, her shadow broke over shafts of morning sunlight on the floor. It was a beautiful October day. The worst things always happened on the most beautiful days.

Whistles screeched out of the gymnasium. Freshmen's sneakers thumped and squeaked. Poor freshmen. She paused, her palm flat on the cinderblock wall, and thought of her sister, Violet. Next year she'd walk these halls of pretension, mockery, delusion, torment . . . No, Lily thought. He would stop it. He would shut them up. And he promised no one would get hurt—just scared. He'd scare the arrogance out of them.

*He promised.*

She pushed up her glasses and moved forward, past the cafeteria's warm, yeasty smell of baking rolls and the long-faced janitor mopping the sticky breakfast floor. She had to pee but couldn't stop, couldn't be late. When she flitted past the outer wall of the auditorium, sweat beaded along her hairline. Her breath came in spurts. The auditorium was where her complete humiliation had happened. Her cries and their laughter still echoed. Her parents would be so dishonored if they knew what she had done. She smashed her hands over her ears and scurried like a mouse away from the excruciating memory.

Finally, she reached the double steel doors. Each one had a crash bar—emergency exit only. They couldn't be opened from the outside. No one used this exit except drama kids after late rehearsals. No cameras monitored these doors. Lily checked her watch. She was two minutes early. Two minutes. Not enough time to go to the bathroom, but time enough for second thoughts.

Her back fell against the cinderblock wall. Her knees bent, and she slipped down to a chair position. She closed her eyes and forced deep breaths to her belly. *This is wrong. This is wrong.* Her leg muscles tightened like they wanted to run. Run, run, run away from this madness, away from this pain. But where could she possibly go? Not to her strict parents. Not her sister or a teacher or minister. She had no real friends. There was only him.

She opened her eyes, checked her watch again: 9:21. Almost. Across the hall, a folded piece of paper caught her attention. She scooted over, snatched it up, and unfolded it. A flyer for the fall play: *Rockwell High School Theatre Department proudly presents* Almost, Maine. *It's love. But not quite.* Notes were scribbled on the back—a phone number, a to-do list, a list of props: ice skates, mittens, suitcase. Important stuff. Someone from drama must have dropped it. It belonged to her now. She refolded it and tucked it in the pocket of her khakis.

It was time. She peered through one of the rectangular windows, past her dark-haired reflection to the parking lot. *Where was he? He changed his mind.* No, no, there he was, her knight in ripped jeans and black hoodie plodding toward the building. His ski-type sunglasses reflected prismatic colors. A duffel bag hung over his shoulder. Her eyes lingered on the bag. Something seemed off. Why was it so big?

Hair raised on her arms. Her legs squeezed together with the urge to pee.

*This is wrong.*

*This is wrong.*

She remembered his voice and shivered. *"I promise."* She placed both hands on the cold metal bar and pushed.

## Keisha

Keisha Washington stood in Alex Robinson's first-floor guidance office holding the book of essays he'd just given her. He wanted her to understand the power of passionate writing. She got that. Authentic writing, he called it. For just a second, the color of his eyes distracted Keisha. She'd heard other girls gossip about her young college advisor's looks and charisma, their mouths twisted into little grins, but that wasn't the point of her visit. She snapped herself out of this momentary slip. Achieving her goals—that's the reason she went to see him. And she didn't need coaching.

"Write your heart out," he said. "Don't worry about demonstrating how smart you are. They'll see your grades and test scores. Write about something that matters to you."

Keisha glanced at the book titles on the shelves behind him, all exploring the theories of educational psychology. His framed master's degree hung on the wall behind his chair; it was meant to impress her, but her mother had an MD as well as a couple of other letters required for a pediatric oncologist and could run circles around anyone in this building.

A small silver-framed photo of Mr. Robinson with a woman smiling up at him sat on his desk. Keisha assumed the woman was his wife. They looked happy with each other. On one wall hung Rockwell High's blue and gold school pennant, featuring the prancing wild mustang which once boosted her school spirit, but now in her fourth year, tested her patience. A bank of bland metal cabinets held the records of the school's thirteen-hundred students. *How does he even know who I am? He must know; that's his job. At least he knows I'm the senior class president.*

She touched the crown of tight braids on her head and rolled her shoulders to loosen the tension she felt. Her face reflected in the open door's window—high arch of an eyebrow, high cheekbones, full lips. *Pharaonic, like Hatshepsut, just as Mom said.* Keisha stood straighter.

The bell rang, followed by the cacophony of hordes of teenagers moving between classes. Lockers ticked open and slammed shut. Sneakers squeaked on the polished floor. "Shut the fuck up!" a male voice yelled over the low rumble. The extra-strong scent of body spray wafted into the room. It reminded Keisha of her friend Samantha, who smelled like a fresh mango. Sam would be waiting for her at her locker; they always walked to the third period together. She had to wrap this up.

Although she generally respected Alex Robinson, Keisha felt a little annoyed that this man thought he could tell her anything about how to communicate powerfully, just because he was a man and the counselor. He stood for a box she had to check to get what she wanted.

Keisha put her hand on her hip. "Well, I want to present myself in the best light right away." She lifted her chin the way she did during a debate when she scored a point.

Mr. Robinson smiled at her, not like he was laughing at her but like he cared. Maybe he wasn't so far off the mark. Maybe she should listen to him.

"You have everything going for you, Keisha. You don't have to work so hard. Relax a little bit. Enjoy yourself."

She couldn't do what he said, though. She knew what had to happen. High school was about preparation, not enjoyment. At seven years old, when asked by doting adults what she wanted to be when she grew up, Keisha always said she would be president of the United States. Not wanted to, intended to be. She didn't smile when she said it. It wasn't a wish. She was certain. Adults laughed and patted her head, astounded by her high seriousness. She ignored them and organized her life to make it happen.

Mr. Robinson sat on the edge of his desk, his handsome face serious. "The point is, you're not arguing a case the way you do on the debate team; you're—"

A sound like thunder echoed off the corridor's walls. Stunned, they both turned toward the open door. "What was that?" they said at the same time.

Feet pounded across the floor. The school's alarm system blared. A body knocked into a locker. Screams erupted. More blasts echoed off the walls. Doors slammed. The sound came closer, louder. Glass crashed onto the corridor floor. Another scream. *Bup bup bup bup.*

Taking two long strides from his desk to the door, Mr. Robinson put his hand on the knob to close the door and lock it—the drill they had practiced a thousand times. "Get down," he said. "Get under the de—" The muzzle of a black gun stopped the door from closing.

Keisha froze. She didn't have time to move. She saw the hand holding the stock. A face, pale and contorted with fury. Shiny, reflective sunglasses.

Alex Robinson stepped back from the door, directly in front of Keisha, and faced the gunman. He held up his hand. "Let's talk."

The sound of the blast, a grunt from Mr. Robinson, and then he sank against her, and she fell under his weight, clutching him. Blood seeped from his chest. Keisha wanted to yell, to say something, but all the words clogged in her throat. She closed her eyes and opened them. The gun barrel pointed at her. In her head, she yelled, *stop it, stop it, stop it,* but no sound came from her lips. Play dead, she thought and closed her eyes.

## Sofia

Before biology class even started, Sofia Hernandez had her eye to the stereoscope counting fruit flies. Her best friend since middle school, Caitlyn Moran, sat cross-legged beside her. A ragged run in her tights went from her heel and disappeared under her skirt hem. She perched on a lab stool, swinging her leg, holding her clipboard and a nibbled pencil to tally the numbers of red- versus white-eyed flies.

Without even telling her, Cat had adorned her hair with a swath of pink color—her new fashion statement. Sofia was supposed to get a blue stripe, but she was probably going to chicken out. Sometimes Cat was too daring for her, but she longed to be that bold. She *had* to be that bold to keep up with her friend. But was it in her?

Caitlyn leaned over and whispered in Sofia's ear. "Guess what was delivered yesterday?"

Sofia looked up from the scope, knowing immediately what Cat meant. "Oh, my God, I hope you brought it to school; I can't wait all day to see it!"

"Yes, I stuffed it in my locker. You're going to love it."

"Did you wrinkle it?"

"The piece of magic that's going to make us famous? Of course not. It's folded up in a fat envelope."

A distant booming sound made the table tremble. Sofia froze in place. More booms. Then popping sounds moved closer down the hall, like people were smashing the lockers with hammers. Caitlyn dropped her clipboard. Their teacher, Mr. Johnson, yanked a skinny boy from the hall into the room and slammed the door, locking it and flicking off the lights.

"Not a drill!" Mr. Johnson shouted, "Get down, get down!"

The wrenching sound was on them, visceral. Sofia knew the steps they had practiced since kindergarten, but she stood paralyzed. *Hide . . . get away from the door, out of the sightline. No, no, no.* The door splintered. Caitlyn flew off her stool. Sofia squealed as someone yanked her to the floor. She pressed her hands to her ears. Shiny red dots splattered across her arms. *Oh, my God. Caitlyn's blood.* Someone stepped on her foot. The firecracker sound kept going, banging, reckless and absorbing. It moved down the hall. The sound throbbed in her ears.

Caitlyn lay with her cheek on the floor. Sofia crawled to her and lay beside her. A strand of pink hair fell over Caitlyn's closed eye. *Is she alive?* Sofia brushed it aside. Caitlyn's wet skirt smelled like iron.

Mr. Johnson was shrill. "Stay down!" He slipped in the bright red blood pooling from Caitlyn's leg. His knee hit the floor.

"Caitlyn, get up." Sofia sobbed and dragged her friend to the wall, away from the gaping door.

Mr. Johnson's coffee breath wafted over Sofia as he leaned down to check Caitlyn's leg. With shaking hands, he pulled off his belt and wrapped it around her thigh, tightening it to try and stop the blood loss. Then he crawled away to check the next kid who was hit. His heavy breathing scared her even though his voice droned, "Stay calm."

Caitlyn opened her eyes and looked past Sofia.

"Cat, can you hear me? I'm here. I'm here." Sofia shook Cat's shoulders. *Look at me, please, look at me.*

Chair legs scraped as whimpering kids tried to huddle together. A kid held a phone up. It glowed white.

*I have to call Papi.* Sofia jammed her fingers into the back pocket of her jeans and pulled out her phone. Her hands shook as she texted her father. Caitlyn moaned.

Sofia cupped Caitlyn's cheek. "Don't die."

## Caitlyn

*I'm on the floor with Sofia. Did my head hit the table? The door was smashed in. Something heavy hit my thigh.* Sofia's face leaned close, black eyes scared. Mascara smudged her cheeks. *Sofia never did figure out how to put it on. I'll have to show her again how to do it. That day when I first put it on her, "Blink," I said, steadying my hand on her cheek, and she laughed.*

"Can you move?" Sofia asked.

She tried to sit up. "Oh, God, it hurts."

"I thought you were dead," Sofia said. Her lips trembled.

Caitlyn remembered a sound, but she couldn't tell what it was. Her leg was on fire. The next thing she knew, she was looking down from the ceiling at Sofia lying next to her on the waxed floor. The pain had stopped.

She slipped into the hall following a thumping noise. A hooded figure spewed bullets from a long gun. She went around to the face. Dark glasses covered pale skin. His temples glistened. The boy's jaw clenched. He stumbled but kept his balance. The gun tucked against his shoulder swayed and didn't stop. Caitlyn moved away. Shadows huddled in the hall. A soul moved through her, confused, broken.

A girl with dark hair sat on the hard floor, head in her hands. She wasn't scared. Not like the others. *I want to touch her, but I have no fingers.* Caitlyn moved out of the building, away from all that terrible noise. It was nice out here. Up. She longed to go up where a prick of light pierced the sky. It was day, yet she could see stars and the most beautiful blue. It pulled her. Calmed her. The blue filled her with a euphoria where nothing else mattered. But then it disappeared, and she was on the hard floor, the pain unbearable.

Sofia touched her face. Heaviness confined Caitlyn. A stench swirled around her.

She turned her cheek into Sofia's palm. *I don't want to leave her, but the blue . . . it didn't hurt there.* Her eyes burned.

"Don't die," Sofia said.

*I'll stay for you.*

## Joe

The call came over the squawk box while Patrolman Joe Hernandez was noting down the license plate of a jacked-up car missing a back tire: *Active shooter. Explosions and gunshots. Rockwell High. All units report.*

His blood pressure spiked. Rockwell High—his daughter Sofia's school. She was inside where the shooter was, and he was too far away. The skin on his face tightened. Instant pressure behind his eyes made him feel as if he were seeing through broken glass. He flipped on his lights and siren, clenched the steering wheel of his county police vehicle, and yanked the car into a U-turn. His foot slammed the gas pedal.

It took ten minutes to get to the school using the highway to avoid the five towns, dozens of suburban neighborhoods, and hundreds of retail stores between him and Rockwell High. Ten minutes of holding his breath, dodging cars, praying to his dead wife. *Protect her, Emilia, keep her safe.* His phone bleeped. He ignored it.

Police vehicles had pulled up on the grass and sat sideways on the half-circle drive in front of the brick school building. Several glass doors led to a grand two-story entry atrium. All the windows were dark. Joe scanned the blocks around the school for the glint of a gun from one of the single-family houses set back on wide lawns. Everything looked eerily still. He leaped out of the vehicle and ran to the sergeant in charge.

"Assign me. I'll go in. Tell me where to go."

Sergeant Davis, a friend since they met at the county police academy eighteen years earlier, put a restraining hand on Joe's chest. Even from outside the building, they could hear the sound of a semi-automatic rifle reverberating off school walls. Inside, gunfire would sound like a cannon. The rumble kept going and going like some crazed energizer bunny. Joe imagined children dying. He pictured blood everywhere.

His phone buzzed in his pocket. He didn't have time for that. "My daughter's in there. I've got to go in."

Davis grabbed Joe's shoulder. "No, man. No one's going in till the chief gives the order."

For a second, Joe succumbed to Davis' authority, looking in the direction he pointed for him to stand. An image of his daughter rose in his mind. She'd looked up from her cereal this morning, her face luminous in the morning light filtering through the kitchen window and blew him a kiss. She was the spitting image of his late wife.

He twisted away from his friend's grip. "Fuck that. I'm going in."

He ran to the school's main door and pulled on the handle. It was locked. He tried the adjacent door. Also locked. He shook his head. *I'm an idiot. They're in lockdown.* No one else could get in the building. In case—*God, don't think about it*—in case the shooter had accomplices. He couldn't help thinking about it—two maniacs with guns roving the halls, shooting everyone. His heart rammed against his chest.

Joe banged on the door window. He pointed to the shining badge on his navy-blue county police uniform and waited for school personnel to buzz him in. Nothing. He couldn't see anyone in the office. They were probably hiding under their desks the way they were supposed to. Panic choked him. The windows were webbed with wire. No point in trying to break them.

His phone bleeped again. He grabbed it from his back pocket as he ran around the building looking for an entry. Halfway down the right side of the building, he spotted a door that had been left slightly ajar. *Someone went in or out of that door. Is that how the shooter got in? Did someone open the door for him?* When he was in school, kids used to leave a door open for friends who were sneaking in late.

Joe ignored his crime scene training. He had two goals: Find the shooter and stop him. And in the process, save his daughter. He sprinted toward the door. It was propped open with a rock. He thought again about accomplices, pressed his back flat against the brick wall, and drew his gun. He couldn't rescue his daughter if he were dead. The phone bleeped. Sweat stinging his eyes, he gave into the phone and looked at the screen. He had three texts from Sofia.

*There's shooting in my class. I'm ok*
*Cat's hit bad*

*I love you*

The last text nearly broke him. His face twitched. He flipped off the safety on his gun with his thumb, grabbed the door, kicked away the rock, and spun into the building. He was in a utility area with concrete floors and cinder block walls. The school alarm clanged in his ears. An orange door right in front of him led to a first-floor corridor.

He listened for gunfire to pinpoint the shooter's position. It was coming from the right, around the corner. The gunman had already passed this exit. His gun moving out ahead of him, Joe yanked open the door and sidled into the corridor. The acrid smell of gunpowder filled his nostrils. Back against the wall, he visually checked all directions. It was quiet. *That asshole's reloading.*

A sound of whimpering came from the classroom nearest to him. The window on the door was smashed. That's how the shooter got in, Joe thought. The teacher must have had time to close and lock the door by the time the shooter got to this corridor. The shooter probably blew out the window, reached in, and unlocked the door. Joe looked down the corridor in each direction again. No gunfire. Maybe he could get these kids out. He pulled open the door and moved into the room, gun first. He heard them suck in their breath together. Someone sobbed.

"Don't shoot us," a girl's voice said, quavering but determined.

A boy, covered in blood and groaning, lay on the floor. Kneeling next to him, a girl used her t-shirt to staunch the blood flow. The teacher was sprawled across her desk. Joe felt for the pulse at her neck. *Dead.* The kids looked at him. He suppressed his own panic. *What is the protocol?* He couldn't remember. All he could think was to get these kids out of harm's way. He had cleared the corridor to this point. The exit was clear. They could get out. *I don't give a damn if I do it wrong, and they live.*

"Come on. Those of you who can walk, you're getting out. Come on. Stand up. If you can't walk, stay hidden. EMTs will come to help you."

Students pulled themselves off the floor. Faces frozen, eyes wide, they watched the door. Some wrapped their arms around each other. Most were weeping.

"Leave all your stuff," Joe said. "Move fast but don't run. Turn left out of the room. Stay near the wall. Take the exit door immediately to the left and go outside. Walk to the front of the building with your hands above your heads. There are policemen there. They'll tell you where to go and what to do."

He turned his face to his shoulder microphone and pressed the button. "Sergeant Davis heads up. I'm sending out students from a classroom on the right side of the school. The shooter has already been here. One dead, one wounded in the room."

He turned to the kids. "What classroom is this?"

"Two-sixteen," they said in a chorus. "Mrs. Brown's science class."

"They're from classroom two-sixteen," Joe said into the mic. "Coming from the right side of the school. We need EMTs in here." He didn't wait to hear Davis yell at him for not following orders.

He swallowed to keep his voice from trembling. "Don't run," he reminded the students. "When you're outside, walk together with your hands above your heads. Don't leave the grounds."

He thought about the count, about missing kids, dead kids, about parents not knowing where they were. *Sofia, where are you?* "Go now."

Joe held the classroom door open and covered them as they fast-walked to the exit. When the last kid made it to the exit door, he went the other way down the hall. He slid along the wall, swiveling his head to stay aware of anything coming his way. Gunfire started again around the corner. *Too close. It's not over.* He waited until the last student would have rounded the corner outside for one second, two, and then he went back to hunting the shooter, to saving his Sofia.

**Lily**

She sat in a puddle of water and her own urine. The sprinklers rained down on her, soaked her white oxford, and matted her hair to her head. Her hands rested palms-up at her sides, her head tilted slightly to the left. Her mouth was open, still wanting to scream but somehow unable. The high-pitched, rhythmic screech of the fire alarm—three slow blasts and a pause—along with its flashing strobe light had hypnotized her and left her paralyzed there on the floor. She had been there ever since she heard the first shots. She had expected the thunderclaps from the bombs. First in the auditorium, then the cafeteria and gymnasium. *Boom . . . Boom . . . Boom.*

But she didn't expect gunfire.

That wasn't part of the plan. The memory of his convincing voice echoed between the alarm: "No one will get hurt. We'll just scare the shit out of them. Burst their privileged suburban bubble. All you have to do is open the door. I'll take care of the rest."

Sirens blared outside. Smoke billowed into the hall and caught in her throat. She coughed. Her eyes burned. Kids screamed past her. One tripped over her foot and landed with a splash. The kid looked at her—a girl, her face a plate of shock. Tears streamed down her cheeks. The girl scrambled to her feet and ran through the doors into the bright day.

He said school shooters were uncreative pussies.

He lied to her.

She pictured his face on a pillow, so close to hers their noses almost touched. His blue eyes. His words. *You are my universe.* She hadn't seen his eyes when he came into the building. He never took off those stupid sunglasses. He didn't say a word, not when she tried to speak to him, not when she latched on to his forearm, pleading, "Wait, wait, wait." He shook her off and continued down the hall. A robot. An eyeless, programmed robot.

He deceived her.

Now his figure appeared through the smoke. He set the long rifle on the floor and pulled a handgun from the waistband of his jeans.

Her body burned with rage. Yes, she thought. *Yes, please end me now.* But he didn't move. He still wore the sunglasses—she couldn't see his eyes. He'd ceased to be human. She didn't know who he was, didn't want to know him or his explanation. She only wanted all of it to be over.

Her mind splintered. The hall tilted and warped. She couldn't form words. A Korean sound came to her.

She screamed it: *"Hae!"*

The word came again, exploding from her gut. *"HAE!"* *Do it.*

He raised the gun to his temple. *No. He doesn't get to die and leave this on me.* Fury raised her off the floor. She took a step forward. "NO—"

A bright yellow object flashed through the air. Her body flinched. She blinked, and he was on the ground. The handgun spun across the floor and landed at her feet. A janitor fell on top of him.

"Run," the janitor yelled at her. "Run!"

**Sofia**

Two police officers stood at the front of the biology lab. "You all have to go right now," one of them said, his voice urgent. All around her, kids stood and formed a line at the door.

Sofia crouched next to Caitlyn. "I can't leave my friend."

The policewoman insisted, pulling on her arm. "It'll be okay. Help is coming. You have to go with us now."

Her hands were sticky with Caitlyn's blood. Sofia gave her phone to the policeman. He slipped it into a bag along with the others.

*Where is Papi?* Sofia stood. The room whirled. Fear streaked her classmates' faces. Caitlyn's new boyfriend grasped Sofia's sleeve. The police wouldn't let him near Caitlyn either. Her mind blanked. *What is his name?* "Eric, I—"

"Hands up, kids, over your heads, please. It's okay; we're moving you out of here," the policewoman said. She spoke into the device strapped to her shoulder.

Her classmates interlaced their fingers behind their heads. The police gave orders. Sofia obeyed. "Stay in a line, don't run, keep your hands on your head." Obedient, like Papi had taught her. But her mind fiercely stayed with Cat.

At the classroom door, Sofia and Eric turned back to check on Caitlyn. A silver tarp covered her body and partially concealed her face. Sofia's teeth chattered. Her body felt empty. Dark footprints stained the floor where they had walked through Caitlyn's blood.

Mr. Johnson went with the students, his hands on his head, now quietly trying to comfort the kids near him. The policewoman came with them, leading them through the smoke-filled wreckage of the hall. A lone girl in a purple t-shirt slumped against the lockers, her backpack still strapped to her motionless body. Sofia could hear her phone *buzzing, buzzing.*

*Caitlyn, don't die.*

Then they were outside on the sidewalk she had walked on this morning so long ago. The air bumped with helicopter blades and pulsed against Sofia's neck. The policewoman kept them moving toward a parking lot. Sofia listened to her, followed, and trusted her. The uniform was a beacon in the confusion. She looked down, wanting her father, following Eric's frayed cuffs. In all the drills before today, Cat was in front of her, glancing back to say, "This is dumb." Sophia chewed on her hair to keep herself from crying. Behind her, someone whined, a low-pitched wail she had never heard before.

The line of kids crossed the parking lot, and they were allowed to release their hands as they sat on the grass. Sofia looked around for Eric, but he was gone. Then she felt a familiar hand at her back. She stood and threw herself into her father's arms. Her cheek pressed against the dark fabric and the metal badge, she sobbed. Papi caressed her head and looked down at her. His thumbs brushed her tears away. He kissed her sweaty forehead.

"Sofy, *mi hija.*"

"Papi, I had to leave Caitlyn. They made me. She's hurt bad." Sofia choked.

"Look." Papi pointed to a gurney pushed by medics. Sofia could see the pink hair. Her father wrapped his arm around Sofia's shoulders. If she were bold enough, she would jump into the ambulance and be with Cat. Papi held her tight, but it wasn't tight enough to make her feel safe again.

## Charmaine

Charmaine Robinson reviewed the discharge instructions with the mother whose four-year-old came to the emergency room with a broken arm, another trampoline injury. She pushed back the curtain to the ER bay and vowed— not for the first time—*I swear, when Alex and I have kids, they are never getting a trampoline.*

The Tri-County Hospital emergency room typically saw cases like this: childhood falls, allergic reactions, an occasional heart attack or stroke victim, and just this morning, a man who had correctly self-diagnosed his appendicitis. Not the gang knifings and drive-by shootings she might have seen had she and Alex settled in the urban district where he grew up, and his parents still lived. She was so happy when he accepted a job at Rockwell High School, just a few safe suburbs away from her own parents. Growing up there, she never missed an episode of *ER* on television. The black nurses and doctors on the program inspired her to become an RN. When she first met Alex, she thought he looked like *ER*'s hot Dr. Peter Benton. She pictured Alex at breakfast that morning, talking about the students he advised, one young woman named Keisha in particular. He was so good with those kids.

A commotion at the Station 1 desk interrupted her memories. "What's going on?" she asked Lori, a fellow ER nurse.

"School shooting," Lori replied. "The ambulances should arrive any minute."

"What? What school?"

Sprinting toward the Med room, Lori didn't answer. Charmaine struggled to comprehend, her mind suddenly frozen by fear. She hoped it wasn't Alex's school. She retrieved her phone and sent him a quick text: *Shooting at your school?*

"Get ready," ordered Dr. Ryan McGann, the attending in charge of the emergency department. "Clear the treatment area." The doctor didn't look like a miracle worker, with his unruly red hair and wiry build, but Charmaine knew he was. She usually worked on McGann's team with Lori. That was one of the things she liked about being an ER nurse, being a respected member of a team. That and the pace, the excitement of never knowing what was going to happen next.

The paramedics rushed in with a young boy on a gurney. "GSW to the back, BP fifty over thirty-five. He's barely holding on," they said. The boy appeared too young to be in high school. *So, Alex would be okay.*

Dr. McGann waved them toward a bay. "I'll take him. In here." The boy looked like a black tag to Charmaine, a patient who had already died or had no chance of survival, but she knew Dr. McGann would try to save the boy anyway. In the trauma bay, when they lifted him from the gurney to the ER table, she saw the gaping hole in his back, the size of an orange. *Oh, my God, what could have caused that? An explosion?* She wasn't the least bit squeamish, couldn't be to work in the ER, but she had never seen anything like that before, not in all her training or in her three years as an RN.

She started to set up a transfusion, but Dr. McGann said, "Hold it. He's stopped breathing." The doctor tried CPR but got no response. He called it: "Time of death 10:22."

The next ambulance had already arrived. Charmaine quickly checked her phone. No word from Alex. She texted him again: *Are you ok?*

"How many more victims? What kinds of injuries?" Dr. McGann asked.

"Dozens more, mostly glass cuts and abrasions," the ambulance driver answered. "They haven't found all the victims inside the school yet. There's an EMT triaging at the scene. He'll call in to let you know what's coming."

Charmaine looked down at the gurney and saw a girl with a pink stripe in her hair, definitely high school age, shot in the leg. She was conscious but obviously in shock. The paramedic had started an IV and packed bleeding control gauze into the hole the bullet made in her thigh.

"What school?" Charmaine asked the paramedic.

"Rockwell High."

Her stomach lurched as if she'd also been shot. For a moment, she thought she was going to be sick, but she took a deep breath and focused on the patient. If she thought about Alex now, she knew she would collapse.

In the trauma bay, Dr. McGann took one look at this new shooting victim and barked, "Red tag," the emergency department's code for a critical patient. "Start a transfusion. Page Dr. Bakshi and get the patient to surgery, stat. The sooner she gets on the operating table, the better her chances."

Charmaine retrieved a bag of O-negative blood—the universal donor. There wasn't time to type blood. This was the "golden hour," the short period after trauma when prompt medical treatment might prevent death. The girl moaned.

"You're going to be all right, baby girl," Charmaine whispered in her ear. When she leaned over her to insert the IV needle into the girl's arm, the image of Alex's sister, who died at about the same age in a shooting, flashed through her mind.

As the orderly wheeled the patient to the elevator, Charmaine asked Lori the girl's name. She wanted to check on her status later.

"Who knows? She didn't have her school ID or a driver's license on her. Probably too young to drive." Lori shook her head.

An hour later, a young man approached them. "I'm looking for my girlfriend, Caitlyn Moran. She was shot at school. Is she here? Is she okay? I don't have a photo because they took our phones. She has a pink stripe in her hair."

Lori and Charmaine exchanged looks. They remembered that pink stripe on the girl they had sent to the OR.

Lori directed the boy to the admissions desk while Charmaine checked her phone again. *Why hadn't Alex texted her?*

"Any word from Alex?" Lori asked.

Charmaine shook her head. "He probably left his phone in his office when they evacuated the school."

"Don't worry," Lori said. "He'll be fine."

Before she could reply, another ambulance arrived.

**Mike**

Mike Moran turned sharply into the hospital parking lot, his brakes screeching, as he pulled into the first empty parking space he spotted. He ran to the emergency room entrance without stopping for breath. The doors swished open. In two steps, the next set of doors complied with his unspoken command.

"Caitlyn Moran," he barked to the lobby receptionist before she could greet him. "She was shot at Rockwell High School today. My wife is already here. Where is she?"

The middle-aged woman's welcoming smile vanished as she lowered her gaze to her computer and typed in Caitlyn's name. "Your daughter's in surgery, sir," she replied. She didn't raise her head to look him in the eyes. "The waiting room is on the fifth floor."

He took the elevator and found Lisa, his wife of twenty-five years, hunched over in a chair with her arms folded in front of her stomach, rocking back and forth. She stood when she saw him and rushed to him. He enfolded her in a protective embrace as she leaned against his chest and sobbed softly.

He comforted his wife with pats and shushes. Mike, a retired U.S. Army colonel, glanced over her head at the others in the waiting room. Ever on the alert to assess any situation, he saw two men in the opposite corner, probably father and son. The older man stared straight ahead; the younger fiddled with his phone. A heavyset woman paced the room as she argued in an ever-louder voice on her phone about an insurance company's coverage. *More victims, just like me and Lisa.*

Lisa's sobs diminished, and they sat down. "Did you get in touch with the boys?" he asked. Connor, their oldest, served as a first lieutenant in the army stationed in Germany. Patrick was a senior at the state university.

"Yes," she answered. "Patrick's driving home now. Connor's going to put in for emergency leave. The news of the shooting has already reached Germany." She retrieved a tissue from her purse and wiped her eyes.

"Have you talked to the doctors?"

"No. She was already in surgery when I got here. All I know is that she was shot in the right leg and has a concussion." She twisted the tissue in her hands like the candy cane cookie dough she made every Christmas.

"Caitlyn will be all right. She's a tough kid." He put his arm around her, and she leaned against him.

A television mounted on the opposite wall blared breaking news. ". . . the shooter used an AR-15. We're now learning the casualties at Rockwell High could be as high as ten dead and many more injured."

The heavyset woman walked past them and gestured to the TV. "Horrible, isn't it?" she said as she left the waiting area.

Mike studied the TV screen. The reporter stood in front of the high school Caitlyn attended. Yellow police tape fluttered behind him. Mike recognized the walkways leading to the front doors, the green side lawns, and the statue of a mustang, the school mascot, rearing up on its hind legs. He couldn't believe this was happening here. For a brief time, he'd wondered if the Sandy Hook shooting in Newtown, Connecticut had ever occurred, or if it was a sham, fake news as some conspiracy theorists believed. Now the same tragedy had struck his family. This was real, as real as war. Lisa covered her eyes and cried again.

Mike spotted the TV remote on a corner table near the two guys. He walked over to them. "Mind if I change the channel? The news is upsetting my wife."

"Sure." The younger man reached for the remote and handed it to Mike.

"My wife never likes to watch bad news," the older man said, "especially if there are children involved."

Mike thanked them and flipped through the channels. The shooting at Rockwell High dominated every local and cable news channel. Finally, he settled on ESPN.

"Okay with you?" he asked.

"Fine," the older man said. The younger guy never looked up from his phone.

Lisa stopped crying when he sat down again. "How long do you think she'll be in the operating room?"

"Shouldn't be long now."

Her eyes bored into him. "Do you think Caitlyn will make it?"

Mike pondered his wife's ashen face. He saw hope there and fear too. She had aged ten years since he left the house that morning. He couldn't imagine how she would survive if her daughter didn't.

"Yes," he told her. He hoped he was right about that. Experience told him the odds were in her favor. During two tours in Iraq, he'd seen automatic weapons shred human bodies. If Caitlyn had caught a bullet anywhere in her torso, there wasn't much hope. She was young and strong, but so were the soldiers who came home in body bags. Being shot in the leg was no picnic. She could lose her leg, but he couldn't think about that now. He just wanted her to live.

A young man dressed in scrubs entered the waiting room. Mike hoped he wasn't Caitlyn's doctor—he looked far too young. The father and son duo rushed to greet him, and the doctor began to speak in a low voice. Mike couldn't hear what he said, but he did hear the younger man say, "I told you Mom was going to be all right, Dad," as the two left the waiting room. Now he and Lisa were the only occupants.

He held Lisa's hand, and they sat quietly, awaiting the surgeon's news. He couldn't imagine life without his daughter, their surprise baby. When Caitlyn was born, he was totally unprepared for the joys a daughter would bring, the hugs and kisses she bestowed while saying, "I love you, Daddy." She was his princess, and he wasn't ashamed to admit that.

She entranced him when she twirled around the room to show off a new outfit and bewildered him when she fussed over her hair, things her brothers never did or even thought about doing. She also had a bit of a tomboy streak and knew how to throw and catch a football. Not quite the girly-girl Lisa preferred, but with two older brothers, what did his wife expect? He spoiled his daughter, he admitted. She was his salvation whenever wartime flashbacks threatened.

Just hours ago, when he was rushing out the door to work, she'd handed him a coffee mug, that ridiculous pink hair falling over her eye.

"Here you go, Daddy. Three sugars, no cream, just the way you like it." She pecked his cheek and danced away from him. "Love you."

*Did I say I love you back? Please God, tell me that I said it.*

The door to the surgical suite banged open, and an Indian doctor with jet black hair approached them. They stood to face him. "Mr. and Mrs. Moran? I'm Dr. Bakshi, the chief orthopedic surgeon." The doctor looked to be around his own age, which pleased Mike. He didn't want an inexperienced surgeon operating on his girl.

Lisa inhaled and held her breath. Neither of them said anything.

"Your daughter suffered major injuries to her femur, but we were able to save her leg. We cleaned the wound, removed several bone fragments, and put in a steel rod to hold her damaged femur in place. She'll be in traction for a while, and we'll have to monitor her, but she should be fine."

Lisa leaned against Mike. He grabbed her around the waist and held tight, fearing she would collapse.

"She also suffered a head trauma that caused a brief lack of consciousness," Dr. Bakshi said, "but a CT scan showed no swelling or bleeding."

"Thank you, doctor." Mike shook the surgeon's hand. His shoulders sagged as every muscle and tendon in his body simultaneously released the tension he had clutched until now. The doc said Caitlyn was going to be fine. For the first time that day, Mike didn't hold back tears.

Later in the ICU, Lisa gasped when she saw her daughter in traction, her leg raised and pins sticking out of the cast. Mike gripped his daughter's hand. "You're going to be fine, Caitlyn. You're going to make it." He smiled for her sake to hide his anguish at what had happened to her.

Caitlyn let out a soft groan. Her mouth moved, but Mike couldn't hear her words. He brought his face closer to hers. Her eyes fluttered open.

"I saw him, Daddy."

**Sen. Mel Woodrow@melwoodrow**
Sending my #thoughtsandprayers to the students and parents at Rockwell High today as news of heinous acts of a lone wolf shooter arrives. I pray for healing and peace for our community.

# CHAPTER TWO

## Charmaine

The girl didn't flinch when Charmaine extracted the fourth piece of glass from her temple. She barely blinked, her eyes fixed on the LED light that Charmaine had pulled close to her face. In the next bay, a boy with a deep laceration in his forearm moaned. Charmaine wheeled her stool over to him and squeezed his trembling hand. He was big, all muscle, probably a football player, yet his cheeks were soaked with tears.

"Hang in there, buddy," Charmaine said. "They're getting you something for the pain; then they'll get you stitched up. You're going to be okay."

She knew it was a lie but couldn't help saying it. Physically, he'd be fine. But the psychological damage would be lasting. Before today, probably the most traumatic event that had occurred in their lives was not getting chosen for the cheerleading squad or losing a football game. A decade ago, she was one of those students, living a middle-class life in what was supposed to be a safe community. Now everything was upside down. But she couldn't think about that now. *Clean 'em up, stitch 'em up and send them home. Do your job.*

Behind her, a team pushed a gurney with another gunshot victim toward the OR for orthopedic surgery. That made number five. Most of the injuries she had treated were non-life-threatening, deep cuts from the explosions and shattering glass. Thankfully, the more serious cases, like the young boy with the hole in his back who died in the ER, were sent to the trauma center at City Hospital. Charmaine never wanted to see a wound like that again.

When she wheeled past the curtain separating the bays, Charmaine found the girl she had been treating curled on her side in the fetal position. She pumped the hand sanitizer, rubbed her hands together, and pulled on new gloves.

"Stay strong," Charmaine whispered as she rubbed the girl's back. "You got this. It'll be all right. You're going to get through this together."

With this free second, Charmaine slipped her phone out of her pocket. Alex still hadn't texted. Her call went straight to his voicemail. She caressed the girl's hair and told herself he was busy comforting his students, just as she was doing here. This urge to help others was a quality they shared and one that attracted her to him. When they first met at a fraternity mixer her sophomore year, his amber eyes had captivated her. If the eyes were truly the window to the soul, as her mother claimed, then Alex's soul was kind, hopeful, and alive with possibilities.

A flurry of noise came down the hall. "Justin," a desperate voice called. "Justin?"

The boy in the next bay sobbed. "Mom!"

The woman sprinted the last few steps and collapsed on her son's chest. Her wave of terror and relief made Charmaine shudder. She turned back to her own patient and finished cleaning and dressing the girl's face. Then she checked her watch and realized her shift had ended forty minutes ago.

"I can stay if you need me," she said to the supervising nurse.

The woman shook her head. "Go home. You've done more than enough."

Relief flooded through Charmaine. She couldn't wait to see Alex and give him a big hug. She needed to know for sure he was well, despite what he had experienced this horrible day. Maybe she could persuade him to go with her for her daily after-work jog. They could run away from the horrors of the day together.

As Charmaine rounded the nurse's desk, Dr. McGann approached her, accompanied by a policeman. "Officer Hernandez, this is Mrs. Robinson," McGann said. For a second, Charmaine was confused. *Why is he introducing me to a cop now?*

"Is there some place we can talk privately?" the officer asked.

The sad, serious look on his face told her everything she didn't want to hear. Her whole body stiffened. She couldn't move, except to shake her head slowly in denial.

"I'm so sorry to tell you, your husband was killed today at the high school."

"No, no, no," Charmaine argued in a voice louder than she expected.

McGann grabbed her hand and squeezed it. She tried to steady herself, but her mind wouldn't stop spinning. "You must have the wrong name. Are you sure it's Robinson and not Robins or Robertson? Alex Robinson?"

Officer Hernandez's deep brown eyes brimmed with sympathy. "I wish I was wrong, Mrs. Robinson. If it's any consolation, your husband died a hero trying to protect one of his students." That sounded like Alex to her, but she wasn't ready to believe him. She wanted details. Unwelcome tears wet her cheeks, but she maintained her composure.

"Where was he shot? I want to know."

The officer looked down as if considering how he should answer her. Then he raised his eyes to hers. "In the chest. In his office."

Panic descended. The cop was telling the truth. This was real. Alex was gone. "I need to see him. Where is he?" She knew she was screaming but didn't care.

Officer Hernandez spoke in a low voice, trying to calm her. "His body is still at the school while the forensic team finishes up its work. Then he'll be transported to the county morgue with the other victims." He handed her a card with the address and phone number of the morgue. "You can see him tomorrow morning."

She began to sob, great heaving moans. Dr. McGann put his arm around her shoulder, and she leaned against his bony chest. "Is there someone I can call for you?" he asked.

*Alex, call Alex. He's my emergency contact, my husband. You know that. But you can't.* She wracked her brain, trying to think of someone. In the three years they'd lived as newlyweds in Rockwell Township, she and Alex had made work friends and neighborhood acquaintances, but no one close enough to share this horrible moment.

"My parents," she answered. "I'll call my mother once I get home." Then she remembered Alex's parents. She'd have to call them, too, a call she dreaded. Years ago, before she and Alex met, their only daughter was an innocent victim of a drive-by shooting. Now their only son was taken from them.

"You shouldn't be driving now," Officer Hernandez said. "I'll take you home."

## Lily

She stood at the window in her bathrobe, her body raw from scrubbing it so hard in the shower. Her hair was still wet, her eyes red-rimmed and swollen. Her small bare feet sank into the same spot in the low plush carpet where she had stood and watched him every night last June.

He'd stood at his window too, in his identical brick townhouse diagonally across from hers, each of them watching and waiting for the other to make a move. He made the first move, holding up pieces of paper with words written big enough to see, just like in the movie, *Love, Actually.*

*meet me*
*in ten minutes*
*at the big tree*
*behind my house*

Ten minutes. That was all the time she had to make the decision to sneak out after midnight and risk the wrath of her parents—and if caught, the wrath would be biblical—just to meet a *boy*. No boy had ever wanted to meet her anywhere. No girl, for that matter. She used to think it was because she looked different, but that excuse didn't work in the diverse Rockwell community. There was something wrong with her, she concluded. It wasn't her shyness or awkwardness. She joined every club or activity available. She just didn't know how to connect to people. Or maybe she didn't come equipped with the human connection circuit. God forgot to install it. She was defective.

She wanted to find a way to fix herself.

Lily had stood at the window that night for eight minutes, heart and mind racing. Then she ran. Silently down the hall past her sleeping parents and sister, down the stairs, out the sliding patio door, into the summer night that smelled of her mother's tea roses.

He had waited in the moonlight, hands in pockets, back hunched but still so tall, staring up at the stars. His hair looked like wet sand that fingers had combed and raked into disarray. His blue eyes blinked with disbelief. "You came?" He smiled like no one on earth had ever come to him. Like she was there to rescue him.

Now she watched the news vans descend, the police weave their yellow tape, and his mother break down in the middle of the street. The world suddenly knew his name.

Aaron Blake Crofton.

Would they soon know hers?

Her body started to shake. Her stomach roiled. She bent over and threw up in the wastepaper basket.

"Lily?" Her sister Violet knocked on the door. "Mom wants you to come down."

Violet sniffled and hiccupped on the other side of the door. She'd been crying. Lily imagined all of Rockwell Township crying, all at once, a great tsunami of salty tears sweeping through the streets and cul de sacs, crashing over the Starbucks and Whole Foods, swallowing the cineplex and Target and Trader Joe's. In this fantasy, there were no survivors. No one to remember what happened here today or who caused it.

"Lily!"

"I'm coming!"

She didn't want to go downstairs to her crying sister and praying mother and CNN blaring through the house. But she had to obey her mother because that's what good girls did. *Good girls did not have sex with boys who turned out to be lying monsters.*

Lily rinsed her mouth, cleaned her wastebasket. Before she went downstairs, she emptied the items from the pockets of her khakis, which were balled up in the middle of the bathroom floor next to her urine-soaked underwear. She smoothed out the puckered drama club flyer and counted two hair ties, one locker magnet, and the broken half of a number two pencil. She reminded herself it wasn't stealing. Finders keepers. She liked the spike of adrenaline she felt finding pieces of other people's lives. All of it went into the tin box she kept in the back of the cabinet under the sink— the new hiding place. When her sister pounded on the door, Lily scooped up the shards of broken glass and dropped them in the pocket of her robe. She had no memory of collecting them, but they explained the cuts on her hip.

Downstairs, her mother stood at the front window, clutching her elbows as she watched the action outside. Stephanie Jeong was a tiny woman with a short black bob and skin as smooth as her rose petals. She wore a camel-colored cardigan, just like all of the mothers at the Korean Presbyterian Church. Lily wondered if the commotion outside would crush this slight woman.

"I can't believe it," she muttered. "That boy next door. Right next door. His mother . . . how could this happen?" She turned and swept her eyes over Lily's robe. "You need to get dressed. Your father will be home early."

Ted Jeong never came home early. Not when Lily had the chickenpox or the flu, or when Violet fell at recess and needed four stitches on her chin. He was a biomedical engineer at a biotech firm—the same company that brought her parents to America almost twenty years ago when their names were Jae-Hyun and Eun-Mi. Ted's priority was his work, not comforting his children. That he left to his wife.

Lily stared dumbfounded at her mother. "Why?"

Stephanie came over and touched Lily's face, something she rarely did but had done once already today, at the middle school where all the students had been herded, where other mothers pulled their children into their arms.

"Why?" Her mother's voice held back a sob. "Oh, my Lily Rose. Because of what happened. Because you're alive."

The warmth of her mother's fingertips stirred something in Lily. Her body began to shake again. She broke away and stood in front of the television. A grim-faced anchorwoman spoke from the screen.

*We're following breaking news out of Rockwell Township, where at least ten people were killed this morning in yet another mass shooting at an American high school. Here's what we know: at approximately 9:25 this morning, three pipe bombs exploded in rapid succession in the school's auditorium, cafeteria, and gymnasium. Seconds later, shots were heard in the school's main corridor. Now we are waiting for a press briefing from the sheriff's department, but it has been confirmed that the suspected shooter is in custody, and sources at the scene are telling us that it was a* school janitor *who apprehended the shooter. If this is confirmed, well, what an unbelievable story of heroism that will be.*

"Why unbelievable?" Violet said. "Because he scrubs urinals, he can't be a hero?"

"Violet!" Stephanie snapped. "Don't be crass."

"People are dead, Mommy. Lily could be dead. I'm allowed to be crass."

*None of the victims' names have been released, pending notification to families, and we've learned that at least twenty students have been taken to area hospitals. City Hospital reports five patients in critical condition.*

Who? Lily wondered. She watched the familiar loop of terror-stricken faces, police crawling around outside the building, and lines of students exiting the school with their hands in the air. It could have been freshmen who just finished gym class. Any teachers? Maybe Billy Johnson, who'd been calling her Cookie Kwan since third grade. Or Sabrina Cox, who used to be Lily's friend, then one day found better friends. Keisha Washington, whose grades were no better than Lily's, who had the same extracurricular resume but got all of the accolades and attention? It would be just like Keisha to immortalize herself by dying like this.

A couple of red-eyed students spoke to a reporter at the scene. They were already planning a vigil tonight. If Keisha weren't dead, she'd certainly be there.

Just as the sheriff appeared on the screen, flanked by a stoic wall of first responders, police, medical professionals, and politicians, a loud hum and flapping sound hovered above the house. Violet rushed to the window.

"A helicopter!" she exclaimed.

Half the screen was now an aerial view of their neighborhood. The other was the sheriff:

*. . . We believe the suspect entered the building through the northeast door, which we found to be propped open with a large rock. This is a door that remains locked*

*during school hours, so we have reason to believe that there may have been an accomplice who opened the door.*

Lily's skin tightened. They already thought Aaron had an accomplice. *I am the accomplice. I let him in. These things happened because of me.* She stared in confusion. The police thought he came through a door propped open by a rock. There was no rock at the door she opened. Would they think it was someone else? Yes, someone else . . . another door. The sheriff's voice garbled as Lily imagined herself as a dragon soaring over the rooftops, circling the cul-de-sac, swooping down and blasting holy fire on the big tree behind Aaron Blake Crofton's house. It burned to a blackened, ashy stump.

*If anyone has any information, we're asking you to please contact the sheriff's department . . .*

She pulled her hand out of her robe pocket and unfurled her fingers. Red hatch marks crisscrossed her palm. As blood pooled over the shards of glass she'd unknowingly been squeezing, it came back to her. The janitor had told her to run, so she ran, first through the smoke, then into the main hallway past the guidance offices and science labs, running and running like in a nightmare, her mind completely shut off. Her foot hit something slick and flew out from under her. She landed hard on her back. Broken glass was all around her. She crawled through it on hands and knees, picking out the most beautifully shaped pieces. There was a sneaker. And a girl . . . slumped against the wall. Her face—

Lily looked back down at the blood in her palm and screamed.

## Caitlyn

Caitlyn woke and saw her father's hand, his fingers wrapped gently around her lower arm, his wedding band, plain and shiny gold. *Where am I?*

"Caitlyn, princess, can you hear me?"

*Yes, I can, but I can't say it yet. My throat . . .*

"Do you hurt?"

Caitlyn nodded and touched her throat. A needle stuck out of her hand. Her leg was in a sling. The rest of her didn't seem to be there. "What happened?"

"You were shot in the leg. The doctor operated. You're in traction. You're one brave girl. You're going to make it."

*Brave?* Caitlyn remembered the terrible sound, being on the floor, Sofia's hand on her face. *Was that real?* She looked at her father, the moist corners of his eyes. He looked so sad.

*Am I going to make it?*

"Where's Mom? Is she okay?"

"She's fine. I made her go get something to eat."

Her father held up a white Styrofoam cup filled with slivers of ice and slipped a piece through her parched lips. *That boy . . . There's something I have to tell Daddy. Was it about Sofia?* Her brain was foggy.

"I saw him, Daddy."

"Who?"

"The boy with the gun in the hall."

"We don't have to worry about that now," he said and slipped more ice into her mouth.

Melting ice soothed her throat. *Heaven.*

"Thank you," the words came easier, "I wish it were ice cream."

He chuckled. "Black raspberry?"

"Absolutely." Caitlyn slurred as she sucked on the ice and managed a smile.

"I don't think they have that flavor in the hospital, but I'll bring you some, come hell or high water."

"It'll melt."

"I'll find a way."

He picked up her hand, kissed the top of her chipped, polished blue fingernails, and looked at her. There were no other eyes on earth like his.

Before the drugs pulled her back into sleep, she saw the boy again. And a girl, alone on the floor.

## Mike

Caitlyn was asleep again. Many things he had considered important before, like the contracts he managed at work, paled in comparison to Caitlyn's distress.

His phone rang. He grabbed it out of his pocket to turn off the sound and saw it was his brother, Sean, to whom he hadn't spoken in years. He hesitated, then swiped to accept the call.

"Mike, I saw the news. Is Caitlyn okay? God, it's so awful."

"Yeah." Mike's head swam. What should he say to a brother he'd cut off because he didn't approve of Sean's openly gay lifestyle? "I . . . she . . . they operated." He couldn't say any more, or he'd break, and that's the last thing he wanted to do in front of Sean, but he wished for the old days when they were close. He coughed. "I appreciate you calling. I'll try to call you later."

Mike gripped his phone and glanced up at the television. After this terrifying day, heart-wrenching stories of the victims played over and over on the news, not just on local stations but national TV and cable networks. Survivors stood strong on camera, vowing to fight for school safety. Politicians offered their thoughts and prayers with promises to fund more mental health programs, promises Mike knew from past experience would not be kept.

Patrick rushed into the room. He had driven home from college. He stood at his sister's bedside and smoothed her hair. "Dad, how is she?"

Mike patted his son's shoulder. "The doctors think she'll make it. Luckily the bullet didn't hit her torso."

The two settled down to watch the TV suspended from the ceiling in Caitlyn's room.

"Look at that liar." Mike pointed to Senator Woodrow on the evening news.

"It's all going to be about gun control from here on, Dad. Again. Same as the last time this happened."

Mike worried that Patrick was picking up unacceptable ideas in college. "I don't believe responsible gun owners like us should be deprived of our Second Amendment right to bear arms," he said.

"Guns don't kill people. People kill people. Right, Dad?" Patrick said. "But don't you at least think there should be background checks?"

Despite Patrick's smirking tone, Mike had to agree. "You're right about that. And they should raise the gun-buying age to twenty-one so crazies like Aaron Blake Crofton can't get their hands on an AR-15."

His buzzing phone interrupted their conversation. Mike recognized the name on the caller ID, a CNN producer who had called twice before pleading for an interview. He let the call dump into voicemail. "Another reporter calling to harass us," he told Patrick. The media wouldn't let his family alone.

The TV news anchor was speculating on a possible accomplice for the ABC Killer, the media's new nickname for the shooter.

"Probably a buddy as screwed up as he is," Mike said. "I hate when they call him the ABC Killer."

"They just don't want to say his name and give him the notoriety he craves."

Mike wondered if that's what Patrick's professors would say. "No, ABC is just a clever way for the media to drive ratings, to make a good story out of our community's tragedy." His phone buzzed again, same caller. Mike answered, and before the caller could say a word, he bellowed, "It's still no. Quit calling me, or I swear I'll get my AR-15 out and shoot you myself."

Patrick's mouth dropped open. "I hope they weren't recording that."

"At least he'll never call again."

**Keisha**

Her parents brought her to the high school field where she normally played lacrosse, where tonight, students were holding the vigil for their friends and teachers killed by the shooter this morning. Keisha couldn't hold those two thoughts side by side. In two days, the funerals would start. She dreaded them.

"Can a person run out of tears?" she asked her mother after she learned her friend, Samantha, had died. Every time Keisha thought of her—that proud smile from across the debate stage when Keisha scored a point, how they could say anything to each other, how they liked the same books—shrieking started in her head. *I can't go there. I can't deal with that.*

Her mother shook her head. "I don't know." She wiped Keisha's face with a tissue, her own eyes glimmering.

She and her parents weren't talking much, just enough to get through each moment. If she needed to, she could walk into their arms for comfort. They were there for her. She knew they were relieved she hadn't been killed and felt guilty about their relief, but she couldn't worry about them now. She couldn't find the words to talk about anything.

Every time she closed her eyes, she felt Alex Robinson's weight against her, saw the blood pulsing out of his body drenching her clothes, heard him groan, smelled the odd metal odor of his death. She'd stayed like that for five minutes, listening to the sound of the shooter diminishing as he moved down the corridor, hearing the old-fashioned, large-faced clock on the wall clicking off the seconds—five minutes that felt like four hundred years—waiting for the school's "all clear" signal. And then she struggled to get out from under him, to sit up, shaking from head to toe.

Later, she thought how she could have tried to be heroic and save him. Why hadn't she? She could have leaped up and grabbed the gun. She could have at least tried to staunch the flow of blood. But she hadn't. She had only tried not to die.

She shielded him for another hour until a policeman found them. He leaned over and spoke softly. "I'm Patrolman Hernandez," he said. "Maybe you know my daughter, Sofia. She's in the drama club. Do you know her?"

Keisha nodded. "Yes," she managed to whisper. "I know her." Somehow, that made him safer, someone she could trust. But still, she couldn't move, couldn't let go of Mr. Robinson.

"It's okay." The police officer gently slipped his hands under her arms and pulled her away from the dead body. "Everything is under control. The shooter's gone. I've got you. It's okay. Come with me."

She kept shaking her head and saying, "No, no, no," but he seemed to know she meant yes, get me away from here, get me away!

He escorted her out of the room and down the corridor. She robotically answered his simple questions. "Keisha Washington . . . I'm a senior . . . We were talking . . ."

He brought her out of the building to an ambulance, where an EMT checked her over. When he realized the blood on her clothes wasn't hers, he said, "You're in shock. But you're going to be okay."

She didn't bother to say she would never be okay. Never again. Ever.

Her parents arrived while she was sitting in the ambulance. Her mother held her chin and scrutinized her face. She examined Keisha's body with practiced hands. "You're not hurt." Her voice cracked. "You're alive." She swept Keisha into a hug that didn't stop until Keisha pulled away.

Keisha's father put his arm around her shoulders and looked at his wife. "We have a lot to be thankful for, Akeelah." He closed his eyes and lowered his chin to his chest.

Hours later, she returned to the school with flowers for Mr. Robinson and Samantha and a candle for the peaceful vigil the student council had put together on social media to alert the student body. *Peaceful* vigil? In her heart, Keisha raged. *How could this happen to us?* Flowers, stuffed animals, and photographs covered the fence around the athletic field. Her heart was going to rip open. *All those faces, dead now.*

Keisha walked up to a woman stapling a photograph of Mr. Robinson to the fence. She ignored all the rules she'd learned about personal space and put her hand on the woman's shoulder.

"I was with him. I was there." She closed her eyes. She couldn't say anything else. When the woman turned, Keisha realized she was Dr. Thompson, the Rockwell High principal. "Oh, I'm sorry. I didn't . . ." The principal held out her arms, and Keisha fell into them, her breath shuddering with her effort not to sob, the flowers crushed between them.

"It's okay, Keisha, I know. I understand. Fourteen of us were killed."

Keisha stepped back and held out the flowers, which now seemed the stupidest, most trivial of offerings. "He saved my life." *God, that's so lame.* She couldn't think of anything else to say.

Dr. Thompson tucked the bouquet into the fence below Mr. Robinson's photograph. "Mr. Robinson talked about you all the time in our meetings. He said you're going to do great things."

That was too much to bear. Keisha leaned against the fence and wept. There was nothing else to do. Later, she planned to stand up on the makeshift stage and talk about Mr. Robinson's bravery and that people's lives mattered, but right now, she yielded to the unrelenting sorrow that rose in higher and higher waves threatening to swamp her sanity.

When she looked up, she saw her mother watching her. Keisha held out her hand, and her mother walked over. The women introduced themselves. She caught snatches of her mother saying, "I'm so sorry," and Dr. Thompson saying, "We're all in shock," and tucked away the thought that a woman could be heartbroken and calm at the same time for later consideration.

She left the adults and found the rest of the student government officers. Some were stony-faced; some couldn't stop weeping. They were learning to talk while they cried, wiping at their faces and noses with the sides of their hands and thinking their way through what needed to be done at this moment and the next. Keisha marveled at them. They were so much stronger than she was. As she watched them, her anger flared. *We deserve better than this. No one protected us; no one made sure we were safe. How can this be okay?*

The crowd grew. Everyone from school was there, their parents and grandparents, police officers, neighbors, the press. The number of people standing in front of her, behind her, watching remotely through a television screen—it was overwhelming. When it was her turn to speak, she choked for a second and coughed. Her voice was too soft. She leaned forward, closer to the mic. She remembered Mr.

Robinson putting his hand up to stop the shooter. She remembered his gentle tone. He must have been as terrified as she was, but he had courage. She remembered how he fell backward into her arms. She harnessed her fury, her sense that the best of them had been betrayed, and sound came pounding out of her, words she hadn't planned and didn't expect.

"Don't send us your thoughts and prayers. Don't tell us 'it is what it is' and nothing will change. This can't be how it is. Enough is enough. Don't tell us your right to own a gun is more important than our right to be alive. We won't let you. Not anymore."

The crowd cheered; Keisha's mother squeezed her shoulder, and behind her, someone sobbed softly. Her eyes spotted the policeman who had pulled her out of Alex Robinson's office and half-carried her out of the building, talking to her softly, telling her she was okay. He stood in the front row watching her intently, occasionally blotting his face with a tissue. *Did he agree with her or disagree? What could she say that would matter to him?*

She drew in a long breath and stopped caring what anyone thought about what she said. "Our friends and teachers are dead because the law says anyone can buy a gun, as many guns as they want. What kind of law is this? How many guns do you need, anyway? Look how many people one gun can kill." She swept both hands out and pointed to the fence. "Fourteen, in fifteen minutes!" she yelled.

She paused for breath and swiped at her wet cheeks. "This can't keep happening. We have to stop it. If the politicians won't stop it, then we'll do it ourselves."

Someone in the crowd booed. "Guns don't kill people, people do!" a disembodied voice yelled.

Her voice broke. Keisha turned her back on the crowd, covered her face with her hands, and stepped into her mother's arms. That was all she could do today, but there was tomorrow and the day after that. She could feel every atom in her body changing, turning her into someone else, someone different from the girl she'd been yesterday, the one who'd been so sure about everything.

## Joe

Some asshole thought this was the right time to argue about gun laws with a young girl in obvious pain. Joe wished he had his weapon, but he had come with his daughter, Sofia, to the Rockwell High vigil as a member of the community, not as a police officer. Showing up armed would have triggered people who were already traumatized. Instantly infuriated by the heckler, Joe looked around, trying to spot him in the crowd. He hated bullies. They had made his childhood miserable.

If he closed his eyes, he could still hear the neighborhood gang taunt him as he walked to elementary school from his family's apartment above the dry cleaners in the town center. "Eh, *pendejo*. You think you gonna cross here? You think you can even walk here?" That was thirty years ago, but the empty feeling in his chest returned the second he thought about it.

Helpless at eight years old, he had wished for invisibility. No one had come to his aid. His parents had already gone to work by the time he left for school. He had taken the beatings in silence, trying not to cry. His head and ribs had hurt, his stomach burned, but that pain was nothing to the ache in his heart. *I was born in this country. I'm an American. I belong here. Why isn't anyone helping me?* Rage had grown in him and turned into purpose. He wouldn't be helpless when he grew up.

Joe had vowed to be a cop and make sure no one was attacked the way he had been as a child. But here he was, still powerless, unable to stop some maniac with a gun from killing kids. His head ached from thinking about it.

Someone put a hand on his shoulder. "Officer Hernandez?"

Joe tried not to startle. He was off duty and in civvies. Who would call him that? When he looked around at the woman who had touched him, she seemed vaguely familiar, as if he'd seen her from a distance a few times, but he couldn't place her.

All around him at the school vigil were his neighbors, children of all ages, school personnel, and way too many reporters with cameras. He looked around for Sofia, who was in such distress she could barely speak or eat. She was completely preoccupied with her friend, Caitlyn, who had endured surgery on bones shattered by the shooter's bullet and survived. His daughter was a mess, and he had no idea how to fix it.

He would have gone to the vigil anyway, even if he didn't have a child in the school, because it was the right thing to do, to stand up for his community the way his wife would have wanted him to do. It seemed a long time since she'd died, a long time since he put aside his hopes to become a sergeant, move up the career ladder, and make a little more income for his family. Now, just when he was ready again to take the sergeant's exam, his life had been turned upside down another time. He didn't like to think it, but it was like fate had it in for him. He stared at the woman in front of him.

"I'm Evelyn Thompson, the principal at Rockwell High," the woman said, her face taut. "I wanted to thank you for being the first to enter the building to save our children." She held out her hand. "The police chief told me. It was very brave, what you did." She pressed her lips together.

Joe took her hand and held it. "It's my job, ma'am." He read her eyes—horror and grief competed with rage. She felt what he felt. Neither of them could say it out loud.

She nodded and touched his arm again, understanding what he couldn't say.

He knew that wasn't enough, but he had no way to speak about his feelings. They were too enormous for words. He had moved his family to this quiet suburban community to make sure they were far away from the gang violence that had made the streets where he grew up dangerous, but the violence had followed him here.

The Rockwell Township neighborhood had been everything Emilia had hoped. The way she'd looked at him when they found their house, her eyes glowing, that meant the world to him. "Joe, this is it," she said. "This is our home." Emilia would marvel about all the beautiful trees and houses, the gardens and shops, she saw on her daily walks with Sofia in the stroller, feeling completely safe.

This was where he'd first thought he could be more. The day he announced he was going to study for the sergeant's exam, Emilia had been painting Sofia's bedroom. "You can do anything," she said. "You're my Captain America." He'd wiped a swoosh of blue off her chin and saw tiredness in her eyes. Only later did he learn what that was.

But the violence had come anyway, disrupting their peace. He hadn't been able to stop it any more than he'd been able to stop cancer from ravaging his wife's body. Sometimes he just wanted to scream.

Angry at his own helplessness, he looked around at his neighbors, at the kids, at the parents—those who had somehow managed to shake off their fear and come out of their homes to stand with their community. Everyone's faces had that shocked look an infant gets in the moments before it wails after being jabbed with a needle—eyes wide, mouth open, unable to even take in a breath. That's what Sofia was going through. He kept waiting for her to breathe again. Joe hung his head, his shoulders slumped. He hadn't kept his daughter safe. He'd failed her and Emilia.

He tuned in to Keisha, one of the girls he'd escorted from the school today, talking from the podium, sometimes shouting, sometimes weeping. Her courage filled him with pride as if she were his child. He was in awe of her ability to translate their pain into words. In his heart, he was yelling, "Right on!"

As far as he was concerned, the only people who should be allowed to carry weapons were the police and active-duty military. Joe didn't care if that position made him the odd man out among his police peers. He didn't need to own a cache of weapons to feel like a man. He'd never thought hunting was fun.

All the wrong people had guns. Every traffic stop, he had to anticipate that either the driver or the passenger was carrying. He never knew when some crazy person would bolt out of a vehicle and shoot him. But he could handle all that fear; he was used to it. What he couldn't handle was some lunatic bringing it into his daughter's school.

Joe brought his mind back to the vigil. He looked around. Was some scumbag with a weapon lurking here among all these grieving people? The accomplice could be here, gloating, with a new plan to hurt more people. His stomach clenched. He swiveled in place, vigilant, his mouth dry. He wouldn't see an assailant in time. Without a gun, he couldn't return fire. The only option was to spot the accomplice before he got a shot off.

It was dark now. People who didn't have candles had clicked on their phone flashlight app. From a distance, he thought, from above them where the police and news helicopters shuddered in the air, the field would look lit by stars. He tried to tell Sofia that the people who died had joined the stars in heaven, but he couldn't even convince himself. "They will be in our hearts forever," he said, but that didn't feel strong enough. Everything in him rebelled at the idea that they'd been forced to leave this earth before their time.

At what passed for dinner tonight before the vigil, the two of them sitting across from each other in their small kitchen, food getting cold on their plates, Sofia had told him he didn't have to go to all the funerals.

"It's okay, Papi. I'll go with my friends. I know you have to work."

"I'm going, *mi hija*; I'm going to the funerals because I'm sad too and because I want to be there for you."

She had burrowed into his arms the way she used to do when she was little. He never wanted to let go of her, never wanted her to go farther than arm's reach away from him. He couldn't bear the idea that she had to go back into that school.

"Papi," she whispered into his shoulder, "I saw on Twitter there may have been an accomplice. What if that guy comes back to kill the rest of us?"

Joe shuddered and held his daughter closer. "I won't let that happen, *querida*." But how could he protect her out there in the world where crazy people shot anyone for no reason?

Now he felt a hand on his arm. "It's over, Papi."

"You ready to go?"

Sofia pointed to people leaving the field and nodded. Every kid on the field had hugged everyone else. He wrapped his arm around her, but she pulled away, and they were silent in the car driving home. Her distance from him made him feel cold. But it was just as well. He didn't want to share the thoughts he was having.

When she went back to school in two weeks, she'd have no more protection than she had yesterday. Oh, sure, the chief would assign some officers for a while, but then what? The incident would get old. All the yelling and TV coverage would stop. Everyone would forget it had ever happened. There'd be competing demands for manpower resources. People would turn their attention to some other crisis. These kids would be sitting ducks. Again. Joe ground his teeth together at the thought.

He decided he would add the school grounds to his patrol, regardless of where he was assigned. Maybe he could convince the chief to put a regular patrol on the campus during school hours. Everyone's feelings were raw. There was an accomplice on the loose who might decide to repeat the shooting. It was time to ramp up security at the school. He couldn't let this happen again.

**Lily**

Late that night, her father tapped on her bedroom door. It was strange to see him in her room, like a fish on top of a wedding cake. Lily sat up and put on her glasses to see him clearly. He perched on the edge of her bed. She had expected him to holler when she didn't come down for dinner or when she refused to go to the vigil. He didn't. It took dead students to bend his rules.

Ted Jeong had arrived in the US twenty years earlier with his father's work-until-you-drop-dead attitude. Was he here to see if she had done her homework even though classes were canceled until further notice? He pushed Lily through school, demanding she excel. Now a senior, she'd met all of his expectations: violinist in the school orchestra, math team, debate team, STEM club, 4.2 GPA. Her father didn't seem concerned that she had failed socially. He wanted her to go to MIT, study science, follow in his footsteps. She just wanted him to take her to Disney World. And she wanted one day to see him bend over in laughter.

He lifted her bandaged hand and held it in his. "Soon, this will all be over."

Lily thought she might cry again, but nothing came. Instead, she said dryly, "A dead girl . . . She didn't have a face, Appa."

In the dim light of the room, he winced. The muscles in his face and neck twitched. Ted kissed his daughter's hand, then silently slipped from the room.

She lay awake until she was certain her family was asleep. Then she took the tin can from beneath her sink, went to the kitchen, and retrieved the glass her mother had picked out of her flesh, wrapped in a paper towel, and thrown in the trash can. In the basement, Lily gathered her tools from all of their hiding places: tubes of acrylic paint in puzzle boxes; brushes in the Jenga box; wire in the Disney DVD cases; glue gun, scissors, and blades in her old violin case. She sat on the floor with her canvas and went to work. Weaving. Creating. Thinking. It calmed her. Realigned her fragmented brain, like the colored squares of a Rubik's Cube twisting back into place.

No one knew about her art, just like no one knew about her and Aaron. His betrayal wrapped like fingers around her throat. She gasped for air. For a moment, she thought about running to her parents, crying, "He lied to me. I didn't know he would do this." But how could they—how could anyone—believe that such a smart girl could be so stupid?

Shame pressed her to the basement floor. No one would believe her. She'd go to prison for the rest of her life. Lying prone on the floor, she committed herself to making sure no one ever found out that she was the one who opened that door.

**Beowolf @RockwellHighNews**
I survived a school shooting. My guidance counselor did not. I was supposed to meet with him about my service hours. Now he's gone. Just gone.

# CHAPTER THREE

## Charmaine

When she saw his body in the morgue, she knew it was no longer her Alex. His closed eyelids hid his beautiful soul. The goofy grin that had made it almost impossible for her to be angry at him for more than a few minutes had vanished. His waxy skin looked cold, and she was glad she was standing behind a glass viewing window so she wouldn't be tempted to touch it. He didn't look like he was sleeping. He looked gone.

Her mother and father stood on either side of her. They had driven to her townhouse yesterday and spent the night. She was glad Alex's parents weren't here to see him like this. The funeral home would be hard enough on them, even after their son's body was dressed and his face made to look almost alive again with makeup.

"Yes, that's my husband, Alex Robinson," she whispered to the morgue attendant standing nearby. Her father grabbed her elbow. She must have stumbled for a second. She steadied herself. The curtains on the window closed. Her mother dabbed her eyes when the attendant gave Charmaine Alex's wedding ring. She looked down at the simple gold band in the palm of her hand and began to cry.

Her mom hugged her until her sobs subsided, then handed her a tissue. Charmaine had always envisioned a life for herself and Alex like her parents' marriage, both spouses working hard at good jobs, Dad puttering around their fifty-year-old Cape Cod with yet another DIY project, and Mom happily tending to the children. Kurt and Tina Parham took to Alex from the moment they met him, and why wouldn't they? He was the perfect mate they had envisioned for their daughter, educated, a churchgoer, a man with good values and good prospects. Now their dreams for their daughter were shattered along with her own.

"We've got to see to the funeral arrangements," Tina, ever practical, said as Kurt drove them home. "Have you thought about what Alex would want?"

Charmaine felt apprehension rising in her chest. She and Alex had never discussed funeral arrangements. Why would they? He was only twenty-six years old, just a year older than she was.

"All I know is that Alex would want his students to be able to pay their respects. He cared about those kids, talked about them all the time. The funeral service has to be here, even though I know his parents will want to hold it near them, where he grew up."

Her mother pointed at her. "It's your call, Charmaine. You're his wife. It's not up to them."

Charmaine didn't have the emotional energy to reply. She knew her mother resented her twice-a-month visits with Alex to see her in-laws. Both of Charmaine's older brothers lived out of state, Greg, the oldest, a master sergeant in the army, and Larry, an IT specialist who worked long hours. Neither came back home very often. Charmaine lived nearby, and her mom thought any free time should be spent with her.

"Oh, what about a minister?" Tina asked.

"I forgot about that." Unlike her late husband, Charmaine was a sporadic churchgoer. She asked her mother to remind her to call the minister at the Rockwell A.M.E. church Alex had attended nearly every Sunday. Occasionally she accompanied him on the rare Sundays she didn't work and couldn't sleep late.

When Alex's parents arrived at the townhouse later that morning, Charmaine was momentarily taken aback by their appearance. Purplish circles under their eyes, runny noses, and stooped shoulders betrayed their utter devastation, and she struggled to hold herself together. Delores Robinson, who had instructed Charmaine to call her "Mama D" at their first meeting five years ago, pulled Charmaine to her ample bosom while they both wept. Her husband gently pried them apart to hold Charmaine in his own sturdy embrace.

"Oh, Pops, what are we going to do without him?" Charmaine sobbed, calling her husband's father by the name Alex gave him as a child, a moniker he treasured. She worried about the health of Alex's folks, who, unlike her parents, were big people who ate too much and rarely exercised.

Charmaine's in-laws and parents barely knew each other, and neither couple seemed comfortable in the other's presence. The older generation had met only a few times during their courtship and then at the wedding three years ago. Tina thought Mama D wanted to be too involved in the wedding plans. "The wedding is the bride's day, and you are not her daughter," her mom had said.

But Charmaine knew Mama D *did* see her as a replacement for her daughter, and besides, Alex was her only surviving child. Charmaine was fond of her in-laws and they of her, but unruffling Mom's feathers proved to be an ongoing challenge. After the honeymoon, she and Alex decided to alternate holidays between the two sets of parents. Now she regretted that decision.

Perhaps they might have all spent every important occasion together as one big happy family if she and Alex had provided a grandchild. Both sets of parents had constantly nagged them about it, but Alex wanted to wait to start a family until after finishing his master's degree last spring. Since then, they had been trying to get pregnant with no luck. Every month when she woke up to blood-stained sheets and cramps, she felt like a failure.

"Don't fret about it," Alex had told her. "We just have to keep trying." His kiss convinced her he was right. They both thought they had all the time in the world.

## Keisha

Massed black umbrellas formed a canopy shielding them from the rain. Shoulder to shoulder, they stood around Samantha's grave, so close they could smell each other's skin. This new intimacy with her classmates—different from locker rooms or sleepovers or huddles on the athletic field—was sorrow, as if their shared sadness transformed them into one organism.

Keisha looked out across the cemetery and spotted police officers standing guard at a respectful distance. She shuddered. Would her entire life now be spent waiting for her turn to die? Leaves blew away from trees, torn loose by the wind. Fall used to be her favorite season, the time that smelled like new facts to learn, new skills to acquire. From now on, fall would be the season of constant surveillance, of always looking over her shoulder. She had diagnosed herself with PTSD. How long would it take to recover, to not jump at the sound of every book dropped or freeze at heavy footsteps in the corridor outside a classroom? The shooting was the one high school event she would always remember, eclipsing all others.

She scanned her friends. They were all feeling the same things. They needed the pressure of each other's bodies to hold them up, keep warm, to move through funeral after funeral. At some point each day, she felt an overwhelming pride that she was part of them. This feeling in her chest had no name, but before the shooting, she would have called it love. It was bigger than that, though. They were her tribe, her family. She was linked to them at the most basic level.

Who could she ask about this feeling? Alex Robinson, her guidance counselor, was dead. Before his death, she hadn't felt close enough to him to ask him anyway. But they were close now. His dying in her arms made them close. That thought catapulted her into her waking nightmare—falling under his weight, feeling his body go limp, the smell of his blood, the hatred on the shooter's face. Memory was a terrorist, attacking her at unexpected times, exploding like a bomb in her face when she was at her most vulnerable.

"Can you run out of tears?" Keisha asked her mother again as they were getting ready this morning.

Akeelah shook her head, her face ashen with sadness. "Eventually, I think, with enough horror, you move beyond them. Sometimes you find your real strength."

Her parents were in the outer circle around the grave, the row of grownups in dark clothes who now guarded them constantly, afraid of some new assault because there was still an accomplice out there. She'd heard her parents whispering that some copycat hoping for instant glory in the online crazyland of mass murderers and haters would come back to finish the job and kill all of them. What about the accomplice, Keisha thought, the person who let the shooter into the school? That was the threat; that was who they had to find and do something about.

Keisha knew there were other bad guys out there. She already had her own trolls, followers who jumped on her every post to mock and threaten her. The spokeswoman for the NRA claimed she was a paid actor. She almost laughed. Keisha turned her head to find her mother's face in the crowd. Their eyes locked for a second. Her mother—her face tranquil, her black eyes clear, her chin held high—was real. That was all she needed to continue.

Her mother worried she was putting a target on her own back by being outspoken. "You're making it easy for someone to shoot you or snap your photo and bully you online."

Keisha didn't tell her mother that was already happening. She had stared into the face of a boy with a rifle aimed right at her and seen her fear reflected in his sunglasses. Her throat burned. Just by being alive, she was a target. She couldn't hide. She had to do something to stop this madness. Speaking out was her way of grieving. Everybody had their own way.

Someone pressed a face against her back. Her classmate's sobs vibrated through her body. In front of her was an open hole in the ground carefully draped with green Astroturf, as if carpet could hide the dirt into which the body of her friend was about to be dropped. She couldn't look at the casket, at the profusion of flowers. *This is so wrong, it's wrong, it's wrong.*

Samantha was one of the first people to die that day. Today, she was going into the ground. Keisha had agreed to say a few words about her. Samantha's mother looked at her and nodded. Keisha closed her eyes for a beat, hoping her voice would work.

She raised her chin. "Each one of these people we bury today is special. Each of them was the whole world to their parents. They were our friends, an essential part of the world we knew. Samantha was close to her mother, helping out in the house. She even got me to help out too. I used to watch her play tennis. What a serve she had. She tried to teach me, but I was hopeless, and she never judged me. She wasn't just the things she did. You always knew with her where you stood, that she cared about you."

Samantha's mother took in a deep, shaky breath and closed her eyes.

"Each high five I got in the hallway, each pat on the back, every smile across the classroom from Samantha meant I was okay. She was my beacon. She lit my way when I was down or unsure. She was part of my tribe. She was supposed to be part of my future."

Her throat convulsed. She stopped speaking and let tears run down her face for the length of time it took for the shooter to kill Mr. Robinson. One second, two, three. "And now . . . and now, she's been ripped away from me, from all of us."

Keisha looked around at all the faces. So many people were here. Kids she had never known or passed in the hall without acknowledging, without even noticing they existed. She was remiss, thoughtless—all those lives she hadn't valued or had simply taken for granted.

"These are our sacrifices, our warriors, our heroes. We didn't know that until now. But we know it now." She took in a deep, shuddering breath. "We better make good on these sacrifices. We better do something important to live up to them." She wiped her eyes with her fingertips. "I love you, Sam. I'll never forget you."

After the preacher said more words over the coffin, Samantha's mother wrapped an arm around Keisha's shoulders. They stood at the gravesite as other people walked back to their cars. "Come over anytime, honey, just like you always do."

Keisha nodded, but she knew after a while, she wouldn't visit. Being in Samantha's house would remind her of the friend she'd lost. That would be too much. She looked over her shoulder for her parents. Her mother came to her rescue, taking Mrs. Goodwin's hand, kissing her cheek. Her father talked quietly to Mr. Goodwin, who looked like a man who had lost his way in a strange city and now stood inert, not knowing which way to turn. Samantha's grandparents flanked him, their faces gray, staring out into the distance.

Keisha threw her arms around Mrs. Goodwin and hugged her until the shaking in her stomach stopped. Then she heard gunfire. She whipped around, looked in the direction of the sound, and dragged Mrs. Goodwin down onto the ground.

## Charmaine

In the afternoon, her parents and in-laws accompanied Charmaine to the funeral home to pick out a casket and make arrangements. Standing in the room of coffins, Mama D asked, "Do you think Alex would want the funeral held in our neighborhood, where he grew up, so his old friends could come?"

Charmaine held her ground. "Sorry, Mama D, but it has to be here, so his students can honor him. He died protecting one of them. So that's how it has to be. His old buddies can drive an hour to the funeral home. It's not that far."

"Charmaine's right," Pops said, and that ended the discussion.

At her mother's suggestion, she took along a white shirt, a tie with the Rockwell High School mustang logo, and Alex's best suit, the one he wore as a bridegroom. He was so gorgeous on their wedding day in that navy pinstripe, his face beaming with pride as she walked down the aisle toward him. She could still feel his love today. Would that feeling last? Or would it die too?

Mr. Brown, the funeral director, a portly man with reading glasses perched on the end of his nose, quietly reviewed his list of specifics. "Would the deceased want to be buried or cremated?" he asked. Charmaine shuddered at the question. The man had just called the love of her life "the deceased." Nor could she imagine keeping his ashes in a box on her mantelpiece. "Buried," Mama D answered, and Charmaine didn't object.

The funeral costs shocked her. How am I going to pay for this? Even though she and Alex both had good jobs and stuck to a budget, student loan payments prevented much saving. She was determined not to accept money from either set of parents, although both offered. Her parents worried about having enough to retire, she knew, and Alex's parents were older and even worse off, with Pops retired from the post office and Mama D working part-time at a library.

"Have you made arrangements for a cemetery plot?" Mr. Brown asked.

"We have a family plot, but it's fifty miles from here," Mama D said.

"There would be an additional charge to transport the body beyond twenty miles."

Mama D patted Charmaine's hand. "We'll pay. Don't worry about that. I'd like to see my two children laid to rest next to each other."

"This should be Charmaine's decision," her mother interjected.

Charmaine couldn't believe her mother seemed to be itching to start an argument. Not now. Cemeteries gave Charmaine the creeps. She couldn't imagine herself visiting every day or every week to kneel at Alex's grave. She decided to compromise. "The funeral will be here, but the burial at the Robinson family plot."

For once, Tina Parham held her tongue.

## Joe

Joe had taken up his post twenty feet back from the new grave. He knew this cemetery well. Emilia was buried here. He looked over his shoulder in the direction of her grave. He hated funerals.

Usually, the county police department only provided a funeral guard for dignitaries, but the chief was checking every box, making sure nothing slipped by him. The goal was to restore order, to recreate the sense of security the community used to feel.

Four marked cars escorted the procession from the funeral home, two officers guarded the vehicle entrances to each cemetery, and three patrol officers, including Joe, covered the perimeter of each gravesite on foot. He felt like a crow in his starched navy blues watching from a distance as mourners gathered. He put a hand on the hilt of his gun, reassuring himself that he was prepared for anything.

Although his child had miraculously been spared, he mourned for the loss of his safe community, where children once were free to walk around its streets unafraid. Safety died the day the shooter killed fourteen people at his daughter's school. His daughter wasn't eating or sleeping. She wandered around their house like a ghost. What a fool he'd been, thinking he had found Eden. He had promised Emilia he would keep their child safe. No place on earth was safe. He couldn't take Sofia far enough away.

His blood pressure rose at any hint that Sofia was in danger. Heat pressed against the skin on his face from inside. He didn't want her to have to live her childhood constantly on alert as he had when he was young. That was thirty years ago, but he could still hear the taunts, feel fear rise in him, drying his mouth, chasing words from his brain.

The first *pop* snagged Joe's attention and brought him back to the cemetery. He spun around, looking for the source. Three more blasts—*pop, pop, pop.* Mourners at the funeral flinched and crouched. A thin wail rose from the crowd. Two officers moved closer to flank the mourners, guns drawn, scanning the area. People in the outer circle around the grave fled across the grass in all directions.

Joe put his hand on his gun and sprinted across the cemetery toward the sound. The officers at the gate moved into the street. A white man dressed in a camouflage outfit from some army surplus store had pulled a black Ram pickup truck in front of the cemetery gates. He stood in the truck bed, an AR-15 slung over his chest. Across the truck, a banner declared: *Your First Amendment Rights Don't Trump My Second.*

Sweat trickled down Joe's back. *This asshole brings an assault weapon to a funeral to mock the mourners! Cabrones.*

The man slammed a cherry bomb against the asphalt. Joe's ears rang. Police surrounded the truck; their guns pointed at the man.

Sergeant Davis yelled, "Put your weapon down. Hands above your head. Step down from the truck."

The man grinned and threw another firecracker at Davis' feet. "I got my rights!"

While the man cursed at Davis, Joe leaped up onto the truck, and wrenched the man's arms behind his back, removed his rifle, and zipped on plastic cuffs.

"You have rights, man," Joe said, "but you don't get to terrorize grieving families. I'm arresting you for disturbing the peace, assaulting a police officer, and whatever else the sergeant wants to throw at you."

The man yowled and strained against the cuffs. "Police brutality. Warrantless search and seizure." He looked around to check whether anyone was making a video on their phone. "Cops are violating my right to freely assemble."

"Shut up," Joe said into the man's ear. Fury made him clench his teeth. "You have the right to remain silent, and I advise you to take that right seriously."

Mourners watched silently from the sidewalk, their faces stricken. Some idiot took a photo. Without a word, the mourners turned and walked back into the cemetery, their arms around each other.

Joe spotted Sofia as they shoved the protestor into a squad car. Her eyes were wide, her mouth opened as if she wanted to scream, but no sound came out. She looked terrified. He had to do something to make her safe, anything. He broke protocol and ran to her, putting his arm around his daughter and leading her away from the group. "It's okay, Sofia, it's okay, we got him. He's just some *cabrón*."

"Papi, could you take me to the hospital? I need to see Cat." She looked up at him, and he knew he'd always do anything she wanted.

"Whatever you need, *mi corazon*, just ask." Still, he felt helpless. He was always after the fact, always consoling, never preventing the harm.

### Charmaine

Condolences came from her sorority sisters and Alex's fraternity brothers, high school friends, and out-of-town relatives who had seen his photo on the network news. She kept the conversations short because they just made her cry. Eventually, she asked her mother to answer the calls and questions about arrangements. She posted funeral details on her and Alex's Facebook pages and hoped that would discourage callers.

Over the next two days, the viewing room with Alex's coffin filled with baskets of flowers, not just from family and friends, but also from the teachers' union, the Rockwell

High PTA, Alex's fraternity, and the hospital emergency room staff. Though beautiful, the scent of the lilies was overpowering, and Charmaine had to ask the funeral director to move some into the hall.

Her parents positioned themselves at the doorway to greet the mourners and ask them to sign the guest book, while Alex's parents sat on chairs facing the casket. Charmaine wandered back and forth between them until her brothers arrived.

Charmaine was grateful Greg and Larry had traveled there to support her. Growing up, she had never been much of a crier with those two around to toughen her up, but they protected her, too. She blotted her tears with the tissue Greg handed her. "I remember the hard time you gave Alex when we first started dating."

"Told him he'd have to fight me if he hurt you in any way," Greg replied, and they both smiled, the first time she'd smiled since the shooting. "Alex was a good guy," Greg said, his voice breaking.

Larry hugged her and whispered in her ear, "Let me know if you need anything, anything at all, the oil in your car changed or money to tide you over. I'm just a couple hours away." She knew she could always rely on him.

Despite Mama D's initial concerns, friends from Alex's childhood neighborhood traveled to the funeral home to offer their condolences to his inconsolable mother. "Both my babies are shot and killed," she said over and over. His arm around his wife's shoulder, Pops coughed, looked away, and shook his head.

Many of Alex's fraternity brothers and Charmaine's sorority sisters had flown in or driven long distances to attend the viewing. Yvonne Parham, her cousin and maid of honor, arrived visibly pregnant, a sad reminder that Charmaine's own hopes for motherhood died with her husband. Ty Swearingen, the best man at their wedding, told her a funny story about Alex she had never heard before, how he was so nervous before their first date that he changed his clothes three times and started to walk out of the frat house without his shoes.

Charmaine laughed. "He never told me that."

"That man was crazy about you from the start," Ty said, something she had always known and a feeling she shared.

As they continued to reminisce about Alex, a determined black girl approached the group. "Mrs. Robinson?" she said, extending her hand. "I'm Keisha Washington. I was with Mr. Robinson when he was shot. He saved my life. I just wanted to say I'm so sorry. He meant so much to us students. We'll miss him."

Alex had told her about Keisha, one of the top students at Rockwell High, senior class president, and champion debater, a role model for black teens. The story of how Alex had stood between the shooter and Keisha Washington to save her young life had been played and replayed in the media. Charmaine didn't want to hear that her husband was a hero. *Maybe he would still be here if he weren't. Maybe he'd be alive, and you'd be dead.* Charmaine shook the girl's hand. "Thank you."

But Keisha wouldn't stop talking. "We held a vigil at the school for all the people who were killed. So many students came by to pay their respects to Mr. Robinson."

Charmaine knew the girl was trying to be kind, but she couldn't stop resentment from seeping through her. *I should have been with Alex when he died, not you.*

"I heard the shooter had an accomplice," Ty said to Keisha. "Do you know anything more about that?"

She shook her head. "It's surreal to think another one of my classmates was involved."

Charmaine wanted to get away from this conversation. Across the room, she spotted a young Asian girl who looked dizzy and walked over to steady her.

"Thank you, I'm fine." The girl didn't meet her eyes. "It's the lilies."

"They are overwhelming."

Before she could say anything else, Dr. McGann approached. Acquaintances she hadn't felt particularly close to streamed in, church members, neighbors, Lori and other co-workers from the hospital, even her hairdresser. Without realizing it, she and Alex had become part of the Rockwell community. People she had never met before— Alex's students and fellow faculty members, the school janitor who disarmed the shooter, strangers who saw the news and wanted to do something—offered their condolences. They all praised Alex. Their words gave her strength. She thanked them, grateful to have an excuse to avert her eyes from the body in the casket, who used to be Alex but wasn't anymore.

## Caitlyn

Her mother put another pillow behind her head. Unlike the ICU, sunlight poured into this new hospital room and washed over her elevated leg. The doctors said they had to monitor her. What did that mean? That they were going to amputate it? She was never going to be able to handle that, her mother either. She knew it was petty, selfish even, but she liked her legs. They were flawless, and why she wore skirts all the time. Tears stung the corners of her eyes. Friends had lost their lives, and she was pining over her once perfect leg. Her long thigh bones.

"How many kids died?"

Lisa turned away and poured a glass of water. "Let's not talk about that now. Let's just focus on getting you better."

*She's not going to tell me.* "Do you have my phone?"

"No, the police still have it."

"Mom, how's Sofia?"

Her mother brushed Caitlyn's bangs aside and behind her ear. "She misses you."

Caitlyn's face flushed. Poor Sofy, they had not seen each other since that horrible day. How was she taking it? She hadn't even heard her voice. "When will I get to see her?"

"Soon. Wiggle your toes, sweetheart."

Caitlyn did what her mother asked. Through the numbness, she could see them wiggle. She could not imagine life without her leg. It was too scary to think about.

"I need to talk to Sofia about our audition." She sighed. "I feel so tired. Can Daddy get something for me? The new fabric is still in my locker at school."

"Of course. As soon as they let us back into the school."

"I never got to show it to Sofia. Will you show her, Mom? It's our big finale dress with the embroidered insects."

"Your what?" Lisa sat back down.

"The last dress in our collection. It's white with beetles and caterpillars and butterflies. Sofy and her grandmother are doing the embroidery. They'll need the fabric."

"Don't worry about this now, sweetheart." Her mother leaned over and stroked Caitlyn's face.

"There are no spiders on it, although we thought about it." Caitlyn felt a twinge of pain in her hip and shifted her position.

Her mother jumped up and adjusted the bed. "Better?" she asked.

Caitlyn drifted, remembering that day, the boom of the gun, the feeling of being up in the blue. The freedom and peace. It pulled on her.

She nodded. "Will you look after Sofia, Mom? That dress, she'll need help."

"You'll work on it together. And I'll take you *both* to the audition."

"I'm tired of the happy talk. I don't think I'll be out of here in time." Caitlyn gestured toward her cast. "Sophia has to drape that dress, sew it all together, her grandmother has to do all that needlework." The pain seared through her leg again, and this time it went higher.

"Oh, my sweet girl, don't worry about everyone else; the most important thing is you get better."

Caitlyn's stomach churned. "I need to talk to Sofia."

**ERDoc @RyanMcGannM.D.**
I object to bullet holes in my patients, I object to children arriving dead in my ER, I object to politicians who put money over lives, to endless funerals. Where is our reason? #EndSenselessViolence

# CHAPTER FOUR

## Sofia

Three awful days after Cat's mom said her friend had made it through surgery, Sofia finally stood at the foot of her hospital bed with Papi, tongue-tied and awkward. She didn't recognize the figure laid out in the bed with tubes coming out of her and her leg in a cast with metal brackets sticking out from the side.

A face turned to her and smiled. "Sofy, you're here."

"Yes," Sofia managed to say. *I can't look shocked. I can't show her I'm freaked out.* Papi tapped his belt buckle with his thumb, the way he did when he was impatient and worried. Sofia squeezed his hand. She could read him like a book.

"Who got you the lame balloon?" Sofia's voice cracked as she looked away from the sunken eyes and pointed to the *Minion* balloon floating at the end of the bed. "Don't they know you're fifteen?"

"It's from my brother, Connor. He still thinks I'm six."

"If only," Sofia said as she flicked the minion's goggles. *We were safer then when Mama was alive.* "Papi, can I sit with Caitlyn by myself?" There were things they needed to say. She could see it in Cat's eyes.

"Sure, *mi hija.*" He took Sofia's jacket and draped it over his arm. "I'll be in that waiting room near the elevator." He squeezed Caitlyn's shoulder, and she smiled at him. "Nice to see you smile," he said and left the room.

The tangle of tubes around her friend reminded Sofia of visiting her mother. She stepped around the bed, afraid to touch Cat, fearful she would hurt her. She pressed her hand on the white blanket at Cat's collar bone and looked into her eyes. She was tired, but Cat was okay. *She's okay.* Sofia touched her forehead to her friend's, and they cried for a while.

Sofia picked up a stuffed panda from the table next to the bed. "Who gave you this?"

"You know who."

Sofia read the note hanging from the bear's collar. It had Eric's name with a heart around it. "That's a bit much."

Caitlyn took the panda back, squeezed it, and tossed it to the foot of the bed. "Now my dad thinks he's my boyfriend." Her skin was pasty, her eyes sunken, but she still winked.

Sofia had seen this before when her mother was sick—the brave face, pretending everything was okay. She never came home. Was that going to happen to Cat? She leaned her head against Caitlyn's and closed her eyes.

"Look. Those pins stick right through my thigh, and I don't feel a thing." Caitlyn pointed to the blue and white cast and the metal bars.

Sofia didn't look too closely. The sight of the contraption made her queasy. "I brought you some of that candy you like from Abuela. She and Abuelo say they love you and to get well soon." Sofia handed Caitlyn a white bag filled with brightly colored lollipops in the shape of roosters, pigs, and hearts. "If you can't eat them all, Abuela said to give them to your doctors and nurses."

"Tell them I love them, too."

Caitlyn put the bag on the metal table next to the bed and took Sofia's hand. They held each other's gaze. "What's happening out there in the world?"

"We're all going to funerals," Sofia said. "I hate it."

"How many died? My mom wouldn't tell me, and she took the remote away."

"Eleven kids, two teachers, and the guidance counselor, Mr. Robinson."

"God. Anybody we know?"

"Samantha . . . Ryan Becker."

"Ryan? He has my math book. I gave it to him that morning, and he teased me about my pink hair. I was trying to think of some way to get him back." Caitlyn put her hand over her mouth.

Sophia twisted a lock of hair around her finger. "I went to three funerals yesterday. Ryan's was one. I don't know if I can stand the idea of going to anymore."

Caitlyn squirmed. "How did the shooter get in?"

"Someone propped open a door. They don't know who."

"Who do you think it was? Has to be someone as fucked up as he is."

"I don't know. I don't want to know. Thinking that one person in our school could be so evil is bad enough."

Caitlyn took Sofia's hand. "I have something to tell you."

"What?"

"That day . . . the shooter. I saw him, up close to his sweaty face, out in the hallway. I was on the ceiling looking down at you and me; then I was in the hall . . . with him, but I didn't feel anything, just this weird calm."

"What do you mean you were on the ceiling?" Papi warned her the drugs might make Caitlyn loopy. She shivered.

"It was like a dream. Do you think it was one of those near-death experiences?"

"You're sounding crazy. Maybe it's the drugs."

"I swear. I also saw a girl in the hall, by herself, crying. I don't think he shot her. I went outside. It felt so right . . . peaceful. I wanted to stay, but you called me back. I had to come back because of you."

Sofia picked up the paper bag and shakily placed it on Caitlyn's chest.

"Okay, I'll shut up for now." Caitlyn settled back, pulled a candy rooster from the bag, and jammed it in her mouth.

"That would be a first."

Caitlyn removed the lollipop, stuck out her red-stained tongue to show Sofia, and placed it on a napkin.

Sofia smiled. "You freak." She smoothed the white sheet. "After my Mom died . . . I would see a wren all the time. It would come to my bedroom window, sit on a branch and look at me. It was like my Mom was there, in that black eye, watching over me. That little wren followed me everywhere."

Caitlyn's eyes opened wide. "I love that story. Why didn't you ever tell me that before?"

"Because I didn't want you to think I was crazy." Sofia remembered Caitlyn in the middle school cafeteria, the new girl in school who, for some reason, sat with her.

"Cool vest," Caitlyn had said. "I have one like it in pink."

Sofia's mom had just started chemo. All the kids she knew were afraid to talk to her. This new friend was exactly what she'd needed.

"I already know you're crazy. We're all crazy." Caitlyn smiled.

Sofia sighed and slid off the bed. "I brought a picture, too. Papi printed it off." She reached into her bag and pulled out a framed photo. "Since you don't have the five thousand photos in your phone with you."

Caitlyn held the photo showing the two girls in the *quinceañera* dresses they had designed for Sofia's fifteenth birthday. She stared at the photo, her smile gone. She looked worn out now.

"Do you think we'll ever sew again?" Sofia asked. "We have only one more dress to finish, and I can't do it alone. There's only a few more weeks before the audition."

Caitlyn closed her eyes. "Dad will get the fabric for you."

They had pored over Fashionista Junior for years before they designed and sewed their own original garments, staging two fashion shows: one in the garage using Papi's driveway as the runway and the other at the school for a talent contest. They couldn't believe it when their favorite TV show had accepted their application to audition in their area. Sofia craved that excitement again, but it was gone.

"I don't know." Caitlyn closed her eyes. "It suddenly doesn't feel important anymore." Sofia felt her throat tighten. "How long do you have to stay in here?"

"A while. I start rehab soon. Being able to go to the bathroom on my own is now my number one goal—it's all my mom talks about. But it's scary. The thought of getting out of this bed . . . My doctor says I was lucky. I don't feel lucky, do you?"

They both looked at the photo of Sofia in a blue and white dress that puffed out to the floor. Caitlyn wore a light pink gown, strapless and sparkly. They had been beautiful.

Caitlyn placed the picture next to a cup of melting ice. "I'm tired."

"Okay, I'll go." Sophia tried to sound cheerful. "I'll come back tomorrow."

They clasped pinky fingers. Sofia didn't want to let go. Not ever.

**Mike**

He stared at Caitlyn as she slept, wondering where her dreams had taken her. At first, her expression was peaceful, exactly the way she'd slept as a baby. But then her face muscles began to twitch. She clasped the bedsheet. Her eyes opened and caught Mike's stare. Groggy from the medication, she said, "Daddy, what are you doing here?"

"Looking out for you, Caitlyn. Your mother will be here soon."

She reached up to hug him, and he lowered himself to kiss her cheek. "You always look out for me, Daddy." But he knew he couldn't always. He wasn't there at the school to protect her from the shooter. He gripped the bed rails, helpless and angry. *Caitlyn is doing well. That's all that matters.*

Mike took a deep breath and released his grip. He shifted his eyes to the flowers and the stuffed panda next to the bed. "Eric? A new boyfriend?"

"He's not really my boyfriend, Daddy," she said, "but I do like him. He came to the emergency room to look for me the day I got shot. Wasn't that sweet?"

Mike just grimaced. No boy would ever be good enough for his daughter.

As soon as Caitlyn was able to eat again and not rely on IV fluids, Mike had gone back to work. The health insurance his employer provided would pay the hospital charges, and Mike didn't feel right about depriving his company, a defense contractor, of his billable hours.

There wasn't much he could do for Caitlyn anyway, and he was assured she was getting good care. The orthopedist visited her almost every day. Dr. Kalish, who was called a hospitalist, which Mike figured was the in-patient equivalent of an ER doctor, examined her at least once a day. She was still on an IV to give her a constant dose of antibiotics— Dr. Kalish said infection remained a threat—and she'd be in traction for a while, to give her leg time to heal.

Lisa spent most of every day in Caitlyn's hospital room, returning home to heat a meal one of their neighbors had dropped off before she, Mike, and Patrick returned to the hospital for evening visiting hours. After four days, Mike told Patrick to return to college. "Caitlyn's doing fine," Mike assured him.

And she was, really. Although on pain medication, Caitlyn was her usual charming self, chatting with the nurses and teasing the orderly about the hospital food. But she was quieter, more subdued, even when her best friend Sofia visited. Mike was used to their giggling and bursts of raucous laughter whenever Sofia spent time at their home, which was often, but now the two girls just talked quietly about the teachers and classmates who died.

## Lily

*She climbed over brick and concrete rubble and through a gaping hole in the gymnasium wall. Smoke still billowed. Exposed steel beams crisscrossed overhead. Light panels and wire dangled and sparked in the darkness. The purple sky and stars shone through the smoke. Had a tornado ripped open the school?*

*Her feet crunched on a carpet of broken glass covering the corridor's floors—the only sound in the still building. She needed to use the restroom, but nothing looked familiar; she couldn't find her way. Around every corner, jagged remnants of doors and desks, books fluttering open without a breeze, all confused her. Some corridors stretched into black; others led to dead ends. She followed the sound of water dripping to her right. A restroom. Finally. She pushed on the jammed door, putting her shoulder to the cold metal, straining, but when it opened, dark green sludge spewed from all the toilets, surging toward her bare feet.*

*Her bladder burned. She sped through the haze in the hallway. In another bathroom, every stall door was locked. A girl stood at a sink in front of the cracked mirror. Her reflection showed no eyes, mouth, or nose, just a shredded mass of tissue.*

*Lily ran from the room. She slipped on the glass and crashed into a body twisted like a ragdoll. She tore off down another corridor, past a pair of Converse sneakers poking out from a circle of crows. Her breath came in spurts, heartbeat racketing through her body. Above her, a face peered through the missing roof. A pink bang hung over the girl's curious expression.*

*Lily averted her eyes, racing down the corridor until she halted before Mr. Robinson. He smiled, handsome and composed, his Rockwell Mustangs coffee mug held in front of him. He lifted it to his lips, exposing a gaping hole in his chest. Lily looked through it, all the way past the debris to the emerald lacrosse field.*

*She spun away from him only to smash into another body—a man in a blood-stained janitor's shirt, his eyes boring into hers.*

*"Run!" he screamed.*

Lily woke in a sweat, the sheets tangled around her legs.

## Mike

Exactly eight days after the shooting, while Mike and Lisa were alone with Caitlyn in her hospital room watching "The Big Bang Theory" on TV, his daughter began to cough. Blood splattered the quilt.

"Oh, my God, what's happening?" Lisa grabbed her daughter's hand. She tried to wipe away the blood dripping down Caitlyn's chin. Lisa's face paled.

Mike, his own heart slamming against his chest, pushed the emergency button on the bed remote, then ran down the hall for the nurse on duty. The nurse called the resident to join her and paged Dr. Kalish. Caitlyn was failing. Mike had seen it before, on the battlefield. Her skin paled, and her eyelids fluttered for a brief second, then remained perfectly still. Helpless, Lisa stepped aside to allow the resident to examine their daughter.

The resident began CPR and kept at it until Dr. Kalish arrived. He eyed the bloody sheets and muttered, "Damn. It's a blood clot."

Mike looked to his wife, who stood frozen with her hand over her mouth and her eyes widened, afraid to move.

## Caitlyn

Her drugged heart beat thickly. She couldn't move her mouth or arms. Her body bucked. Blood splattered against the white quilt her mother had brought from home and had earlier spread over her like wings.

Her mother was in a panic. Her father smashed the nurse's button and ran from the room, hitting the wall with his balled fist on his way out. She couldn't speak to tell them something was drastically different. Her chest collapsed; her lungs burned.

She wasn't going to make it. She knew something they didn't; her heart knew. It pushed hard, but it was finished. Pain flashed across her shoulders.

She rose up to the ceiling. Up here, the pain was gone. She could see everything now. Below, a medic pounded her limp body. She watched her mother sink to the floor. *I love you, Mom. Daddy.*

Her heart was down there, motionless. Her lungs wanted to expand but couldn't. She could see the dark room with the beeping lights below her from her calm place on the ceiling. A monitor screeched. The balloon bobbed; the panda fell to the floor.

She wasn't supposed to die. Her doctors said she was improving. People wanted her to live, but she couldn't help it.

*"I'm up here,"* Caitlyn said to her parents. They couldn't hear her.

*Oh, they'll all be so sad.* She wished she could tell them, move her mouth and say last words, something beautiful for them to remember, but she couldn't. Her heart broke. Her father pulled her mother up to stand next to him. She wanted to caress them.

She went upward filled with wonder, out through the ceiling, and up through all the rooms where people were sleeping or talking or thinking. Bliss washed over her. She ascended away from the chaos, saw the gravel roof of the hospital, and a landing pad for the emergency helicopter. There was the beautiful blue sky, deep cobalt this time, almost the color of Sofia's *quinceañera* dress. A blue like no other.

She passed through the color, moving toward a distant glow, but there was something she had to do before she went there. With all her might, she pushed herself back to where her body was. Her parents were gone now, and a clean, white sheet covered what remained of her earthly self.

She slipped along beside the young hospital aide, who pushed a wobbly-wheeled gurney down the hall. He hoisted her body into a long drawer with the help of an aide with red, slicked-back hair.

"It's Caitlyn Moran," the orderly said, "the last one."

"Shit," the red-haired aide said. "What a fucked-up world we live in." He shoved the heavy drawer shut until it clicked.

Caitlyn felt she was also part of these guys. She could feel the beat of one heart heavier than the other, not synchronized. They moved away. She stayed. She had no pulsing blood, no eardrums to hear, retinas to see, yet she did it all and more. Caitlyn could sense others here in this space filled with metal drawers but didn't want to go with them. She had more to do.

**Dirtywork @billyscrubs**
Last ABC victim died today. Long way down the corridor to the morgue. Can't take much more of this. Hope that's the end. #neveragain

# CHAPTER FIVE

## Charmaine

Alex's body was in the ground. His parents had returned home after the burial. Mom and Dad and her brothers stayed with her through the weekend, but then everyone had to get back to their jobs.

On Wednesday morning, Charmaine found herself utterly alone. By habit, she woke up at six, and also by habit, rolled over onto Alex's side of their king-sized bed, groping with an outstretched arm for the warmth of him before fully waking up to reality. She missed the "good morning, beautiful," he always said to start their day. Sighing, she got up and padded downstairs to make coffee.

How unlike this day was from before, when she and Alex were comparing schedules for the week ahead, grabbing a quick breakfast, and sharing a long goodbye kiss before hurrying off to work. Today she went through the motions, pouring herself a glass of orange juice and a bowl of cornflakes, which she had no desire to eat. Her breakfast sat untouched as she sipped her coffee and turned on the television for company.

Flipping through the channels, she found the breaking news unbearable. The school shooting had claimed its fifteenth victim. When a young girl's photo appeared on the screen, Charmaine recognized the girl with a bullet wound to the leg she had seen in the emergency room. "Oh, my God," she said aloud to the television.

The news anchor segued into the search for the accomplice. An unknown accomplice still at large made Charmaine nervous. Her face fell, but she didn't cry. She had shed so many tears these past few days; she was all cried out. She would never cry again. She was just numb.

She remembered the first time Alex told her about his sister. They'd been dating only a few weeks and were walking across the campus of the large state university they attended. She was telling him a story about a day she and her high school friends skipped school to hang out at the suburban shopping mall near her house.

"The neighborhood you grew up in sounds a lot different from mine," he said.

That surprised her. He was a fraternity guy, wasn't he? "Really? How?"

"I grew up in the city. You'd probably think my neighborhood was a ghetto."

"Oh, it couldn't have been that bad."

"It was bad sometimes, Charmaine. I've never told you about my big sister, Lizzie." He steered her to a low wall outside the liberal arts building, and they sat down. He held her hand.

"I didn't know you had a sister."

"She died just before her high school graduation when I was still in middle school. She was hanging out with some friends and friends-of-friends, people she didn't know, a couple blocks from our house when a car full of gang members pulled up and started shooting. They were aiming for some guy but killed Lizzie instead."

Tears welled up in his eyes. Charmaine saw that after all these years, he was still devastated. She hugged him and whispered in his ear, "I'm sorry."

He could have been a doctor or a lawyer; he was certainly smart enough and hard-working but becoming a high school guidance counselor was his goal. He'd seen too many young hopes diminished and dreams abandoned, and he wanted to change that. He paid his own way through college with student loans and good-paying construction work on summer breaks. "I'll never be the richest man in the world," he told her, "but I can make a difference in so many lives, especially young black lives."

As she came to know him better, she realized they were different in other ways. He was religious, and she wasn't. Maybe if she had been, she would be comforted at the idea of reuniting with Alex in heaven one day, but that thought, even if true, which she doubted, didn't comfort her. She wanted him with her now. How could a loving God take him away from her in such a terrible way? No church could comfort her or replace her husband.

Charmaine clicked off the TV remote, poured her breakfast down the garbage disposal, and left the dishes in the sink. She hadn't taken a shower yesterday and probably wouldn't take one today. What was the point? She went up-stairs to their bedroom closet and turned the clothes hamper upside down, retrieving his dirty shirts and inhal-ing his scent that lingered. Taking one of the shirts with her to bed, she lay back down. She reached for their wed-ding photo on the nightstand and hugged it to her chest. She wanted to remember Alex like that, not like the man-nequin in the coffin.

The day of his college graduation, he had proposed. She didn't accept right away. "You're just asking me now be-cause you're afraid I'll find a new boyfriend once you get a job." His smile told her he knew she was just teasing him.

"You're right," he answered, "I want to make sure you're mine."

"You don't have to worry about that. I'm yours forever."

They set their wedding date for the following June when she'd have her RN. When he received the job offer from the Rockwell Township high school, she was relieved he wouldn't be teaching in the inner city, where she feared he wouldn't be safe. How naive she'd been to think she was protected from gun violence.

Her thoughts wandered to her financial worries. She would have to sell Alex's Kia to pay for the cost of the fu-neral. It turned out her husband had two small life insurance policies that together equaled a year's salary. Af-ter that, she wasn't sure she could afford the rent on this townhouse on her paycheck alone. Maybe she'd have to move or get a roommate. Maybe she should get a dog for protection as well as company. She'd gone from her parents to a dorm to a sorority house to married life. She wasn't used to living alone.

If only they'd had a child, she wouldn't be alone. They thought they were being responsible by waiting until Alex finished his masters. They thought they'd have no trouble getting pregnant, but apparently, they were wrong. *Thanks again, God.* Yes, it would have been another financial hard-ship to be a single mother, but other women have done it.

She felt guilty having these regrets and worrying about money when she should be mourning her husband's death. But, as her mom said, "Life goes on, Charmaine. You have to go on, too. It will be hard without Alex, but it's what he'd want you to do."

She knew Mom was right. The world was still spinning on its own timetable. People got back to their everyday lives, even if hers would never be the same. Dr. McGann said to take whatever time off she needed. She didn't know if she would be able to work in the ER or even as a nurse again, to witness pain and death on a regular basis.

She picked up her cell phone to scroll through the photos of her and Alex together. In one selfie, they were both wearing caps with the Rockwell High mustang logo at a high school football game, which, for some reason, she remembered the Mustangs won. She didn't remember when she took the photo of him cooking in their townhouse kitchen, but he was hamming it up for the camera, waving a large spoon over a pot of spaghetti boiling on the stove. She loved seeing his big smile and sparkling amber eyes again. She could almost feel his arm around her shoulder and his lips nuzzling her neck.

She called his cell number just to hear his voice; "Hey, Alex here. What's up?" She called it again.

"When is it going to stop hurting?" she asked herself aloud. What would Alex want her to do?

The doorbell rang. Throwing on a robe, she went downstairs and opened the door just in time to see the brown truck driving away. She picked up the envelope left on the doorstep. It was addressed to Alex. Inside were two tickets for a Bruno Mars concert. On Valentine's Day.

**Lily**

They were back, the blonde woman and short man from the FBI. They were canvassing Lily's neighborhood, investigating Aaron Blake Crofton's motive for killing fourteen people—fifteen now that Caitlyn Moran died suddenly last night. They had to rule out terrorism first, though Lily wondered how shooting thirty-six people could not be considered terrorism.

Setting off three pipe bombs was definitely terrorism. Lily knew Aaron was going to do that. She let him into the building. That made her a terrorist. She could go to prison.

Her whole life suddenly depended on this moment with the blonde woman and short man.

"What grade are you in, Lily?"

"I'm a senior," Lily replied. "Didn't my parents tell you?"

The man, Special Agent Warren, checked his notes. Special Agent Radson smiled and said, "We like each person to answer for themselves, to give us their perspective without influence." Lily categorized her as the Good Cop.

The first time they came, a day after the shooting, they talked to Lily's father, mother, and sister. But Lily, her father insisted, was *not in a state* to talk to anyone. Lily figured they really left because of her mother's incoherent wailing. The second time, the family was on its way to another funeral. Stephanie, who never missed a chance to pray, insisted they attend all of them, even though they didn't know any of the victims personally.

Except Mr. Robinson. Lily knew the guidance counselor well. The day after the disastrous debate, he had called her to his office and tried to get her to talk about what happened. She'd laughed it off and left the room before she cried. His funeral had the most lilies. She nearly fainted from the smell of them, and it was Mr. Robinson's wife—of all people—who steadied her.

"Did you know your neighbor, Aaron Crofton?" Special Agent Warren asked.

Lily kept her back straight and looked him in the eyes. There were over eleven million articles on the internet on how to tell if someone is lying.

"No," she said.

"Did you ever talk to him at school?"

"No."

"Is he in any of your classes?"

Lily took a sip of her tea. "I'm in all honors and A.P. classes. Aaron Crofton is not in any of my classes."

The two agents looked at each other. Special Agent Radson scratched her neck. Her nails were trimmed so short Lily couldn't see the white crescent tips. Being the Good Cop was apparently more stressful. Lily knew the stress of being good.

"What about on the bus?" Radson asked. "Did you ever see him on the bus?"

"I don't ride the bus," Lily said. "In middle school, I told my mother that kids said the word fuck on the bus. Ever since then, she's driven me and my sister to school. She doesn't want us to be around bad influences and vulgarity."

Lily glanced over her shoulder and caught her mother as she leaned back into the kitchen. Stephanie was supposed to be cooking, not eavesdropping. The ridiculously strong smell of ginger wasn't fooling anyone.

"Did you ever notice any unusual activity going on at the Crofton house?" Warren asked.

"What do you mean by unusual?"

"Loud noises or arguments coming from the house. People coming or going at odd hours."

The air in the room pushed down on Lily's shoulders, but her back did not bend, not a single vertebra tilted. *People coming or going at odd hours.* She was that person, night after night, all summer long. Even when school started, though not as often, and on a few occasions in broad daylight when her mother had taken Violet to her piano lesson. Had any of the neighbors who'd already been questioned by Warren and Radson noticed? Lily had been careful, cutting through the backyard and the small common space between their houses, always looking over her shoulder, always watching for a light to pop on—especially in her parents' bedroom. She was afraid of being caught by her father, not the FBI. Her stomach clenched. Aaron's room had been searched. Maybe they'd already found her fingerprints on the covers of his graphic novels. Had they found her DNA in his bedsheets?

Her throat dried. She took another sip of tea. "Sometimes I'd see him standing in his window. Like he was looking for someone."

"Who do you think he was looking for?"

Not me, Lily thought, as if she could erase the last few months. She watched her life reversing like she had pushed a button on the remote control. She walked backward out of the school, backward out of his room, down his steps, across the common space. That first night the world's axis reversed, and she circled the big tree in the opposite direction.

"You came," he had said, so surprised.

She felt a bird flapping in her chest. The grass was air beneath her feet. She wanted to say something flirtatious, something she'd heard other girls at school say to boys. What would Keisha say?

Lily picked a piece of bark off the tree. "Such an epic romantic comedy gesture." Her voice floated like a feather into the summer night. "How could I say no?"

He followed her around the trunk. Their fingers trailed each other's. "I'm glad," he said. "My next move was to hold a boom box above my head and blast music. But I don't know if they make them anymore."

She looked up at him over her shoulder, an attempt to flirt. "It's a good thing you didn't. You would have woken the whole street. And my father would have shot you."

*Was it all an act? Was I his pawn from night one?*

No, Lily didn't want to be that girl. When she realized her eyes had drifted from the investigators, she blurted, "A girl. I just remembered, one night last summer I couldn't sleep, so I went down to the kitchen. I saw a girl cutting across the backyards. She was going in the direction of Aaron's house."

Radson scribbled on her notepad. Warren moved an inch forward on the sofa and asked, "What did she look like?"

"It was dark. Past midnight," Lily answered. "I couldn't see her very well. I think she had dark hair."

"Was she tall? Short?"

"I think short. Like I said, it was dark. I didn't have my glasses on."

The agents exhaled in unison. Their silent pause concealed all thoughts. Did they believe her? Would they look for another girl with dark hair who would be stupid enough to give herself to a mass murderer?

Radson flipped over another sheet on her notepad. Her face turned grave like she was about to deliver terrible news. "We know it's been difficult, but can we talk about October fifteenth?"

Lily froze in mid-sip of her tea. "Why? You have the shooter."

"We do," Warren said. "But the legal system is an extremely complex matrix. Even a minuscule detail can help an average defense team. We owe it to your classmates and teachers who died to be as thorough as possible."

All of Lily's muscles tensed. She concentrated on the teacup, setting it on the saucer as if it might explode. When it was safely on the coffee table, she folded her hands in her lap and nodded.

Warren went first: "Do you remember seeing Aaron that morning?"

"No."

"Did you see or hear anything suspicious before the pipe bombs exploded?"

"No. It all happened so fast. It was confusing. I didn't know what was happening."

"Where were you when it started?" Radson asked.

The questions felt like an insect crawling up Lily's pant leg. She was desperate to leap off the sofa, but she kept her muscles tight and voice steady. "I finished my A.P. stats test early and went to the restroom."

"Which restroom?"

No one had seen Lily that morning. It wasn't unusual. She could go all day unnoticed at that school. She could stand in the back of a classroom naked and screaming, and no one would notice. The subtle shift in the questions coming from Special Agents Warren and Radson made Lily wish she had an alibi. Mrs. Vandell could confirm she left class early to use the restroom. Would they think she really left to open the door for the kid they were calling the ABC Killer? The invisible insect skittered across her skin. She remembered from the news that police had found a door propped open by a rock. Not her door. She mapped out the school in her mind, all the doors, windows, corridors, and restrooms of that insufferable place, and picked the least suspicious one.

"First floor," she said. "By the front office. I stopped in to see Mr. Robinson about getting my transcripts. My father wants me to apply to MIT Early Action."

"Your father wants you to?" Radson said. "Do you want to?"

The insect crawled around her waist. Inched up her side. She tried not to squirm. "What does that have to do with Aaron Crofton?"

"Nothing." Radson forced a smile.

Special Agent Warren leaned an elbow on his thigh. His eyebrows almost met. Lily imagined an expedition of miniature cosmeticians had cut a swath between them. He asked, "Did you see Mr. Wilkins that morning?"

"Mr. who?"

"Wilkins. The custodian."

Heat rose to Lily's cheeks. Mr. Wilkins, the hero. The only one who had seen her. But it was smoky in the hallway. Could he identify her? Lily stared at them blankly. "No."

The agents paused again. Radson eyed the bandage on Lily's hand and asked, "What happened to your hand?"

Lily lifted her hand and turned her wrist, examining it as if it didn't belong to her. "I was running . . . I slipped on—there was . . . all this blood. There was broken glass. It heals, but every time I play my violin, the cuts open again."

Her mother rushed into the room. "That's all," she announced. "We have to go."

Stephanie Jeong's presumed authority over these federal agents seemed to stun them. They snapped to their feet. Lily plowed both hands through her hair, where the insect had migrated. It was time to leave for Violet's piano lesson. Because death, and pipe bombs, and federal investigations could not stop piano lessons.

Special Agent Radson handed Lily a business card. "If you think of anything else, *anything*, you can call or email me. Call anytime."

As Stephanie showed them to the door, Lily bolted for the staircase. The urge to strip herself of these clothes, to scrub her body clean, overwhelmed her. She ran up the first few steps then halted just before the landing. Her sister sat there stone-faced, her arms folded over her chest.

"Move," Lily ordered.

Violet glared. "Why did you lie?"

***

Just past two in the morning, Lily packed up her paint and brushes, her glue and wax and blades, and tucked them all away in their hiding places. She checked the funeral flowers she had pilfered and hung to dry behind the water heater where no one would find them. The upside-down flowers looked like orphans, so fragile and afraid. Soon they would take their place in her masterpiece. They would be beautiful again.

She crept back upstairs, but instead of her own room, slipped into her sister's room. Violet slept on her back with one arm above her head. Moonlight bled over her delicate features. She was a sleeping fairy. A sprite lost in some fantastical dream. Lily climbed on top of her and clamped a hand over her mouth.

Violet's eyes shot open in terror.

"Do *not* make noise," Lily instructed. "If you wake Mom or Dad, you'll regret it."

Her sister's expression morphed to pure annoyance. Lily lifted her hand, but only to press both of Violet's shoulders into the mattress.

"Get off me," Violet hissed.

Lily didn't budge. She knew she'd never find another moment to corner her sister without her mother's nosy interference. "Tell me what you meant earlier. Why did you say I was lying?"

Violet squirmed beneath her and quickly found the strength to push Lily aside. "You're crazy. Leave me alone; it's the middle of the night."

"Not until you tell me what you think you know."

"You lied to the FBI." Violet sat up and twisted the leg of a worn sock monkey that she still slept with. "The freaking *FBI!*"

"I did not!"

"I saw you. You know that boy." Violet pointed to the window.

Lily shifted onto her hands and knees. The bed bounced beneath them. "When did you see me?"

"One night last summer. I woke from the weirdest dream where I was in the backseat of the car, going to piano lessons. Mom stopped at a red light. I looked out the window, and there was an alien with a beet-shaped face and huge blank eyes staring into the car window. It freaked me out. I got up to pee. I heard a noise. It was you. I watched you sneak outside and go over there."

Lily shook her head. "You didn't see me. You were dreaming. It was all part of your stupid alien dream."

"If it was a dream and you're not lying, then why are you harassing me in the middle of the night? And why are you acting so crazy?"

"Why am I acting crazy?" Lily caught the feral sound of her voice—too loud in the small room. She leaned closer to her sister and spoke through gritted teeth. "My school was shot up by a psychopath. I saw a girl with her face shot off."

"I know. That's why Mom is making you go to that group therapy thing."

Lily collapsed onto her sister's pillow. "Group therapy? Like that's going to help. All those crying people in a hospital where kids died. I don't want to go. She can't make me go."

"Of course she can." Violet laid her head next to Lily's. Her voice softened. "Why did you go to Aaron's house that night? Did you know he was going to do this?"

*That night.* One night. That was all Violet knew. Lily slipped her body beneath the covers. Words floated out of her, but they didn't belong to her. She watched them swirl with the dust motes in the beam of moonlight. "I didn't know. I had no idea. He had just moved in. He didn't know anyone. He asked me to come over. I felt sorry for him. But he was weird. I told him I couldn't be his friend; my parents wouldn't allow it. He called me a cunt. I never saw him after that."

Lily recalled Aaron's words, his arms wrapped around her, his breath warm on her temple: *"Parents project their fears and failings onto their kids. Then wonder why we're so fucked up."*

"You could have said that to the FBI," Violet said.

"No, I couldn't. Because Mom was listening. If she knew I went to a boy's house in the middle of the night, she'd kill me. And then Dad would bring me back to life and kill me again."

Violet rolled onto her side to face Lily. "I don't believe that."

"Then you're an idiot. They're tyrants. They don't understand what it's like. They think they're protecting us, wrapping us in their strange world instead of letting us be in the real world. They think they're molding us into brilliant young women. But they've molded us into nothing."

"That's not true."

"It's true. I don't know how to make friends. If I make a friend, I can't keep them. No matter how hard I work, no matter what I do, I'm invisible. I'm nothing. Nobody sees me. Aaron saw me. That's why I went over there. If people find out . . . my life is over."

The room fell silent. Exhaustion slammed against Lily. She pulled the covers up to her chin and closed her eyes. Violet curled next to Lily. Their cold feet twisted together.

Violet whispered, "You're not nothing."

Lily tried to let the words into her heart, but her chest felt like an empty cell. She wished she could tell her sister everything, but Violet wouldn't understand. And she couldn't be trusted. Lily could trust no one with her secret. In a few hours, she'd have to go back to school. How would she walk down those halls where the carnage occurred and not let her secret slip? Her stomach knotted.

Her whole life, she wanted to be somebody, to be recognized, to feel important.

Tomorrow she would have to perfect being nothing.

**Joe**

Two weeks after the shooting, the school reopened, and classes were back in session. On his third lap driving around the school, Joe spotted a tall, thin boy in a black hoodie carrying a long fabric case under his arm. The boy loped across the grass toward the school as if he were on a mission. Joe's heart jumped. *Is that the accomplice? Coming to finish what ABC started?*

He screeched the police car to a stop, leaped out, and ran toward the kid, yelling, "Stop! Police. Stop."

The kid turned around and looked at him, his face blanching beneath his long sandy bangs. He waited for Joe to catch up to him. "Yes, Sir?"

"What's in the case?"

"My violin." The boy's voice trembled.

Joe put his hand on the hilt of his gun, but he didn't pull it. "Open the case."

The boy made a series of faces, his eyebrows raised, his mouth open, but he squatted, put the case on the ground, and unzipped it. Inside was a shiny violin and a bow. The kid looked up at Joe.

"Okay. You can zip it up. Why aren't you in school already?"

The boy put his palm against his cheek. "Dentist appointment. Do you want to see my note?" His empty hand tapped his pants pocket.

Joe remembered the rock holding the side door opened. A flash of panic ran through him. Was a door left open for another shooter? "How were you going to get in the building?"

The kid reached in his pocket and took out a note. He shook it in the air. "I buzz in the front and go to the office with my late excuse. Do you want to see it?"

Joe thought he detected a sneer, but he waved his hand. "No. Go on."

The boy turned away, and Joe walked back to the vehicle, his heart still thrashing against his ribs. Only when he was behind the wheel did Joe realize he had re-traumatized the boy by stopping him like that. This wasn't the solution. He couldn't stop every teenager with a backpack or instrument case. Again, he felt helpless.

Without thinking how it would look to anyone outside on the school grounds, he threw his head back and howled, letting the sound of his anguish ricochet against every surface in the vehicle. He slammed his fists against the steering wheel. Finally exhausted, he sank back in the seat, his head lowered as if he were praying. There had to be something he could do to make things right again.

At dinner last night, a quick meal of reheated casserole his mother brought over, he asked Sofia if she wanted to leave the area. It was the first time he'd tried to have a conversation with her since her best friend died. She wasn't talking at all. She wasn't herself. She didn't even pick at her food anymore. She just sat in front of it like it was a penance she had to perform. Dark circles under her eyes told him she still wasn't sleeping. She stayed in her room most of the time. He had no idea what to do for her, how to save her from her grief. Emilia would have known what to do. She always knew how to make Sofia feel better, how to make her laugh, or distract her with her favorite TV show. Without Emilia, everything was ten times harder.

"We could move anywhere. I can get a job on a different police force in any state. We can go someplace safer. A small town out west, maybe, or up north. How about Vermont? I've heard it's really nice there."

"Vermont? *This* is my home, Papi. I lost Caitlyn. I can't lose everything else." She put her face in her hands. "Besides," she said, lifting her wet face, "if we're not safe here, we're not safe anywhere." She picked up her fork and dragged it through the salad but didn't take a bite.

Joe swallowed. His daughter was teaching him now; they couldn't just run away. "You're right, *mi alma*; we have to change the way things are." But first, he had to get his daughter and himself through her best friend's funeral.

**FirstPrincipals @EvelynThompsonEDD**
Another funeral today. We don't know the full measure of
this catastrophe until it hits our own school and we see all
those lives destroyed in front of our eyes. Rockwell High
mourns but we will persist. #RockwellStrong

# CHAPTER SIX

## Mike

After all their hopes had been raised, after he and Lisa were sure Caitlyn was going to not only survive but be all right, be able to walk and run again, in a minute, she was gone. "A blood clot as a result of her injury reached her heart," Dr. Kalish told them. "We did everything we could to prevent it. I am so sorry."

"No," Lisa had cried. She'd pounded her fists into Mike's chest. He wanted to punch, too, the doctor, the resident, the wall, anyone or anything. Instead, he hugged his wife and tried to comfort her as his tears mingled with hers.

Nothing in Mike's life compared to the cruelty of his daughter's death. He had always fought against cruelty, whether confronting playground bullies as a boy, arguing with racist high school classmates, or retrieving body parts in Iraq after the Humvee behind his was hit by an IED. But none of those incidents compared to the loss of his daughter. He was her father. He was supposed to protect her.

He was outraged that the shooter survived while he would never see his beloved Caitlyn grow up. Sure, the killer would be convicted in a court of law, but this was a no death penalty state. Aaron Blake Crofton would live out his life in prison at taxpayers' expense, the same taxpayers whose families he had ripped apart. He might even take online college courses while behind bars or write a book about his miserable life. *Was that justice for Caitlyn?* Mike wanted revenge, but he didn't know how to get it.

For now, he had to focus on the funeral arrangements and the heart-wrenching task of selecting a cemetery plot. Thank God for Patrick. His youngest son came home from college and just took over, getting meals on the table and fielding phone calls from relatives, friends, and the media. Mike didn't know Patrick had it in him. He sometimes worried about his younger son. Not at all like his big brother, Connor, who had followed in their father's footsteps, Patrick wanted to be a writer, a profession that probably suited him. Still, Mike couldn't let go of his worry that

Patrick might be gay, like his Uncle Sean, even though Lisa told him that would be okay.

They postponed the funeral for two days to allow Connor to fly home from his army base in Germany. Mike picked him up at the airport. "I'm so sorry I told you not to come before . . ." He couldn't finish his thought: *before Caitlyn died.*

"It's all right, Dad," his son replied. They gave each other a tentative hug, neither comfortable with a touchy-feely display of emotion.

Nine years apart in age, Connor and Caitlyn had never been particularly close. Although Mike was sure his son cared for his little sister, Connor had just ignored her most of the time. He had no interest in the childish things that interested her. Patrick, on the other hand, would sometimes take the time to play soccer with her or drive her to the mall. Lisa often said Patrick considered his seven-years-younger sister a substitute for a pet, which she refused to allow in her orderly house.

Mike and his older son arrived home to find Patrick fixing dinner in the kitchen. After greeting each other with insults and friendly punches—*some things never change*—Connor asked, "Where's Mom?"

Patrick opened the refrigerator, retrieved three cans of beer, and handed them around. "She's lying down. Took a sedative. I hope it's working."

They drank quietly for a while. Mike was never one to talk much about his feelings, and his older son was cast in the same mold. Finally, Patrick said, "I miss my baby sister already. I miss her silly giggles and all her drama." He quickly wiped his eyes.

"She was such a kid, and we didn't have much in common before I was deployed overseas," Connor admitted. "I always thought we'd get to know each other better once we were both adults."

"Don't get me wrong, boys, but I always thought I wanted only sons until Caitlyn came around. A daughter is . . ." He choked up. They finished their beers in silence, each occupied with his own memories.

By training and temperament, Mike was a problem solver. He quickly determined he didn't have to worry about his sons. Each would deal with his grief in his own way. But it scared him that Lisa, whom he had often jokingly referred to as the commander-in-chief of their household, had completely fallen apart. His wife was a mess. There was no other way to describe her. The woman known for her spotless home now didn't care if there were dirty dishes in the sink or laundry littering the bedroom rug. He didn't care about the dishes or the laundry; he cared about Lisa. He just wanted his wife to be the way she'd always been.

When they had to select the clothing Caitlyn would be buried in, Lisa stood in front of her daughter's closet and rejected every outfit Mike brought out. Each one recalled a memory of Caitlyn. "No, not the *quinceañera* dress," Lisa said. "Too fancy. But remember how happy she and Sofia were that day?"

Patrick held up a blue plaid dress. "That's what she wore the first day of school," Lisa said. "No, not something that reminds me of the school."

Feeling frustrated and helpless at the same time, Mike blurted out, "We've got to pick something, Lisa."

Lisa stared at the bulletin board hanging on the wall, filled with fabric swatches and sketches for her project with Sofia. "I can't. I just can't." She grabbed the shabby Paddington Bear, Caitlyn's childhood favorite, from her daughter's bed and sat down, hugging the stuffed animal to her chest.

Patrick must have overheard the commotion because he suddenly appeared.

"I've got this," he said. Sliding the hangers over the closet rail, he appraised each with a critical eye. "Here's one with the sales tags still on it. Never worn." He held up a Kelly-green dress for their approval.

*That should do it. No memories attached.* "Very Irish. I like it," Mike said.

"What do you think, Mom?"

"That's the dress she bought to wear to a party Eric invited her to. I think Caitlyn would approve." That was the first Mike had heard about a party date, but what did that matter now?

In a way, going to the funeral home provided relief from their house, which felt increasingly claustrophobic. Every room was filled with reminders of Caitlyn, her fashion magazines on the coffee table, her lip gloss in the bathroom, the kiwis that only Caitlyn ate rotting in the fruit bowl. For the first time since Caitlyn's death, Lisa dressed herself in something other than sweats and put on makeup.

Lisa began sobbing the minute they entered the flower-filled parlor. "Your child in a coffin is something no parent should ever have to see," Lisa whispered. Mike knew eleven other Rockwell High parents had endured that sight. And, even if they hadn't lost their own child, everyone at the school was traumatized. More than a week after the school community thought all the victims had been laid to rest, its citizens had to relive the tragedy once again.

"Mom, look at all the flowers," Patrick said. "Everybody loved Caitlyn." The parlor glowed with pink roses and carnations, coneflowers, and asters, a tribute to the girl with the pink stripe in her hair.

It seemed that all of Rockwell Township came to the funeral home. The cruelty of Caitlyn's death affected the entire community. They had assumed the fourteen previous funerals the week before were the end of their tragedy, the worst behind them, only to be proven wrong. Mike watched teachers and students console one another as they solemnly signed the guest book, experts now in funeral protocol.

Eric, the boy who had brought Caitlin a stuffed panda in the hospital, came with his parents. He looked stricken, like he couldn't believe she was dead. *He'll find another girl to fall in love with, but no girl is going to replace my daughter.*

Sofia and her father came early and stayed the entire time. The girl looked shell-shocked as she stared at the casket. "Caitlyn loved that dress," she said. "I'm glad she got to wear it."

Smiling at Sofia's newly colored swath of pink hair, Mike choked out a reply. "Thank you for being such a good friend to Caitlyn." Sofia sat down next to Lisa and clutched her hand. This appeared to comfort his wife.

Joe Hernandez shook his hand. "I'm so sorry, Mike. The girls were such good friends. I understand a little what you're going through. I lost my wife, you remember. Let me know if there's anything I can do for you, anything at all."

Mike thanked him and introduced Joe to his sons. "This is the policeman who was the first to enter the school to go after the shooter. If it wasn't for him, Caitlyn might not have survived that day."

"Thank you for all you did, Officer Hernandez," Patrick said.

The cop bit his lip. "I wish I could have saved them all."

A tall man with a full head of hair and immaculately dressed in a tailored suit and silk tie walked up to them. "Uncle Sean?" Patrick said. They hugged. Their interaction made Mike a little queasy. He worried Patrick would be influenced by his uncle instead of by himself.

"I wanted to pay my respects, Mike," Sean Moran said. "Caitlyn was such a lovely child. I hope it's all right with you that I've come."

"Of course," Mike replied, patting his brother's back.

"It's been what, three years?" Sean asked.

Mike nodded. He regretted depriving his brother of Caitlyn all that time.

Sean shook Connor's hand. "I'm going to say hello to your mother."

*Good move*, Mike thought. *That's enough of my brother for now. I've got all the emotion I can handle at the moment.*

Parents of other victims approached Mike to introduce themselves. He struggled to resist their sorrow and hold back his own tears. The viewing hours were almost over when a petite black woman, too young to be the mother of a high school student, walked up to him.

"Mr. Moran, I'm a nurse. I was working in the emergency room when your daughter was first brought in. I wanted you to know she was so brave."

"Thank you, Mrs. ..."

"Robinson. Charmaine Robinson. My husband was a guidance counselor at Rockwell High." Her voice broke. "He was also killed." Her pretty face crumbled, and she covered it with a tissue.

Connor stepped in and encircled her in his arms. "It's all right," he said as she leaned against him and sobbed. "We're all going to get through this."

Mike said nothing; his lips stretched against his teeth. *How are any of us going to get through this when that bastard is still breathing? When whoever let him into the school is still breathing?*

## Sofia

Sofia had been ten years old at her mother's funeral. She'd hid her face in Papi's musty suit. The fabric tickled her nose and absorbed her tears. In the coffin, her mother's face was stone, one dull hand on top of the other. Sofia didn't want to kiss her. Mama wasn't there. Wallpaper roses had decorated the inside of the casket. Abuela kept mumbling to herself, her fingers moving back and forth over the coffin's edge. Papi took Sofia's hand and led her away. Her new shoes were too big and clunky, and she had to shuffle over the bouncy carpet so they wouldn't fall off her feet.

That was five years ago. Today Papi wore the same suit with gold buttons he had worn to Mama's funeral. She didn't put her face against him. *Was his suit still musty?* Sofia sat close to the back of the church. She didn't want to get any closer. *Amazing Grace* floated out from the organ pipes. Instead of singing along with the other mourners, Sofia stared at the pink balloons attached to Caitlyn's casket.

A soft voice, like Caitlyn's when she was telling a secret, whispered to Sofia. *That's not me in the casket. I'm in you. I'm with my parents, my brothers. I'm spread.*

Sofia looked up and around her, her eyes startled and wide. *Cat, is that you?*

*Yes. I'm here. I need to tell you something.*

*Is that really you? If you're not in the casket, where are you?*

No answer.

*What do you need to tell me?*

"Sofia, look at me." Papi shook her, and she looked up. "What is it, *mi hija*? I was talking to you, and you wouldn't answer me." Her father took her hand. "The service is over. They're taking the casket out. It's time to go."

Sofia watched the pallbearers carry the casket. *Cat, don't leave.* "No, Papi, I don't want to go to the cemetery." How could she bear to see her friend being put into the ground?

Papi stroked her hair. "Okay, I'll be in the car." Sofia nodded and watched him, her familiar, reassuring Papi. His steady walk gave her strength, even though she felt like half of her had disappeared.

As the church emptied, a small girl hurried up the aisle toward the altar. Her dark hair swished over thin, pinched shoulders. *Who is she?*

## Lily

This funeral had more pink than white. Pink roses, carnations, asters. Very few lilies. People wore pink or splashes of pink on their black clothes. Many girls had dyed a stripe of their hair pink in tribute to Caitlyn Moran. And when Lily had pleaded with her mother to skip this funeral, Stephanie pinned a pink ribbon to her blouse and said, "You're going."

Now Lily shuffled down the crowded aisle, careful to avoid the family—the mother who could barely stand, the father with the military posture and blank face, two bewildered older brothers. Exiting the church, she got separated from her own family. When she spun around to find them, she knocked into Keisha Washington.

"Sorry," Lily muttered.

Keisha stood six inches taller than Lily, but today, her slumped shoulders made their heads nearly touch. For a moment, Keisha studied Lily with her red-rimmed eyes. First, she seemed startled; then, her expression changed swiftly to recognition and discomfort. They hadn't spoken since the shooting—actually, since the debate. The whole scene seemed to be playing in Keisha's mind. Lily saw it too, standing at opposite podiums, Keisha's confident voice hitting like a jackhammer, her body growing with each point she earned until she lifted her giant boot and brought it right down on Lily's head.

"Hey, Lily," Keisha said softly. "How're you holding up?"

It was strange to witness Keisha in this subdued state. Before October fifteenth, Keisha Washington was always on her game. Aaron changed everyone. Unsure if she meant since the shooting or debate, Lily stammered, "Okay, I guess."

"Yeah, it's still so . . . surreal." Keisha's gaze fell to their feet. Her fingers traced the bumps of her braids. "That day keeps playing in a loop in my head. I keep hearing the shots. Keep feeling Mr. Robinson's body in my arms."

*The shooting, she's talking about the shooting.* Lily adjusted her glasses. Keisha was with Mr. Robinson. Lily told the FBI she had stopped in his office at the time the bombs exploded. How long before their stories were compared?

"He died, Lily. Right in my arms." Keisha held out her hands, palms up, and repeated, "Right in my arms. But he didn't die for nothing. I'm going to change things. I have a plan. A demonstration at the gun show next week. Something has to be done. Kids can't be target practice anymore."

There it is, Lily thought, a spark of the old Keisha, the girl who thinks she can change the world. Since elementary school, they'd been in the same academic circle but never the same friend circle. Lily used to wonder why she never earned friendship status with Keisha. When wondering became too painful, when she blamed it on her own defective social mechanics, Lily switched her motive. If she couldn't be Keisha's friend, she would be her competitor. But even in that, she failed. Now Lily watched Keisha search the faces in the churchyard, probably looking for one of her friends. Instead, Keisha turned back to Lily, her expression sharp with curiosity.

"Who do you think did it?" Keisha asked.

"Did what?"

"Let a homicidal maniac into our school."

The words spiked Lily's chest. She flicked her eyes away, up to the church steeple that seemed to bend and warp, aiming its pointed cross at Lily's heart.

"Maybe it was no one," Lily said. "I heard a door was propped open with a rock. Maybe he's the one that propped it open. The FBI will figure it out."

Keisha huffed. "It's been two weeks. When they questioned me, they didn't seem to know what they were doing.

They'll never figure it out. But I bet I could. I know these kids better than they do."

Lily's cheeks burned. Keisha doesn't know all of these kids. *She doesn't know me. She never tried to know me.* Lily fought the urge to grab hold of Keisha's braids and yank them out of her head. *I bet Keisha wouldn't have fallen for his lie.* A hand touched her elbow. Her father stood at her side.

"Come on, Lily, we have to go."

Lily met Keisha's eyes and said flatly, "You don't know these kids at all."

Her hands shook as her father whisked her toward the car. She tried to exhale her anger away, but air stuck in her lungs when she remembered she told the FBI she'd been with Mr. Robinson. How long did she have before Special Agents Radson and Warren knocked on her door again? She imagined opening the door to find all these grieving families laying their dead loved ones at her feet.

Lily halted. "*Wait!*"

Her father turned, impatience flickering across his silent face. "What is it, Lily? We have to go."

"I forgot something."

She pivoted and hurried back toward the church doors. She ignored her father's voice and pushed herself through the whimpering crowd, which was flowing in the opposite direction. At the church steps, the crowd thinned. Lily broke free. She sped up the stone steps, down the red-carpeted aisle, straight up to the wall of flowers at the altar. The church was almost emptied of people. She plucked a pink rose off its stem and squeezed the soft petals until she felt her skin splice open beneath the fresh bandage. She kneeled beneath the wooden cross and cried.

"Please," Lily whispered through her tears. "Please . . ."

A girl's voice said, "The flowers are pretty, aren't they?"

Lily stiffened her body but didn't turn. She pushed the rose into the pocket of her skirt. A moment later, a young girl kneeled beside her. From the corner of her eye, Lily noted the row of friendship bracelets on the girl's wrist. Her voice had a soft echo like she was speaking from a cavern.

"They're taking her to the cemetery now," the girl said, "but I can't go. I can't watch them put her in the ground. Did any of your friends die?"

Lily turned slightly and caught a waterfall of pink hair cascading over the girl's shoulder. Another Caitlyn tribute. "Yes," she said.

"I'm sorry."

Silence fell between them. Lily was afraid to move, afraid to leave this girl alone beneath Jesus.

"She was my best friend," the girl continued. "It doesn't seem real yet. Like she's going to run in and drag me out into the sun. Like we're going to Sweet Frog for frozen yogurt, and she's going to pile gummy worms on top of hers, and I'm going to tell her how disgusting it is, but then pick them off and eat them, too."

At a loss for words, Lily said quietly, "I'm sorry."

"I couldn't go back to school yesterday. I don't know if I ever can. So many people died there. What if there are ghosts?"

Lily looked directly at the girl. "There's no such thing as ghosts."

"But what if there is?"

"We'll send them all to Principal Thompson's office."

The girl's slight smile seemed to hurt her face. She stood and offered her hand. "I'm Sofia."

Lily stood. "Lily."

"They said they're having a support meeting at the hospital next week," Sofia said. "Sort of like therapy or something. Are you going?"

"My mother is making me go. I don't want to."

"I think I'll go. Maybe you could try it."

"I don't think it will help," Lily said.

Sofia looked over her shoulder as she walked down the aisle. "It might."

**Caitlyn**

Without a body, Caitlyn could go anywhere. She rested in the minds of people, several at a time, visiting them, comforting them. It was not always successful, and her peaceful mind accepted that with an open heart.

Her father needed her the most but was the least receptive to her visits. He burned inside. Her coolness of being and presence caused him to grit his teeth, pull back. Mom, though, sweet mom . . . Caitlyn would slip into the rain on her bedroom window or into birds within her sight. She would ride the sighs in her breath and caress her with the breeze and touch her wet, tired cheeks.

She spent most of her fragmented self with Sofia, answering her questions. Sofia was an open gate.

"What was it like to die?" Sofia asked as she lay on her bed in her room with the door closed against the world.

*There was pain; then there wasn't. I could feel it. I knew I was dead.*

"God, it must've been awful."

*It was for a while. Awful for my parents. I was on the ceiling, where I could see everything below me. I was calm, blissful, wonderful. I wanted to tell my parents I was all right. I want everyone to be safe and happy again.*

"How?" Sofia asked.

*By reaching out.*

"I thought I imagined you. That you're just in my head . . . that I'm insane."

*You're not insane. I'm there too, the part of me that's in you.*

Sofia buried her face in the pillow. "So, I'm not talking to you?"

*I have something to tell you. Remember the girl you talked to at my funeral? She was the one I saw in the hall during the shooting. Remember . . . when I told you I left my body?*

Sofia drew in a breath and raised her head, listening.

*That girl had her face in her hands. She was there that day, alive among the dead. Why was she there? Why hadn't she run out the door right next to her?*

"She was probably in shock like the rest of us." Sofia's head dropped back to the pillow. "Why does it matter? Why did we go to school that day?"

*Because we did, and so did that girl. I felt her pain. It was different from the others. She gave off a different color.*

"What do you mean?"

*She wasn't scared the way we were.*

**SenMelWoodrow @melwoodrow**
Very sad that the FBI has not identified the accomplice.
What are they doing with our taxpayer money? Our students and families deserve better. We all need closure so
we can get back to our normal lives.

# CHAPTER SEVEN

## Charmaine

The day after she attended Caitlyn Moran's wake, Charmaine got out of bed and went for a run, something she hadn't done since before Alex died. Her leg muscles throbbed, and her heart pounded until the endorphin buzz that had long ago addicted her to running broke through.

Calm and clarity descended. *I have to go back to work. I'll go crazy just moping around like I have been.*

Back at the townhouse, she called Dr. McGann to tell him she was ready to return. "Are you sure?" The concern in his voice made her realize, as she had at the funeral home, that she was part of a community who cared about Alex's widow.

"Yes," she answered. "I'll see you tomorrow."

The next morning, when her co-workers greeted her with hugs and asked how she was getting along, she secretly hoped they wouldn't repeat this litany every day. She found it another painful reminder that her life had irreversibly changed. When the first patients began to arrive, her discomfort vanished. From then on, everybody focused on the task at hand, saving the lives that they could, easing pain. She needed that, to be necessary and competent again as part of a team working together. In the ER, she was no longer alone or lonely.

The day saw their usual assortment of cases, a middle-aged white man with a mild heart attack, a preschooler with a high fever, and people with no insurance who came to the emergency room for illnesses that could have been prevented. She was standing at the desk awaiting her next patient when the medics brought in the victims of an automobile accident.

A black male lay on a gurney. Blood stained his collar. For just an instant, she thought it was Alex. Her breath caught in her throat, and she thought she was going to faint. She escaped to the nurses' locker room to cry, all her effort to deal with her grief undone.

Lori came in soon after. "You okay, Charmaine?"

"Yes. I'll be fine." She blew her nose. "Just need a minute."

Lori sat down beside her. "Are you seeing a grief counselor?"

Charmaine shook her head. "I don't think I can afford that."

"Doesn't have to cost you anything. The hospital social worker organized a support group for families and friends of the shooting victims. It's going to meet in our Conference Room G every Thursday evening at seven. You should go."

"I won't know anyone there."

"They're all suffering like you, Charmaine. I think you can help each other. Everyone has to figure out their way through this."

**Mike**

Although Patrick volunteered to withdraw from college for the semester to "look after things at home," Mike convinced him to go back to school the week following the funeral. Connor had already flown back to Germany. Just he and Lisa were left to occupy their 2,200-square foot, four-bedroom colonial, a fully decorated house that seemed empty without the sounds of Caitlyn's constantly pinging cell phone, the drone of her sewing machine seeping through her closed bedroom door, and her laughter echoing in his heart.

He escaped to the gun range on the weekend. Pretending the target was ABC, he aimed and pulled the trigger. *What was wrong with that boy?* The bullet pierced the target's head. *Why didn't anyone notice and confine him to a mental hospital?* He shot again and hit the paper ABC's heart this time. Many nights, he dreamed about taking his own AR-15 to the jail where ABC was being held and shooting him just like that, in the chest, a kill shot. It was what the boy deserved, crazy or not. That would be the right thing to do, but even the right thing wouldn't bring Caitlyn back. He shook his head to clear his mind, raised his pistol, and shot again.

On nights when he couldn't sleep, he left for work early and visited Caitlyn's grave. The headstone hadn't been installed yet, but the mound of earth above her buried coffin marked the spot. He let himself cry there, with no one around to witness his grief as the sun came up. A few times during lunch hour, he bought flowers at the grocery and took them to the cemetery. "These are for you, Caitlyn," he said aloud, "I miss you." He waited for a reply—that didn't make sense, he knew—but he longed to hear his daughter's voice again.

He didn't tell Lisa about these visits, and he saw no evidence that his wife had been there. The grave was a reality she wasn't ready to acknowledge. They'd been married so long he expected their reactions to Caitlyn's death would be similar, but they weren't. Lisa retreated, cutting herself off from the world, including him.

He wished Lisa could escape to a job every day like he did, but their frequent moves and young boys had made it impossible for her to have a career of her own during the first ten years of their marriage. When Patrick started first grade, she took a job in an interior design firm. Although she loved the work, when she became pregnant with Caitlyn a year later, she quit and never returned to the workplace. Mike didn't care if she worked outside the home or not. With his military pension and civilian salary, they were better off financially than they had ever been. But if a job would help her recover, he was all for it. He just wanted her to be happy and feared she would never be happy again.

The anxiety medication her doctor prescribed didn't seem to be having an effect. He could no longer recall what Lisa's eyes looked like before their current red and puffy state. His wife was barely holding on, turning into a woman he didn't know. He had often bragged to his army buddies that he found the perfect military wife in Lisa. She had always been up to the challenge, packing for the several household moves dictated by his army career, settling the children in their new schools, coping on her own during his two tours in Iraq. She had run an efficient household, raised three well-behaved children who never got in trouble, and managed their finances.

Now things he had taken for granted no longer applied. Dust appeared on the hardwood floors and unused dining room table. No milk waited in the refrigerator for his morning cereal. He ran out of clean underwear and was forced to figure out how to use the washing machine to do his own laundry. He dealt with it. Most nights, she hadn't fixed a meal, and he got them pizza or carryout from the local Greek restaurant.

He was surprised when he came home one evening to find the kitchen table set and a meal of roasted chicken with rice and beans waiting on the table. "Looks delicious," he said, giving Lisa a kiss. He noticed his wife had combed her hair and put on lipstick, signs her spirits were improving.

"Sofia brought it over today. She said it's a traditional Cuban dish. Her grandparents made it for us."

Mike sat down at the table and dug into the hearty meal. "This is good," he said, *the food and your mood.*

"Sofia is a sweet girl. We had a nice chat," Lisa replied. "I finally got that fabric to her. It felt good to talk about Caitlyn. Sofia misses her too."

Mike reached across the table and patted his wife's hand. He didn't have to say a word. She knew what he meant.

"Anyhow, Sofia said a support group is starting at the hospital for families and friends of the . . . the victims. I'd like us to go."

Mike put down his fork. He had never been in counseling or a support group of any kind in his life, not even after his second Iraq tour. He didn't want to talk about his feelings. He preferred to tough it out, strong and silent. Like Clint Eastwood.

"Do you think that will help?" he asked. He meant, *that won't bring Caitlyn back.*

"Yes. I felt better after Sofia and I talked."

He'd do anything to relieve his wife's sorrow. "Okay," he said. "When do they meet?"

**Sofia**

Sofia tripped over the last stair and stumbled toward her bedroom. "No, Papi, I'm not going back to that school, not ever!" She slammed her door and flung herself on her unmade bed. The idea of going back to school was hard enough when Caitlyn was alive and in the hospital. Now Caitlyn was dead, and she was never going back. Ever.

Sofia had planned to be brave when she thought Caitlyn would be there with her. It was how she coped with the idea of going back. She would help Caitlyn adjust, push her in a wheelchair, make sure she caught up on classes. She had signed them up for the entrepreneur business club so they could learn how to sell their fashions.

Sofia hugged the two fabrics Mrs. Moran had retrieved from Caitlyn's locker to her chest. Both were white—a sheer organic voile and sweet-smelling hemp. The hemp skirt would be the backdrop for an abundance of brightly colored beetles, butterflies, and bees that would swarm from the hem and thin out at the voile bodice. They had wanted to honor the insects of the world. Today she wanted to burn that fabric, blacken the pure white, and forget about the collection of garments they had already made, hanging limp in Sofia's closet.

"I can't go back!" Sofia buried her face in the fabric.

Papi tapped at the door. "You have to. You're not the only one who lost someone."

"But I lost my best friend. No one feels like I do. No one hurts as much as me." Sofia lifted herself up on her elbows.

Papi knocked harder, his wedding ring tapping against the hollowed wood. "Listen, Sofia, there are plenty of people hurting just like us. Think of the Morans; they lost a daughter, a sister. What do you think I felt when I lost your mother? She was my best friend in the world. My whole life changed when she died." He choked and cleared his throat. "But I had to go to work. I had to take care of you. Now you have a job to do. You have to help others get through this."

Sofia hiccupped. How could she help others when she was broken? "The Morans don't have to go to the place where Caitlyn was killed and pretend to care about crap like fruit flies, or dates of wars, or math. How am I going to walk down those halls? How can I eat lunch like nothing happened?"

"You don't have to pretend. The place will never be the same for anyone. You walk down the halls knowing the worst nightmare happened there. You go to your classes and be with each other, knowing that it has changed forever."

"But Papi, what if that person, the accomplice, is still there? Maybe there was more than one person who opened the door. I never want to go back if those guys are there. No one should have to go back."

"We'll find them, I promise. We're all watching."

Sofia slipped off her bed. Her face burned. She unlocked the door and let her father open it. He pulled her to his chest. She gave up, pressed her temple into his lumpy buttons, and let him pat her back. But his quickened heartbeat told her that he was scared, too.

## Lily

On Wednesday, the school held a morning assembly outside in the stadium because the auditorium was still under repair. So were the cafeteria and gymnasium, where Aaron's pipe bombs had damaged the floors and walls. News vans circled the school, along with a huge police presence. Rockwell High was under siege again.

Knowing she wouldn't be able to survive the maudlin remarks from the principal and counselors, the moment of silence, the constant sobbing, Lily skipped the assembly and roamed the halls instead. She found herself at the auditorium where yellow tape blocked the entrance doors. Aaron had a weird yellow phobia, and now it was everywhere, like ribbon reminders of his carnage. Lily peeled off one end of tape and opened an auditorium door. The smell of burnt carpet escaped the dark interior. She took a few steps inside and inspected the damage. Several seats and a patch of carpet had been removed, but the stage was unharmed. Lily walked down the aisle, remembering every step she had taken the day of the debate. She was not prepared that day. For the first time in her life, she was not prepared.

"Jesus, Dad," she had pleaded after dinner the night before. "It's only the beginning of October. I have time to make up this grade—"

"Don't argue and don't say Jesus like that. No more drawings and no more distractions. You need to focus. Now more than ever if you're going to apply for early admissions."

She had received one B on a stats test, and her father had confiscated her art supplies, packing them all in plastic bins, duct taping the lids, and stowing them high on the metal shelves in the garage. Lily looked to her mother for help, but Stephanie turned to the sink and furiously scrubbed the dinner dishes. Violet shrank out of the room with one hand over her mouth. Was she laughing? Lily tore at her napkin.

"This isn't fair! It's one grade, my senior year—"

"Enough!" Her father's palm slammed the table. His sharp voice cut through Lily. "I suggest you save your arguments for your debate team meeting tomorrow."

Lily leaped from the table, her chair legs screeching over the ceramic tile floor. She barricaded herself in her room and stewed until she knew her family had gone to sleep. At midnight, she sprinted through pouring rain to the unlocked sliding glass door in Aaron's walkout basement. He was down there, still awake, his shirtless body a silhouette in the blue light of the television. He calmly set down his game remote and held her tear-streaked face in both hands as her rage spilled in torrents on his basement floor.

"I hate him; I hate him, I *hate him*. How could he do it? My art is the only thing I enjoy, the only thing that keeps me sane—"

"Shssh." Aaron brushed her wet hair off her forehead. "I will fix this. I promise."

His fingers on her skin medicated her like a shot of morphine in her veins. Lily calmed for a moment, then a surge from deep inside pushed her to her toes. For the first time in all of their clandestine meetings, she kissed him first. She could not stop. Aaron peeled off her wet clothes. That rage pulsed through her, transmitted to him, made them move their bodies in ways they had never done. Lily's mind blanked. Her heart splintered. The pain stopped.

She never slept that night. The next day each school period was a daze. She wondered if this was how it felt to be hungover. Her regret mounted with each bell. Self-loathing kicked in around the fifth period. What was wrong with her? Was she trying to throw her life away to spite her father or have sex with a boy?

After classes, Lily moved down the auditorium aisle unprepared and unnerved by Keisha Washington's cheery presence. Keisha held court at her team's table, wielding her lacrosse stick like a scepter. Her smile captivated her audience; her laughter pooled over the auditorium seats like a cool lake for Lily to drown in.

The steps to the stage felt like climbing a mountain. Lily reminded herself today was just a Lincoln-Douglas format practice. She was given the negative side, disputing that talent was more important than hard work. It should be an easy argument to win. Obviously, hard work was more important. She was a walking example. But she didn't practice last night. Could she still smash Keisha?

The faculty adviser, Mrs. Ferra, told everyone that today's practice would be like a dress rehearsal for the weekend's debate against South Hills High. "Do your best," she said. "But relax."

"Good afternoon, faculty, students, and guests," Keisha began, the words falling confidently from her lips. "Today, I'd like you to consider something about yourself. What is it that you love to do? What is it that you'd say you're good at—a skill, or sport, or hobby, or yes, even a *job* that you like to immerse yourself in? Something that you're passionate about, that you *want* to do, no matter how difficult. Something that makes the hours on the clock disappear. That passion, that drive, that love for what you do, that is your God-given talent shining through you, and today I am going to prove that talent is far more important than hard work."

As Keisha continued her opening statement, Lily felt herself shrinking in her chair. She thought about what she loved to do more than anything. Her art. Her passion was boxed and taped up like a hostage in her garage. And her years of hard work—of late-night studying, doing extra credit on weekends when everyone else was out partying—gave her nothing but an emptiness in her heart the size of a canyon.

When Keisha finished, she lifted her chin in an I-dare-you-to-top-that gesture. Lily rose and spouted her prepared statement, but she was completely detached from her words. Her speech was rushed, her voice shaky. She only seemed capable of projecting anger. She tried to reign herself in but felt like she was flailing in the deep end of a pool, far from anything to grab onto to save herself.

They continued back and forth, affirmative and negative rebuttals. Lily struggled in her arguments while Keisha's chin continued its superior lift. *It's just practice. Relax.* Lily wanted to relax. She wanted to laugh with ease like Keisha Washington, skirt by on her talents, paint a piece of work so beautiful, so powerful it would make her father fall to his knees in tearful praise. And she wanted to sleep. More than anything, she wanted to lay her head on Aaron's shoulder and sleep forever.

Drama kids began to filter into the back of the auditorium ahead of their rehearsal time. The dozen debate students lounged in the front rows with barely any attention on the stage. Even Mrs. Ferra was on her phone. Lily was invisible at her best *and* her worst. Nothing she did mattered. When Mrs. Ferra announced the winner, Keisha pumped her fist in victory.

"Let's review some points—"

"No," Lily said. The word came out and hung on the stage like a spider dangling from the lights.

Mrs. Ferra looked up from her notepad. "Excuse me, Miss Jeong, did you have a question?"

"No," she repeated.

"No . . . what?"

Lily's mind left the stage and went back to last night, in her kitchen, her father's almost victorious expression as he packed away her paints and brushes and other tools. The *scritching* sound of the tape as he yanked off long strips and plastered them to the bins. And then it was as if he picked her up and stuffed her in the next bin, tucking her arms and legs in tightly so that she couldn't kick or punch the lid open. *Scritch . . . scritch.* She couldn't move. She couldn't breathe.

*"No! Noooo!"*

In the auditorium, Lily pounded the podium, her screams hitting the walls all the way in the back of the room. She gasped for breath and caught the eyes on her.

The astonished faces. The snickers that soon turned into laughter. Not everyone laughed. Some just looked at her with pity.

Now in the empty auditorium with the missing seats, Lily heard an echo of that laughter. She thought about her meltdown on the untouched stage. *He didn't throw the pipe bomb far enough.* Lily pressed her thumb into her palm, berating herself for having such an evil thought. She hurried out of the room, not bothering to replace the yellow tape.

Her path took her to the boarded wall where the glass had been shot out of the administrative offices, the fresh paint where bullet holes had been spackled. She stood on the spot where she had slipped on a puddle of blood. The freshly waxed floor gleamed. A shadow moved across it. Lily's eyes shot up just as a figure moved into the biology lab. Her feet unconsciously drew her toward the room. She stopped just outside the door. Inside, a girl played with the focus of a microscope. She wore a peaceful smile. A swath of pink hair covered one eye. She looked at Lily and said, "I almost died here."

A chill raked Lily's body.

"Hey!"

A police officer appeared at the end of the hall. He moved toward Lily.

"What are you doing out here? Shouldn't you be at the assembly?"

Lily stood frozen as the man approached. His mouth moved, but the pulse in her ears drowned the sound of his voice. Now he was beside her, trying not to look intimidating even though his eyes were as hard as granite.

"I said, I need to look inside your backpack."

As Lily handed over her backpack, she glanced into the biology lab. The girl was gone. She must be hiding, Lily thought. Or was she really there at all? When the police officer finished his search, his face muscles relaxed. Lily read the shiny nameplate above his right pocket: Hernandez, J.

"I'm sorry," Hernandez, J. said, "it's the policy for the time being."

Until the investigation into the accomplice is concluded, Lily thought. The policy had blared through the loudspeakers with the morning's announcements.

"What are you doing out here?" he repeated.

Lily's mind raced. The new policy also said absolutely no one was allowed in the hall without a pass. Everyone had to be accounted for at all times. Sign in and sign out sheets in every classroom. *For everyone's protection.* Her hand suddenly throbbed. She held it out and caught her breath. Bright red blood seeped through her tattered bandage. She hadn't realized her nails had been digging fresh wounds this entire time.

"I was going to see the nurse," she said. "But I stopped . . . this was where . . ." Her eyes watered. "This was where I saw a girl who was shot."

Hernandez gently cradled her hand. His skin was warm, his eyes now soft with concern. He leaned slightly, bringing his eyes closer to hers, like he wanted her to believe him when he said, "It's okay. You're going to be okay."

A small sense of relief and victory swirled through Lily. But more than that, she felt exhausted. She walked with the police officer wondering how long she would be able to keep this up.

**FirstPrincipals @EvelynThompsonEDD**
So proud of my Rockwell High students and faculty, pulling together, coming back as one community stronger than ever. We can face anything together. #RockwellStrong

# CHAPTER EIGHT

## Keisha

The convention center was wall-to-wall people, men and women, old and young, well dressed and in grunge. Whole families came here together to buy guns, the way they went to the county fair or a street festival to have fun. Keisha could smell funnel cakes frying. American flags and patriotic slogans hung from the ceiling. Four hundred booths displayed weapons of every caliber and action for sale. A gun for every season, she thought. The smell of gun oil and sulfur wafted through the huge hall. Her head spun, and her skin felt cold.

She had convinced her drama friends to do this by showing them her research about the gun show loophole. They hadn't believed her at first, but she'd pulled up the Gun Control Act on the federal government's Alcohol, Tobacco, and Firearms agency's website and pointed to the words on the screen. "Check it out."

*An unlicensed person may sell a firearm to another unlicensed person in their state of residence, and similarly, an unlicensed person may buy a firearm from another unlicensed person who resides in the same state.*

"What does that mean, exactly?" Steve asked.

Keisha put her hands on her hips and gave Steve her X-ray look. "It means we can buy guns from an unlicensed seller who lives in our state, which, according to the ATF, will be about a quarter of the sellers at the gun show. We happen to live in one of the thirty-three states that doesn't regulate gun sales between unlicensed sellers and buyers. And neither does the federal government. So, no background checks, no age requirement, no ID, no record of the sale."

"We just walk up to a booth and buy guns?" Steve asked.

"Yes, from sellers who aren't federally licensed. If they'll sell us guns, we buy them with our parents' credit cards."

The plan included recording teenagers buying as many weapons as they could using only a driver's license and a credit card. Their parents would be furious, but that was a small price to pay to make their point. After they bought them, they'd turn the guns into the police to be melted down. Steve would wave his magic techie wand, and they'd have a powerful movie they could put up on social media. It seemed so logical at the time.

Now, as she stood at a black-draped table in booth 352 and hefted an AR-15 into her arms, it seemed like a crazy idea.

The seller helped her adjust her grip on the long gun. Keisha looked over her shoulder at Steve, who was recording the transaction on his phone. She didn't smile. *Is this surge of power what ABC felt?*

She looked around to see if she could spot anyone else from her group in the crush of people at the show. A few days ago, she'd sat through her first classes following the shooting. Every second was agony—a memory, an image, the fear in her body kept her from focusing on learning anything. All over the school, kids stopped anywhere, alone and in groups, and sank to their knees. Keisha found herself at Samantha's locker, weeping. Within seconds friends had wound their arms around her. Contact helped.

Her friends had fanned out across the convention floor, testing their theory that within three weeks of a school shooting, they could buy weapons to commit mass murder without anyone asking any questions. After thirty minutes, they were supposed to assemble outside at the front of the convention hall. They planned to go live with their message.

"Think of this as an experiment," Keisha explained when the group squirmed at the idea.

She hadn't been able to convince Sofia, who just shook her head and looked at the floor. "I won't hold a gun," Sofia said. "I can't do it." Keisha didn't push her. She totally got what Sofia was saying.

"It suits you," the saleswoman said. "We have it in pink."

Keisha's head jerked around. "A pink gun? I'll take it."

"Do you want ammo? I can show you how to load it."

All the breath went out of her. She wanted to wail. But she couldn't break down. That would screw everything up. "No. I don't need ammo." She passed the woman her mother's credit card and waited to see what would happen.

"Do you want a carry case?" the saleswoman asked. "Hard or soft? We've got a pink camo to match the gun." Her tone was the same as if she were asking if Keisha wanted sprinkles on her ice cream cone. *Pink camo. For hiding in a candy-colored world.*

"Soft," Keisha said, barely able to get the sound out of her mouth.

The saleswoman didn't ask for an ID. She inserted the credit card, held out her iPad, and pointed to the line. "Sign here with your finger."

Keisha signed her mother's name.

Ten minutes later—the time it took to thread her way through the crowd—she was outside the building, doubled over, worried she would pass out.

Between them, ten kids had bought twenty weapons. They stood next to each other, the weapons out of their cases, held in the air or slung across their bodies. Two kids unrolled the banner Sofia had designed in their school colors. *Do You Hear Us Now?* Steve filmed them standing there, silent, the breeze rippling the banner, and then posted the video on every social media platform. They all shared it to their followers and waited for it to go viral.

"We're up to a hundred-thousand likes on Insta," Steve said five minutes later as TV vans rolled up in front of the convention center.

Gun show buyers walking into or out of the building taunted them. Police cars arrived. The show organizer came outside and told them to move along. The convention center was private property, and they didn't have permission to be there.

The students walked as a group to the parking lot and performed a perfect parade circle, just as they'd practiced. A crowd of people formed around them. Passersby took sides, shouting at each other. A young woman with her blonde ponytail pulled through the back of her baseball cap, stuck her face in Keisha's, and shouted, "You fucking bitch. We have a right to our guns. You don't belong here. Go home."

Two uniformed police officers walked up to Steve. "You gotta move along, kid."

Steve nodded cordially and ignored them. He looked around at the crowd pushing toward them. "It might get rough here," he whispered to Keisha, but he kept recording.

The shouting increased. Onlookers pushed each other; the officers turned to confront the crowd. A national cable news reporter thrust a microphone in Keisha's face. Even though her stomach quaked, Keisha said to the reporter, "Enough is enough. Today we've demonstrated how easy it is for kids to buy weapons that kill children in the places where we're supposed to be safe. We can't allow one more child to be shot at school."

An image of Alex Robinson flashed across her mind and channeled her rage. "We can't allow one more teacher to die, saving the lives of students." Her voice broke, and she struggled to get her breath.

Steve, his chin stubbled by his first beard, stepped up to the microphone. "We've had enough families waiting for a call or text that never comes." His face turned red, but he stood his ground. "Our children and teachers are dying. We need to change our laws. One child is worth more than all your guns."

Keisha stepped away and let other kids talk into the microphones. She didn't need to be the spokesperson. People kept shouting in her face. She brushed them off without replying, but blood pounded in her ears. The next event they planned would be a rally at the school. Hopefully, all this attention would draw a friendlier crowd.

She checked her phone. Twitter had bundled her thousands of notifications into one. Keisha smiled. People cared. She read the first reply.

@onemanarmy: you uppity bitch. Get your fuckin face outta the camera before I off you myself.

Her breath stopped; her skin turned ice cold. She scanned the parking lot; a shooter could be anywhere. *Who are these people?* The crowd pushed Steve into her. She remembered the weight of Alex Robinson's body falling onto her. She clung to Steve, and together they caught themselves before they fell. *He's as scared as I am.*

"Fuck." Steve brushed his hair out of his eyes. "That escalated quickly."

Keisha straightened her shirt. "What were we thinking?"

"We were thinking of our dead friends."

"How are we going to survive this?" Keisha signaled to their group to head to their cars.

Steve grimaced. "I dunno. Maybe the support group." He shook his head and swiped at the side of his eye with the back of his hand as if his tears betrayed him. "Hard to imagine that'll make it any better."

## Sofia

Sofia pulled on her seat belt and latched it. Her chest felt weak from crying, her eyelids burned. Papi sat quietly behind the wheel, started the engine, and pulled out of their driveway to go to the support meeting. What was she going to talk about at this meeting? No matter what anyone said, nothing was going to fix her.

*Caitlyn, will you be at the meeting?*

*Yes.*

Sofia picked at the edge of her shirt. She remembered the clothes they made together, the times they laughed. Sofia rooted through her backpack, looking for a pad and pen. *I want to write down what you say, so I know it's real. It goes so fast.*

*Your mind makes this happen, Sofy, yours and mine. You can't write it down.*

"Sofia, you doing okay?" her father said.

"I'm okay." They passed the McDonalds, where she and Caitlyn would go for fries and a milkshake after soccer games. Sofia pictured Caitlyn's hand dipping fries into the shake, her pink fingernails.

Her throat was tight. The picture changed to her mother trying to breathe. Sofia turned and looked out at the sidewalk, the one that led to her school. She hadn't noticed how cracked and dirty the sidewalk was. Plastic bags were stuck in the tall grass she used to admire as she and Caitlyn biked to school when they were on a fitness binge. Her town looked ugly now. Probably it was always ugly.

"I'm sorry for all this, Sofia. I know it's tough." Papi stopped at the light in front of the hospital entrance and waved pedestrians across the walk. Sofia hadn't noticed them and didn't know them.

"Are you sure you don't want me to go with you?"

Maybe she did want him to go with her. The door to the hospital glowed a sickly yellow from the lights inside. She wanted to do this on her own. "No. There'll be people I know. The Morans will be there." Maybe some kids from her class would show up. And Lily, the girl kneeling at the altar who seemed to care so much about Cat's death, might be there.

*Cat, what did you mean about Lily being a different color?*

*I don't know . . . not scared, but like she knew something we didn't.*

"Sofia?"

As soon as she looked at him, her connection to Caitlyn snapped. She was suddenly cold. "I'll be fine, Papi."

He pulled up to the curb. "Okay, text me the second you're done. I'll be in the parking lot." He smiled and smoothed her bangs off her forehead. "I know you miss Caitlyn."

Sofia leaned over and kissed his scratchy jaw. He cupped her elbow and pressed a kiss to her temple.

"You're my angel," he said.

Sofia slipped out of the car and headed for the hospital door.

## Lily

They had to bring in extra chairs to accommodate all of the people seeking comfort, or maybe it was attention they wanted, Lily thought. A large circle of chairs surrounded a second one. Lily sat as far away as possible from anyone she knew.

Some students slouched in the metal chairs; others leaned forward, their heads dipped to their phones, looking completely detached from this world. Keisha Washington, fresh from her gun show stunt that made the national news, talked to a gaggle of drama kids. That girl was every-where, at all times. Was she cloned?

Lily pulled at the collar of her turtleneck to relieve her sense of choking. She felt hot and cold at the same time. She scanned the room for a window to crawl through to escape this torture.

Eyes caught hers. She didn't recognize the man at first, especially since he was wearing a bright blue sweater and tan pants, not his usual gray work shirt with the Rockwell High mustang logo. But it was him, Mr. Wilkins, the custodian who made it to the cover of *Time Magazine*, who meekly said into every microphone thrust at his face, "I didn't think about it, I just acted . . . I'm no hero."

Lily flicked her eyes away. Did he recognize her? She imagined herself in a lineup of short girls with dark hair, staring at her reflection in a one-way mirror, Mr. Wilkins unseen on the other side, flanked by Radson and Warren. What hell awaited if Wilkins could pick her out?

As the room filled, Lily moved silently in a crouched position from her seat to the door. She could duck out and nab a soy latte from the Starbucks in the hospital and wait in the lobby until her mother came to pick her up. But in the hall, she stopped dead. There was her mother, planted in her own seat, her mouth turned down in disappointment but not surprise.

"Get back in there," Stephanie said.

Lily huffed. "It's too hot and crowded."

Stephanie stood and began to unbutton her daughter's cardigan. "People are hurting like you are. People who can help you."

"People you never let me mix with before," Lily said as her mother peeled off her sweater. "Now, all of a sudden, they can help me?"

"Now is different." Stephanie draped the freed sweater over her arm and held Lily by the shoulders. "I pray and pray. Our church family prays and prays. But this is too big. You need more." She picked up her daughter's hand. "Just try."

Lily sulked back into the hot room. Someone had taken her seat. She leaned against the wall, folded her arms across her chest. A girl turned her head and looked at her. The girl from the last funeral. Sofia. She smiled at Lily then turned back to the mourner next to her. Lily tuned them out and focused on the ceiling tiles until someone touched her elbow—Mr. Wilkins.

The skin on Lily's face tightened. She couldn't breathe. Mr. Wilkins motioned to his now empty seat. Smile, she thought. Be polite. Be innocent. Her mouth twitched. She wasn't sure if it amounted to a smile, but he nodded at her. Lily took his seat and dropped her eyes to her lap, wishing for an invisibility cloak.

## Mike

Mike gritted his teeth as he drove to the hospital. The place where his daughter died was supposed to be highly rated, so why couldn't the doctors save her? The thought of Caitlyn's demise, alive and laughing one second and then all too suddenly gone, made him furious. Rage prickled his skin.

Of all the places in Rockwell, why did the support group have to meet here, the site of Caitlyn's dying breath? He wanted to pound the dashboard and peel rubber. Angry most of the time now, he controlled his emotions around Lisa. Taking a deep breath to simmer down, he glanced at his wife in the passenger seat. She stared straight ahead, a blank expression on her face. He knew that look. She was lost in her own memories.

He didn't have great expectations for the first support group meeting tonight, but he hoped it would help Lisa. Women liked to talk about their feelings and were better at expressing their emotions, but he was brought up to consider such revelations unmanly. Lisa sometimes teased him about that.

"I see your tears," she said when he first laid eyes on his newborn daughter. Caitlyn was a beautiful baby, not all red and wrinkly, but soft, with wispy blonde hair. Her eyes were closed, and she squirmed slightly in Lisa's arms. "I'm glad you have your girl," he told his wife, but he didn't know what he would do with a daughter. He played ball with his sons, took them fishing, and soon he would buy them their very own hunting rifles. But a girl?

"I really wanted a daughter this time," Lisa replied. "Don't get me wrong, I love Connor and Patrick, but boys are a handful. It will be fun to have a little girl to dress up and go shopping and bake cookies with." She must have noticed a frown on his face because she joked, "I think you're going to like having a daughter. It will be a nice change for you." He didn't know then how right Lisa was.

He pulled into the hospital lot and parked. Lisa was biting her lip, a sign she was uncertain. "Ready?" he asked. She nodded. As they walked to the entrance, he tried to make conversation to assure her. "Wonder how many will show up tonight?" She didn't respond, just shrugged.

They found Conference Room G, a nondescript room with chairs arranged in concentric circles. *Just like AA groups in the movies or on TV. Never thought I'd be in one.* A table in one corner held bottles of water. There were no pictures on the walls. The room was already filled with teenagers and adults. He didn't recognize any of them except for Charmaine Robinson, the nurse who came to Caitlyn's wake, and Eric, the boy who wanted to be his daughter's boyfriend. Sofia spotted them and came over to greet them. Lisa smiled and hugged her daughter's best friend. *Maybe this won't be a complete waste of time.*

A forty-something woman with frizzy gray hair stood up. "I'm Debby Rosenberg, a social worker here at Tri-County Hospital. Welcome to our group. All of you have experienced the horrible event at our high school, and some of you have lost loved ones. We're here today to share our feelings and help one another cope with the tragedy we've been forced to endure. I thought we'd begin by introducing ourselves and the friends or family taken from us. Who wants to begin?"

Mike folded his arms across his chest. *Not me.*

**Charmaine**

Charmaine hadn't expected Keisha Robinson to come to the support group, and she resented her presence. After all, Keisha hadn't lost a parent or a sibling, let alone a husband like she had. She rubbed her chest to ease the sudden burning sensation. Charmaine had never been jealous before, but she was now because she wasn't with Alex when he died. Keisha was, and Keisha made sure everyone knew Alex died protecting her. That wasn't right. If Charmaine had her way, Alex would be a living husband, not a dead hero.

One by one, the others in the group introduced themselves. Each one's life had been shattered by some crazed stranger who had ripped away the people they loved. Their futures were changed in fifteen minutes. Charmaine nodded to Mike and Lisa Moran, who both looked devastated, like they were still in shock. The phrase "the walking wounded" sprang up from her subconscious. *Yes, that's what everyone in this room is, wounded but still standing.*

As Lisa talked about her daughter, Charmaine was struck by the similarities between herself and Caitlyn. Both were the youngest in a family of three children, and both had two older brothers. But Caitlyn never got the chance to go to college or find her mate or start her career, like she had, just as Alex would never become a father. *And I'll never be a mother.*

When it was her turn to speak, Charmaine said, "I went back to work, and that helps me get through the day. Evenings, though, are tough. I hate cooking for one. I hate eating alone and sleeping alone. I miss Alex. I want my husband back." And although she had been determined not to weep, her spirit broke.

"It's all right to let our feelings out. That's what we're here for," Debby, the social worker, said.

Mike shifted the discussion to a less emotional topic. "Anyone hear more about an accomplice? The news says another student was involved."

"Thirteen-hundred kids go to that school," one mother said. "How would they find them?"

"Who were Aaron's friends?" Mike asked. "Who did he hang out with?"

Keisha leaned forward. "Aaron Crofton didn't have any friends. He was an obnoxious loner who didn't belong to any group but always had something nasty to say."

"At the last football game, he was behind the concession stand with that pothead, Jared," another kid said. "Jared would be my guess. He's hated everyone since second grade."

The girl who almost fainted at Alex's funeral said, "It could have been someone from another school. Or maybe the news is wrong, and there wasn't an accomplice."

Ignoring her, Keisha blurted, "I lost twelve classmates, some were friends, and some I barely knew. I'm sorry I didn't know them all. And I lost my guidance counselor, too." She looked at Charmaine as if asking permission to continue. Charmaine was relieved Keisha hadn't said Alex's name. *That isn't her right. Alex was my husband.*

"I'm sad, but I'm mad, too," Keisha continued. "Last weekend, some of my friends and I went to a gun show and were able to buy twenty guns. Twenty! We can't vote or drink beer legally, but we got our hands on automatic weapons that belong in a war zone, not a school zone."

Several others around the table nodded. Mike shifted in his chair. "I'm glad someone else besides me is mad," he declared. "I'm retired military. I own an AR-15 like the one the killer used. It's a nasty weapon, and you're right; it's made for the battlefield and no place else except maybe a shooting range. It's made to kill." Lisa touched his arm, but Mike kept going. "But here's what makes me really angry. Even when a jury finds him guilty, the so-called ABC Killer will live, a privilege he denied my daughter." His voice broke as he continued. "I want to take my AR-15 and kill that bastard myself. And his accomplice, too."

Charmaine gasped. She wasn't the only one to do so. Some of the kids recoiled. Keisha squeezed her eyes shut and gripped her chair arms. Charmaine didn't believe more violence was the answer, but she didn't know what was. A young girl whose name she couldn't recall said, "Caitlyn wouldn't want that, Mr. Moran."

Lisa began to cry. Mike put his arm around his wife's shoulder and said, "I'm sorry, honey. Sofia's right. I'm sorry."

Mr. Wilkins shifted in his chair and stared at Mike. Across the room, Keisha leaned over and put her head in her hands.

No one said anything after that. Finally, Debby broke the eerie silence that had descended on the room. "This is a safe place for all of us to express our feelings. We've made a good start here tonight, but this is just the start. I hope you'll come back next Thursday. We'll meet every week for a while and then maybe cut back to every other week when you're ready."

As soon as the meeting broke up, Charmaine hurried to her car. Despite her pace, Keisha caught up to her. "Are you going to come back next week?"

"Yes, I think so."

Keisha's eyes bored into her. "This group is fine, but I want to do more than just talk. I want to do something, take some action, start a movement so this never happens again. Would you help me?"

Her youthful passion touched Charmaine, but she didn't know how to respond. Her grief had taken hold of her, and she wasn't ready to let it go for some activist idealism. She needed time to mourn. She unlocked her car without replying.

And then Keisha said, "I think it's what Mr. Robinson would have wanted us to do."

Charmaine slid into the driver's seat. "I think I know what my husband wanted better than you do." She started the car and left Keisha standing in the parking lot.

As she drove, she reconsidered. *Was that what Alex would have wanted? Could this obnoxious girl be right?*

**Mike**

"I know you didn't mean what you said about killing anyone," Lisa said as they drove home from the support group. "It felt good to talk, though, to know we're not the only ones. Didn't it?"

"Yes," Mike lied. He wasn't going to deprive his wife of the small bit of comfort the evening had provided her, although his reaction couldn't have been more different. They already knew they weren't the only family whose children had been killed. He didn't need a support group to tell him that. Hearing all the stories of lost lives and lost promise and seeing the agony on the faces of those left behind made him angrier than ever. Why wasn't anything being done about so much senseless murder? ABC had an accomplice, someone who opened the locked school door and let him in to carry out his destruction. He was just as guilty to Mike. *I'll kill him, too.*

He shouldn't have admitted his intentions to the group, though, because it upset Lisa. Nothing anybody said tonight, however, convinced him there was fairness or justice in this tragedy. Somebody had to make sure that there was. It was up to him.

**Intheknow @WRWL-TV**
Breaking: FBI is interviewing female persons of interest in the Rockwell shooting. WRWL also learned today the ABC killer has a history of behavioral issues, including alleged harassment and stalking. Were administrators at Rockwell High aware when he transferred in?

# CHAPTER NINE

**Joe**

A buzz like thousands of flies, bodies moving everywhere, on the stage an angry voice amplified across the gym by five wall-mounted speakers—the kids were using rock concert technology for their after-school rally. Joe shook his head in amazement. Young people seemed to know so much more than he did at their age. They were accomplished in ways he would never be. Professional-looking posters and banners lined the walls of the school gym.

*Protect Kids Not Guns*

Everything these kids had ever learned was marshaled into their effort. Pain at the back of his throat made it hard to swallow. He closed his eyes for a second and let himself feel proud of them. It shouldn't be like this. Childhood had been ripped away from them. His hands clenched, and he blinked to clear his vision. They had lost the joy of being young, just the way he had.

*One Child Is Worth More than All the Guns*

He tuned in briefly to the boy speaking, heard the catch-phrases now familiar after a school shooting—the outrage, the shock, the terror and sorrow—and tuned out again. He was here because he'd been assigned to protect them, but he would have come anyway. His daughter was somewhere among the hundreds of kids in the gym. Joe's head swiveled almost automatically from one spot to another, his eyes on the lookout for the smallest clue that someone planned to harm them again. He read a poster and drew in a sharp breath.

*The Scariest Thing in School Should Be My Grades*

These teenagers, his daughter included, would always feel threatened when they gathered together. They would never shake their fear, would always look over their shoulders, would constantly watch the doors. The more he thought about it, the more enraged he became. How were more speeches going to solve the problem? No one in authority was listening, but the community gathering together, in defiance of their own fear, gave them power. He could feel the electricity in the air. They were buoyed by it.

He shook his head. How long would that feeling last? Soon the world would forget this happened to them and move on. His eyes rested on another poster.

~~RunHide~~*FIGHT*

Joe spotted a figure in a dark hoodie and pants crouched in the far corner by the doors leading to the boy's locker room. He moved swiftly along the wall to intercept him. When he stood over the kid, he found a girl staring back at him, a target drawn on her face in red lipstick.

He sucked in his breath. He wanted to scream, to grab the kid by the shoulders and shake her, but he had to control himself. He was an adult, a cop. He had to live up to his training.

"Please stand," Joe said. "Hold out your hands, palms up and open."

The girl stood up slowly and withdrew her hands from the pockets of the hoodie.

"What's your name?"

"Hannah. Hannah Taman." Her voice shook. "I have my school ID."

Once again, Joe realized, in the name of protecting them, he was terrorizing a child. "Do you go to Rockwell High?"

"No. I go to the country day school in Carderock but I . . . I'm with them. I believe in them. We're afraid at my school, too. I wanted to be here, but now I feel like an outsider, and I don't know what to do." She hugged herself and stumbled.

Joe nodded. "Will you come with me? I'll introduce you to one of the leaders." He scanned the gym for Keisha Washington and spotted her at the foot of the stage. "Come on. She'll put you to work." He smiled at Hannah. "It'll be okay. I promise."

*We Are Humans Not Targets,* he read from the poster above the stage.

Walking back to the post he thought gave him the best vantage point in the gym, his mind flashed through images—the open side door at the school, the girl he thought was a boy, the boy arriving late at school. The FBI was interviewing girls. It dawned on him: *The shooter's accomplice, maybe that accomplice was a girl. Maybe she was his girlfriend.*

He stopped walking while he thought through his idea. He wasn't in line to see the FBI report, and the county detectives weren't talking, so he had no idea where they were in their investigation or whether they'd found the accomplice. That was way above his pay grade. But if there was an accomplice, she could be in the gym right now, hanging around with the very people she helped terrorize.

The thought nearly made his heart stop. *I have to find her.* The minute he thought it, he remembered the girl he found in the corridor the first morning they were back at school. *What was she really doing in the hall that morning?* He thought about it for a second—a girl who doesn't do what she's supposed to—and shook his head. *Probably coincidence,* he concluded and turned his attention to someone else.

**Keisha**

Her parents were having an adult conversation over dinner. They were trying to be normal. Her father, a state senator, was talking about some bill he was pushing through the legislature. It was stalled in committee, he said. He ran the flat of his palm over his close-cropped head. That was his self-calming mechanism. Her mother nodded encouragingly, making small sounds, "Uh-huh, mmm." That was all her father needed to keep talking. When the state legislature wasn't in session, he talked about his law practice, how his day in court went. This was how they always behaved as if the world had gone back to the way it was before.

Keisha tuned them out. The sound of them talking, the back and forth, occasional laughter, the clink of forks against plates, her father sipping his wine loudly—it nauseated her.

Nothing was happening. No laws were changed. This afternoon they had this big rally at school and congratulated themselves about their success, but it didn't do anything. Nobody gave a damn that her friends and teachers were killed. Everybody had moved on to the next subject. Outrage only lasted a minute these days. Twitter was back to its usual obsessions with politics and cats. Social media simply glamorized people's pettiness and self-absorption. The most self-absorbed people became celebrity influencers. Everyone was saying, "Look at me, look at me, aren't I special."

She put her hand over her stomach to ease her queasiness.

"Aren't you feeling well, honey?" her mother asked.

Her father leaned forward and patted her shoulder. "Everything's going to be okay, sweetie."

Instantly, she was furious at them. They didn't understand. They just pretended to understand. They were complete hypocrites, like everyone else. "You don't get it, do you?"

"Get what, honey," her parents said in unison.

"It's over. A guy killed Samantha and fourteen other people, and it's over. No one cares anymore."

Her mother stood up and came around to Keisha. She hugged her and said, "Of course, we care. The shooter was arrested. He's going to be arraigned. He'll go to jail. That's a statement that our country won't tolerate these shootings."

"And what about the accomplice? Everyone's talking about it. One of us helped him kill everyone. They knew what he was going to do and let him in a side door. And he's been sneaking around every day, in school with us, trying to get over. We don't even know who it is." Her skin crawled. She wanted to shriek at the top of her lungs.

Her father crossed his arms over his chest and puffed out his lower lip. That was the one look of his she hated. She turned her face away from him. "We don't know the facts yet," her father said. "The FBI will figure it out," he said. "They'll get the accomplice. You don't have to do their job."

Keisha jumped up from her chair, pushing it back, pushing away her mother. "Getting him isn't the point. It's that he's there, among us, pretending he's one of us when he must hate us. What did we do to make him hate us so much? How could someone hate us enough to kill us? I'm so confused. I don't know what to think or do."

She ran up to her room and slammed the door. I can't trust anyone, she thought. *Not even my parents. The world is a wasteland. What is the point in trying to change it?* She put on her earphones, turned up her music, and tuned everyone out. *I'll figure out who the accomplice is, just like I said to Lily.*

## Sofia

After the rally, Sofia went to her room, exhausted. Papi had taken her to the Thai place for dinner, but she couldn't eat anything. He wanted her to talk to him about the rally, about the shooter, did he have a girlfriend, but she couldn't talk either.

She rolled into a ball on her bed, closed her eyes, and almost instantly felt Caitlyn's hand wrapped around hers. It was her; she was alive.

*I thought you were dead. Caitlyn, why did you hide from me?*

*I didn't. You're dreaming.*

Sofia felt Caitlyn's hair brush her cheeks. She looked into the blue-green eyes of her friend. They sparked tiny clusters of light. They were in the sky. The wind this high up pushed through the night and rustled their blue and pink gowns. The Rockwell High roof was below them. The dark roof rose up and down. It was breathing.

They swam in the air. Stars shot little streaks of light at each other.

*We're flying.*

*No, Sofy, we're not.*

Sofia felt heavy. She kicked her bare feet against her gown. Caitlyn let go of her hand and shook it away.

Sofia reached out as she fell.

Caitlyn looked so sad. Her pink hair lifted in the wind. Her gown rustled. She parted her lips but said nothing.

Sofia fell toward the roof. She would hit it soon, go through it and smash onto the hard floor. She kept falling. Caitlyn was small now, like a kite floating above her. Sofia dropped through the roof like liquid and landed next to a girl in the hall, weeping into her hands. The girl looked up.

Sofia's cell phone pinged, waking her from the dream. She sat up in bed. It was dark in her room. Where was her phone? She saw a screen light on the floor. The screen read

8:11 a.m. A text from Papi: "You were sleeping so soundly, I didn't want to wake you. I'll be at the range if you need me."

She thought of the dream. *What are you trying to tell me, Cat?*

## Joe

Joe was on his second target at the public shooting range, where the police department had a contract so officers could practice and maintain their proficiency. All his shots were in the perfect kill grouping, center mass.

Police didn't practice to disarm or cripple. They shot to kill. He'd never questioned his training; its goal was to keep him and innocent bystanders alive. Besides, he'd never actually shot anyone during all his time on the police force.

He was relieved now that he hadn't killed the shooter that day. By the time he got to him—past the blood on the floor, the bodies sprawled every which way, the fear in the kids' eyes—the punk had been knocked out by the janitor. All he had to do was cuff him and haul him out to the squad car. That janitor was a brave guy who deserved the glory he was getting.

*I would have killed that kid and been glad about it. Something is wrong with me.*

Somewhere out there, another young punk hyped up on hate was practicing the same kill shot with a semi-automatic rifle and a plan to kill as many people in fifteen minutes as he could get away with. The more Joe thought about all of this, the more confused he got. That line about how a bad guy with a gun could be stopped by a good guy with a gun—that line he'd swallowed like a kid getting his first taste of birthday cake—was nonsense. Since the shooting, he had days when his whole career seemed like nonsense. Maybe, like his daughter, he was going crazy.

Joe made sure his Glock 22 was unloaded and put it down on the bench, pointing at the target. Others were still shooting. No one missed. But target practice didn't teach you that in the heat of the moment when someone aimed a gun at you, calm precision went out the window, replaced by adrenalin, fear, and fury. Adrenalin was bad for accuracy. Fury was bad for decision-making. This idea politicians had that teachers and what one moron senator called "talented preschoolers," should be armed was a stupid, cruel joke. Politicians were full of shit. It was hard enough for an officer with eighteen years' experience to know when to shoot and when not to.

He pulled off his earmuffs, placed the gun in his bag, and walked out of the indoor range. In the lounge, he sank onto a tufted leather bench to retie his sneakers. Two white men, probably cops or military by haircut, build, and swagger, joked with each other a few feet from him.

The taller man with the close-shaved head put his hands on his hips. His voice boomed. "Did you see that little bitch at the gun show, that black girl with all the braids and the big mouth? I wanna hit that."

The other guy laughed. "Yeah, that dyke. Serve her right. Shoot the lot of 'em, I say. Clean up the state."

Joe straightened. Heat rushed to his face. They were laughing at Keisha, making her the butt of their disgusting joke. He wanted to crush them with his bare hands.

"Hey, man." Joe worked hard to control the heat building in his chest. "That kid's been through a lot. Give her a break." It was too mild a rebuke, and he knew it.

"Fuck you, man," the shorter man said. "Who the hell do you think you are? This is a private conversation. Stay out of it." He turned his back on Joe.

But Joe was in it now. Blood pounded in his head. His pulse raced. Every bully whose abuse he'd ever endured zoomed through his mind. "I'm a county police officer, Joe Hernandez. Who are you?"

"None of your fucking business. I don't care if you're fucking Moses. Keep your nose out of my concerns."

Joe took their measure. One of them was a foot taller than he was. The other carried twenty more pounds than he did. Neither of them was wearing a weapon, but this was a shooting range, and weapons were nearby. That didn't matter. He just couldn't let the slur pass.

"These kids deserve our protection," Joe said, trying to keep his voice even. "Your comments are disgusting."

The taller man sidled up to Joe and banged into him with his shoulder. Joe stood his ground. The man leaned into him, nose to nose, like some kind of Marine Corps sergeant intimidating a recruit. "You beaners are all the same," he said, quiet menace in his voice, "always looking for an easy way out. You don't belong here. Go back where you came from."

Joe grabbed the man's arm, twisted it behind his back, pressed him down to the floor, and put a knee on his back. The man's face turned red, and he yelped.

"I was born here, amigo," Joe said. "And I belong here."

The guy's friend whipped around and slugged Joe in the head, knocking him backward. Joe staggered, shook himself, and came at the second assailant. At that moment, he saw Mike Moran exit the range. Mike stopped moving, took one look at what was happening, and stepped in.

He put one hand on Joe's chest and the other on his opponent. "Hey! Cut it out," he snapped in the commanding voice they'd been trained to respect. They stopped moving.

Joe came out of his daze. He thanked Mike, grabbed his bag, and walked out of the building. This altercation would be reported. It wouldn't be good for him, but he didn't care. The two men who represented everything he hated were bloodied and cowed. That was enough for today. He was redeemed; he'd deal with the consequences later.

Mike followed him out to the car. "You okay, man?"

"Yeah. No problem. Just trying to clear my head." Joe waved.

Mike saluted. "Like all of us."

Joe managed a smile.

**Beowolf @RockwellHighNews**
I used to think I could be heroic. Every drill since kindergarten, I thought I'd be the one to charge, to stop him. I grew up thinking it would never happen in my school. Then I heard the sound of a gun close up. Everything I thought I knew about myself and the world changed.

# CHAPTER TEN

## Charmaine

Charmaine hadn't checked her Facebook page for almost a week. She didn't know which upset her more, the expressions of sympathy still coming in from old friends who had just recently learned of Alex's death or the happy postings of other couples enjoying their everyday life. But faced with another Friday night spent flipping through the cable channels while eating Rocky Road ice cream for dinner, she picked up her phone and started scrolling.

A fraternity brother of Alex's had posted photos from their college days that made her smile—Alex playing touch football, dancing with her at the frat's annual ball, and watching the brothers compete in a hot dog eating contest. She relived these memories as if they were still part of the ongoing present, not as remnants of an unrecoverable past. She smiled and realized that, for once, she wasn't weeping.

Scrolling through her own page, she noticed a friend request from Connor Moran. *Who is that? Probably another reporter harassing her for her story.* When she saw his photo, she remembered the soldier who comforted her when she broke down at his sister Caitlyn's wake. She accepted the request. When she didn't hear back from him right away, she remembered the time difference. It would be the middle of the night in Germany, where he was stationed.

The next morning, she drove to her in-law's house for lunch, something she and Alex had done every other Saturday. Although they talked on the phone several times a week, she hadn't seen Pops and Mama D in the month since the funeral. She still wasn't sure she could handle the emotions this reunion would undoubtedly stir, but here she was. She found a parking space just a block away from the Robinson's city row house, took a deep breath to steel herself, and walked to their stoop.

Mama D answered the door and embraced Charmaine. "How you doing?"

Charmaine blinked to hold back tears. "I'm hanging in there."

"Us, too."

Pops got up from his recliner in their living room to greet her. Family photos decorated every wall and table: Alex and his sister Lizzie when they were little and studio portraits of the parents and their children. She paused before several scenes from her wedding with Alex. "You were a beautiful bride," Pops said. She smiled. "And Alex was so handsome."

Then she noticed a new addition to this gallery, a laminated and framed newspaper article about Alex's heroism during the shooting. Tears erupted, and she wiped them away. Pops patted her on the back. "I know," he said.

Mama D's voice wobbled as she struggled to keep from crying. "I have to check on lunch," she said, escaping to the kitchen. She had fixed her usual delicious if unhealthy meal, pulled pork sandwiches, macaroni and cheese, and pecan pie, Alex's favorite, for dessert.

They sat down at the same square kitchen table, with metal legs and a Formica top that Alex had once told her he remembered from his childhood. Only his chair was now empty. Everything in this house was a reminder to her that Alex was gone. She didn't think she could come back again anytime soon. Her own grief was too raw.

"Eat, girl," Mama D ordered. "You're getting way too skinny."

Over lunch, they told her stories about Alex, most of which she had heard before, about the time he broke his arm falling out of a tree, about the first tennis tournament he won, and how he told them about Charmaine before he brought her home to meet them. She knew they needed to share these memories but listening to them just made her numb.

She watched Mama D fill containers of mac and cheese and a piece of pie to take home, like she always did for Alex, and felt nothing.

"I'm glad you came by to visit," Pops said. His eyes watered. "I didn't want to lose you, too."

She reached across the table to touch his arm. "I'll always be your daughter-in-law."

Mama D piped up. "No, you're our *daughter*, the only child we have left now."

Charmaine knew then that she'd have to come back to visit them, no matter how painful for her, no matter how many memories, happy and sad, she had to experience. It was what Alex would have wanted her to do.

On the drive back, Bruno Mars' "Just the Way You Are" came on the radio, the song Alex serenaded her with at their wedding, and she started to cry. The sorrow she had been holding in all day released itself. She realized connections with other people like her in-laws were helping her deal with her husband's death. Her parents, Lori and her co-workers, the support group, even Keisha, the girl she resented, reminded her she was not alone.

When she got home, she opened a Facebook message from Connor Moran. "How are you?" it began. "I hope we can stay in touch. My mom is in a dark place, and I know you both recently went to a support group. Maybe you can keep an eye on her, tell me how she's doing. If that's too much to ask, it's okay."

Charmaine felt sorry for this guy, unable to watch over his parents and brother from thousands of miles away. He couldn't just drive to see them and share memories, as she had done today with Mama D and Pops. She typed her reply without further thought. "I think the support group will help us all. I'll keep you posted."

## Joe

The day after his fight at the gun range, Joe stood at attention in the captain's office. This was the first time he'd ever been called in for discipline. He didn't know how to act. All his other encounters with the captain had been for commendations.

Humiliation flooded through him as he stood there in front of the man's desk like a kid being reprimanded for fighting in the schoolyard. Every bad moment he'd ever had in school came back to him. It was all he could do to keep his head up and his back straight. He was an idiot to tangle with those men. Maybe he should be going to those support group meetings with Sofia. He was losing his mind.

Captain Medgar leaned back in his swivel chair and rested his hands on the arms. "I gotta do something about this mess," he said.

Joe nodded and cringed inside. He'd never even thought about the fallout on his department.

"Sorry, Joe, but you're suspended without pay for ten days. I gotta take your badge and gun." Medgar pointed to the desk.

Joe put his identification and weapon on Medgar's desk without saying anything. All his reasons were bad ones, and even if he was justified, it didn't matter. There were rules.

Word of Joe's fight at the gun range had spread like wildfire through the force. Everybody had a point of view. Tension built as cops took sides. He got it. The captain had to do something to reduce the level of animosity. The guys Joe punched were officers from the neighboring county sheriff's department. Word was, he'd started it. Maybe he did, but they deserved it. He understood, however. Medgar couldn't let it stand that one of his men had assaulted fellow police officers, even if they weren't pressing charges and they were assholes.

Without his official ID, Joe felt like an orphan in a strange land where he didn't know the language. If he wasn't a police officer, he couldn't do anything about anything, couldn't protect anyone, or enforce the law. He was as powerless as any other person facing criminals, and he didn't like this feeling at all.

Medgar kept talking. "You know this suspension is gonna affect your career, Joe. I know you were prepping for it, but you can't take the sergeant's exam right now. We gotta let some time pass, maybe a year after you're reinstated. Let things cool down a bit."

Joe just wanted to get the hell out of the office. He raised his chin to say something and then shrugged. What was the point in saying anything? He had no defense. He tried to school some bigots, and the bureaucracy came down on him instead of them. It was easy to see the way the wind blew. The racists were winning.

The captain went on and on. Joe barely listened to him trying to justify his decision. He was thinking of his wife, first what she would think of his being suspended, and then just of her lovely face looking up at him from the breakfast table, two toast crumbs in the corner of her mouth. His hand twitched. He wanted to brush the crumbs away with his thumb.

And then Medgar said, "I know you're caught up in the Rockwell High School shooting because of your daughter. Be a good idea for you to keep your nose clean, you know. So there aren't any questions about your professionalism."

An electric shock ran through Joe. *If I'm suspended, what business is it of yours what I do with my time?* He didn't tell Medgar what he thought. He just nodded and said, "Yes, sir."

Captain Medgar droned on. "And I want you to hear it from me. The shooter is pleading guilty. There won't be a trial, just the arraignment. Everything will be done between his lawyers, the prosecutor, and the judge. The kid will make a statement of guilt in front of the judge for the record, and the judge will determine his sentence. No jury, no trial. His defense is saying victim testimony would unfairly prejudice his sentencing and that no jury in the state would be impartial. But he'll go to jail for the rest of his life on fifteen counts of premeditated murder."

Blood rushed to Joe's face. Words flew out of his mouth without his wanting to say anything. "It's not enough."

Medgar looked startled. "He'll be in jail for life."

Joe clenched his teeth. "He'll still be alive." There was no way he could convince the captain that life without parole for ABC was too good for him. He had no say in the matter at all. As far as Joe was concerned, the law had failed, but there was no point in wasting his breath. He turned to leave the office.

Medgar called after him. "I expect to see you back here, ready for work, in ten days. Right?"

Joe stopped at the door and half-turned back to look at Medgar. "Yes, sir, right." He saluted.

He walked across the floor, avoiding side looks from his fellow officers. A couple of the officers waved. In the hallway, his friend Chen bumped his shoulder and slapped him on the back. "Keep up the good fight, Joe. See you soon."

Obviously, everyone knew what the captain had done and why.

In the parking lot, Joe wondered how the day could be so sunny. He needed a good storm, dark clouds, heavy winds, something to match his mood. What would he say to Sofia when she saw he was lying around the house every day? He had to figure something out. His sweet girl was already coming apart, mooning over that dress she'd been making with her friend. He wasn't going to tell her he was suspended. He'd just tell her he was on a different schedule. For a second, he was glad his wife was dead and didn't have to share his embarrassment.

Driving home, he thought of the one good thing that would come of his suspension: he could patrol the school perimeter every day for hours and keep an eye out for trouble. And he'd be back at work in time for ABC's arraignment to make sure that son of a bitch got what he deserved.

**Mike**

Ernie Polanski poked his head into Mike's office doorway. "Mike, can you get together for lunch today?"

"Sure," Mike replied. "What's up?"

His boss hesitated just a second too long. "Nothing to worry about. Come to my office in about thirty minutes."

Mike nodded. "See you then." He waited until Ernie disappeared down the hallway, then got up and closed his office door. Mike prided himself on his gut instincts, and the hair rising on his neck told him something was off. Ernie occasionally had lunch catered in for his entire senior management team to discuss client problems or upcoming business opportunities, but except for his first day on the job, Ernie had never taken him out to lunch in the three years since.

Was there a problem with his job performance? He knew he wasn't himself, the competent manager he'd been before the shooting. He got distracted by seeing Caitlyn's photo on his desk. He often found himself indulging in revenge fantasies toward ABC in the middle of the workday. Maybe his coworkers complained he wasn't paying attention in staff meetings.

They went to lunch at a nearby Chinese restaurant Ernie liked. His boss ordered two Tsing Tao beers, one for each of them, another unlikely occurrence that put Mike on edge. Mike wasn't a big fan of Chinese food, so he ordered what Ernie did, twice-cooked pork.

The waiter brought their beers, and Ernie lifted his in a toast. "Cheers," Mike replied in kind, and they sipped silently for a minute. Finally, Ernie said, "So how are you doing, Mike? How are Lisa and your sons?"

*So that's what this is all about? He's checking up on my emotional health. Bet HR put him up to this.*

"Doing about as well as could be expected," he replied. "Lisa and I appreciated the flowers the company sent."

"I know. Lisa sent me a thank you note." Mike hadn't known that. In her own way, Lisa was trying to soldier on, too.

"Look, Mike, I know you're going through a hard time now, and I hate to bring this up, but there are problems with the DIA contract." Mike was the lead project manager for the Defense Intelligence Agency business, one of the company's larger customers.

Mike froze. He wasn't aware of any problem. Maybe that *was* the problem. His job had become his refuge from mourning, a refuge he couldn't afford to lose, even if he hadn't always succeeded at escaping his grief. He didn't know how Lisa managed all day with no deadlines and deliverables forced upon her. He would go absolutely insane if he couldn't distract himself with work.

"The contract officer called me this morning," Ernie continued. "Said we have four overdue deliverables, including the quarterly sector analysis. What's going on?"

"I just finished up the quarterly this morning," Mike replied. "I got a little behind, what with everything."

"That's what I thought. You should have told me. I'm assigning Dave to help you out until you get caught up."

"Thanks, Ernie, I appreciate it."

"Listen, Mike, if there's anything the company can do, let me know. We have an Employee Assistance Program and counselors available if you and your family need it."

"Thanks, but I've got that covered," Mike answered. "There's a support group of victims' families and friends that's started meeting."

"That sounds good."

"It's helping Lisa." Mike paused. He didn't want to tell his boss what he really thought, but he couldn't stop himself. "I just wish the police would get off their asses and catch the accomplice. And that we had the death penalty in this state so ABC would get what he deserves. Why should he live when my daughter and fourteen others are dead?"

Ernie looked down at the table and wiped his mouth with his napkin. "I got no answer for you, Mike. Wish I did."

## Lily

Orchestra warm-ups were always excruciating to Lily, but today the sound cut into her head like a buzz saw. She tried to ignore the ghastly noise other students were spewing and concentrate on her own instrument. After a few gentle pumps and tugs, she tuned the A and D strings together to a perfect fifth. Her eyes closed.

*G. D. A. E. A. D. G . . .*

Mr. Howell tugged his ill-fitting vest over his round belly then started the class with a few scales and arpeggios. They went straight to Handel's *Concerto for String Orchestra*, the piece they had been rehearsing for the winter concert. His impatience seemed to startle the other students. Getting back to normal was not coming easy. The students didn't want to jump into the water. They wanted to stand on the shore and let the water lap at their ankles while they vented, reminisced, and occasionally wailed. Lily had heard all of their speculations as she walked the halls: Who was the whack job, spineless, potentially lethal accomplice who let Aaron Crofton into the building? Why hadn't the police caught him/her? Would the fucker strike again?

Lily appreciated the teacher's discipline. Sometimes when she played, the violin melded to her jaw and shoulder and became another limb. She absorbed the notes like morphine. They took away all pain, shrinking her until she was tiny enough to climb inside the instrument. It became her cocoon. By the end of the piece, she emerged a butterfly, light as air, beautiful, ready to fly to a faraway place.

But today, they were only a few bars in when a student office assistant appeared at the door. As she handed Mr. Howell a note, the girl looked directly at Lily. Lily's fingers turned to rubber. Her bow slipped. The sound she produced hurt her ears. Mr. Howell instructed her to go to the office.

Lily's body quaked as she navigated the corridors of Rockwell High. Dr. Thompson waited for her in front of the admin offices. Plywood covered the glass walls that had been shattered by bullets. The smile Dr. Thompson forced turned Lily's stomach to lead. She followed the principal to the faculty conference room and stopped dead. Special Agents Radson and Warren sat at the long table.

Was this it?

Mr. Wilkins was kind to her at the support group session. Did the cloud lift on his memory? Had he identified her, or did Aaron finally give her up?

Warren stood. "Come in, Lily."

Lily took small steps toward the chair Warren pulled out for her. All at once, she wanted her mother, or a lawyer, or to finish her concerto. She wanted to play dress-up with her sister, eat rice cakes and watch *Cinema Paradiso* again. She wanted to drive a stake through Aaron Blake Crofton's heart. More than anything, she wanted to wake up from this nightmare.

She pinched the skin on her elbows.

*Wake up!*

"Hello, Lily. It's nice to see you again." Radson smiled with her warm Good Cop face.

Lily stopped a few feet from the table. "What is this? More questions?"

Warren motioned to the seat. Last semester's yearbook was on the table. "We wanted you to look at some photos," he said. "To see if you perhaps might recognize the girl you saw last summer going to Aaron Crofton's house."

"I told you it was dark," Lily said. "I didn't get a very good look."

Radson pulled out the chair beside Lily's and sat down. "We know, but sometimes seeing the person's image again helps."

Lily wavered another few seconds before sitting. What choice did she have? An innocent person would cooperate. She straightened her posture, flipped open the book, and went to work like she was taking the S.A.T. Her eyes trailed over last year's seniors. The homecoming and prom queens, football players, the drama club's production of *Grease*. Already the photos looked dated. She scanned the eager freshman faces. Now they were sophomores, walking the halls shell-shocked and morose. Lily stopped at one girl's photo. Her face looked familiar. Yes, she was the one in the biology lab the other day. She read the name: Caitlyn Moran. No, Caitlyn died. Lily's mouth dried.

"May I have some water, please?"

"Of course." Special Agent Radson left the room and quickly returned with a water bottle. Lily didn't touch it for fear she would leave fingerprints. She remembered the agent's name on the business card: Elizabeth. Did she go by Liz, or Beth, or Betty? She looked like a Beth—soft when she wanted to be. Today her hair was down in gentle blonde waves over her shoulders. Lily wondered what it would be like to have blonde hair like Agent Radson. Or Aaron. His hair was always a mess. She'd comb it with her fingers, but it would spring back into disarray.

Warren cleared his throat. "Take your time," he said, though his voice conveyed *hurry up*.

Lily went back to the yearbook, but the photos began to blur. Aaron had crept into her mind and wouldn't leave. She remembered sitting on his bed, his head in her lap. Her fingers moved through the waves of his hair.

"What scares you most?" she'd asked.

"The color yellow."

She laughed. "Shut up."

"I'm serious. The shrink I had freshman year called it xanthophobia. So, unless you want to see me have a panic attack, don't wear yellow around me."

"How do you ride the bus?"

"I smoke a joint before school and tell myself it's mustard, not yellow."

Lily stroked his hair. "Where does that fear come from?"

"Who knows. Maybe my daycare center had yellow walls or some shit like that."

They were listening to a playlist of alt-rock songs and drinking beer. Lily detested the taste but tolerated it to get to that floaty feeling. It was late afternoon, forty-five minutes until Lily's mother and sister would return from piano lessons.

"What about you?" he said. "What are you afraid of?"

"My mother with low blood sugar," Lily replied. "She turns into a piranha."

Aaron looked up at her, boyish and sincere. "I have some Lexapro you can give her."

"A medicated Stephanie sounds even scarier." The beer and the music and the strands of Aaron's hair in her fingers relaxed Lily. She felt herself fluttering open like the pages in a book left open in the breeze. "Actually," she said, "there isn't one thing that scares me most. Everything scares me. Being here is terrifying. But leaving may be worse. Leaving means going back to reality."

Aaron suddenly flipped over and knelt above Lily. He brought his face close to hers, touched her hair. "I want to be your reality." His voice drummed in her heart. "I don't want you to ever leave. You can stay in this room forever. My Rapunzel." He kissed her in a way that reached all the way to her toes. "I'll take care of you. I'll love you. I won't let anything hurt you." He kissed her again and set her beer bottle on the nightstand. He lowered his body. She loved the weight of him, the feeling of security it gave her. She lifted her chin for another kiss, but his lips twitched into a funny grin. "And I'll tickle you."

His fingers were suddenly crawling ferociously over her sides, her belly, under her arms. She laughed, squirming beneath him on the bedcovers. She laughed until tears filled her eyes. "Stop it!" His fingers wouldn't stop. Every nerve ending felt on fire. Her body twitched and convulsed. Her laughter stopped. "Aaron, *stop!*" She had to pee. She couldn't breathe. Gasping for air, she gathered all her strength and pushed him aside.

She rolled off the bed, stood, and straightened her rumpled clothes.

"I said stop. What is wrong with you?"

"I'm sorry." In an instant, he was on the floor, on his knees in front of her. He wrapped his arms around her waist and buried his face in her belly. "I'm sorry. Please don't be mad. Please don't hate me."

Lily didn't want to be mad or hate the only boy who ever wanted her, but that powerless, trapped feeling had left her shaking. She had no words. She smoothed his hair.

"Don't ever do that again."

Now in the school conference room, Lily felt Agent Warren's patience thin. Radson was at the window on her phone. Just pick a girl, Lily thought. Pick any girl who looked stupid enough to fall for Aaron Blake Crofton. She figured this whole exercise was a ploy anyway. She was their person of interest. They were just waiting for her to crack. She slowly turned another page.

*Keisha Washington.*

Her finger stopped on the girl's name. Too bad she had a solid alibi.

But maybe . . .

Radson was back at Lily's side. Warren seemed to be holding his breath while Lily's finger didn't move from Keisha's name. After a minute, she fell back in her seat.

"It could be dozens of these girls. I'm sorry. I can't be sure."

## Keisha

Dr. Thompson looked up at Keisha from her desk, her eyebrows raised, forehead furrowed. Keisha put her hand on her hip and waited. She learned long ago that adults took a long time to process requests. The principal was no exception.

"Look, I just thought that if we could see who was absent during the first period, we could narrow down the list of possible accomplices." She shrugged one shoulder—her self-deprecating move.

Thompson shook her head. "The list won't prove anything. We never got to take second-period attendance. And," she stood, indicating the audience was over, "I wouldn't show it to you anyway. There are privacy issues."

"Well, somebody's got to do something!"

Dr. Thompson smiled. "The FBI is doing something. They are interviewing, checking the veracity of statements, and working with us to find the accomplice. You're safe. You can go back to being a student."

Keisha shook her head. "You adults move too slow. We're all dying a little bit every day. Don't you see that?"

Thompson came around her desk and put her hand on Keisha's arm. That night at the vigil when they hugged— that feeling of solidarity, that they were in this together— was long gone. They were back to the usual administration versus students mode. School staff were the adults; they knew best. She was just a kid. That attitude really sucked.

"I refuse to be a sheep," Keisha said, her eyes flooding, "I refuse to stand around and wait for it to happen again."

She turned on her heel and stomped out of the principal's office. On her way out, Keisha caught Dr. Thompson sharing eye contact with all the front office staff. There were more than two eye rolls.

## Sofia

The art room was filled with students reassigned from classrooms still being fixed. Sofia barely knew some of the kids. Her regular seat taken, she took one in the back. The collage she had worked on with Caitlyn was still displayed on the wall. She didn't want to look at it. It was wrinkled and dusty.

Keisha stood at the front table, guiding everyone in making banners and signs for another rally. She was a magnet. Everyone gravitated to where she was. The teacher ripped large sheets of thick paper from the roller and mixed paint. The excitement in the room rattled Sofia. People seemed almost happy. She didn't want to make signs. She moved to an empty table clutching a blank sheet of paper, a cup of red tempera paint, and a brush missing half its bristles. She laid the paper out and taped it down.

"Can I paint with you?"

Sofia looked up to see Lily, the girl she'd met at Cat's funeral. "Sure."

Lily carried a can of black paint as thick as tar. She dipped a wide brush into the can and laid a thick shadow starting in the top left corner of Sofia's paper. Sofia watched as Lily moved with intent across the white surface, dragging her brush back and forth until she had covered the whole page black. When she stopped, they looked at each other. In silence, Sofia lifted her paint can above the dark paper and poured a red pool in the middle. Lily's breath stuttered; the corners of her mouth lifted. She dipped her delicate fingertips in the red pool and splattered dots.

Then both girls smashed their hands down on the wet paper and swirled and mixed until murky brown covered every inch and the paper fell apart under their palms. A musical sound rumbled lightly in Sofia's chest, reminding her of how it felt to laugh.

"Do you like art?" Lily asked.

"Kind of. I design clothes and sew them." Sofia pushed the paint around one last time and picked up a paper towel. "Caitlyn and I have made things forever. Do you know the Fashionista Junior TV auditions are coming here next month?"

"No." Lily balled up the wet masterpiece and threw it away. She held her painted hands away from her body and walked over to the sink.

Sofia nudged the faucet on with her elbow. "It's a show on Netflix about teenagers making a fashion collection. It seems so lame now. Cat and I were trying out. We were making ensembles all year. We had one more to complete."

"Cool." Paint the color of dried blood ran off Lily's hands into the sink.

"Yeah. Cat had the fabric for our last dress in her locker that day."

"Do you still want to make it?" Lily asked.

"No. I don't know. I don't think I can without Cat."

Lily dried her hands with a paper towel and held one out to Sofia. "You should do it."

"Mrs. Moran says Cat would have liked me to finish it."

"Do it." Lily picked up two clean sheets of paper and placed them side by side. "I can help if you want."

"Maybe." Sofia studied Lily, the only person she had laughed with since Caitlyn died. She needed a friend, but something stopped her.

## Keisha

Keisha had always been a favorite with the cafeteria ladies. She remembered to say please and thank you, she asked how they were, bantered with them, recalled their birthdays, wished them happy holidays, asked about their kids and grandkids.

Her mother had taught her this technique. "A smile and a kind word can get you a long way, honey." She'd watched her father chat his way through more than a few pressed-chicken dinners, as he called them. It was time for that training to pay off.

She leaned over the counter and smiled at Mrs. Abernathy. The woman in the gray uniform with a net over her white hair smiled back. "What can I get you today, Keisha? Want a salad?"

Keisha nodded, not caring that she was holding up the line. "You know, I was wondering if you all heard anything the morning of the shooting? Or maybe you saw something?"

Mrs. Abernathy put her fingertips to her lips as if she were holding in a secret. She closed her eyes longer than a blink. "I was out back, Keisha, having a smoke." She shook her head. "I know I'm not supposed to smoke out there, and I think those FBI agents think I'm the accomplice because they know I lied to them about what I was doing at the time. I prop the door open with a rock while I'm out there even though that's against the rules." She hung her head. "They can tell things like that—when you lie. They know."

Inwardly, Keisha groaned. "They're not going to suspect you, Mrs. Abernathy. You're the salt of the earth. Was anyone late getting to work? You know," she smiled and winked, "Miss Shelby is late sometimes." Mrs. Abernathy grinned. They all covered for Miss Shelby. Each day she thrilled them with stories of her madcap love affairs. "She might have seen something when she was coming in, like who opened the door for him?"

Mrs. Abernathy rolled her lower lip and shook her head. "She didn't say, not to me, anyway. But the FBI talked to her, too. They'll know."

Keisha nodded. This wasn't working. There had to be another way. She should just talk to the janitor. He's the one who stopped the shooter. Maybe he saw who let that maniac into the building.

"Thanks, Mrs. Abernathy. You've been awesome. Have a great day." Keisha took the salad and walked down the line. She'd have to talk to the janitor after classes were over.

Two hours later, she spotted Mr. Wilkins in the hallway. She waited for the hallway to be empty and walked over. "Hey, Mr. Wilkins."

Mr. Wilkins looked up at her and half-smiled. "Hey." He was cautious with teenagers.

"I was wondering, since you're the hero who stopped the killer that day, if you saw who let him in the school?" Keisha prided herself on not being one to hold back.

Wilkins laughed. "If I'd a seen him, I woulda told everybody."

"Yeah, well, that's true." Keisha looked around, mildly embarrassed and hoping no one heard this exchange. "But what did you see that day?"

Wilkins mopped the floor for a bit. "Whatever I saw, I'm still thinking about it. I saw a girl in the hall. I told her to run."

"You saw a girl? Who was it?"

"Too smoky, too much going on. I don't know."

Keisha opened her mouth to ask another question. Wilkins cut her off. "Got to do my work here." He turned and pushed his bucket in the other direction.

**Intheknow @WRWL-TV**

BREAKING: ABC shooter to plead guilty in Rockwell High massacre. Sources say the FBI is closing in on identifying the female accomplice who opened doors to the ABC shooter enabling him to kill 15 and injure a dozen more on Oct.15.

# CHAPTER ELEVEN

## Mike

It was all over the news. That son of a bitch was going to plead guilty, and there would be no trial, just an arraignment, and sentencing. ABC didn't have the guts to face a jury. He was a coward through and through.

Mike's anger consumed him. He couldn't concentrate. After he heard the news on the radio during his morning drive to the office, his usual escape hatch, his work, didn't distract him. His co-workers must have heard about the plea deal, too, because everyone gave him a wide berth. No one called him into a meeting or stopped by his office to ask his help. He closed his office door and sat staring at his monitor, pretending to be thinking about his current projects when all his mental energies were focused on somehow making ABC pay for what he had done, what he had taken away. Caitlyn was dead, and Mike's family would never be the same. It was time to make a move. *The murderer is safe in jail now, but I'm going to take him out the day he goes to court.*

His office mates stared at their monitors and pretended not to notice when Mike left work early. He got in his car and headed for the courthouse, located in the small town that had served as the county seat for decades, once a marketplace where farmers brought their crops, eggs, and meat to sell. Encroaching suburbs had transformed the town. Now ethnic restaurants and fashionable boutiques lined its streets. An entire city block housed the county government complex, three buildings arranged in a U-shape around a broad plaza with a clock tower at its center. On one side of the courthouse stood a historic structure rumored to have once been a house of ill repute. A second-floor balcony extended across its entire width. On the other side, a five-story, nondescript building housed the county offices. The courthouse itself, a magnificent red-brick edifice with columns supporting a two-story portico, dominated the trio of buildings.

Mike parked his car a few blocks away and looked around. Trained in army reconnaissance, he took note of his surroundings as he strode to the government plaza. Cars were parked before row houses on the otherwise deserted street. On sentencing day, he knew news vans would crowd the area, blocking traffic and making a quick getaway impossible.

Still on the alert, he entered the plaza and counted his steps until he reached the courthouse door. About a hundred feet, too far away for a pistol or revolver if he was shooting from the street. He'd have to get closer for a kill shot. He'd been to the courthouse once before for jury duty, a drunk driving case in which he was happy to find the defendant guilty. He entered and found the security screening as he remembered, just like in an airport, with an armed guard and metal detectors. There was no way he could get a gun in there. He'd have to kill ABC before he entered the courthouse door. He turned and walked back out to the plaza.

Then he remembered the jury had access to a side door leading to a narrow alley, a door that could only be opened from the inside like the one ABC entered to get into Rockwell High. If the police took ABC into the courthouse through that side door, it would be almost impossible to hit him. For a moment, he doubted his plans. He clenched his fists, wanting to punch something, anything, but instead, he forced himself to calm down and think. They wouldn't use the hidden side door, he concluded. The headline-grabbing prosecutor, who had already hinted he might run against Senator Woodrow in the next election, wouldn't be able to resist the pull of the media gathered on the plaza. Mike could almost see the dramatic coverage of the killer walking toward the impressive front door of the courthouse.

He looked all around the plaza, considering his options. He could probably get into the office building with a gun, but its windows were sealed, and he wouldn't want to draw attention to himself by breaking one open. The balcony of the historic building was a perfect sniper spot, and he decided to explore it. Now a library, the building had no security screening, but he discovered the door to the balcony was blocked by high shelves packed with books.

Frustrated by these restrictions, Mike ventured back to the plaza, and there it was, right in front of his face, the clock tower standing about fifty feet from the courthouse door. He could brace his right arm against it as he aimed and duck behind it for cover if fire were returned. He wasn't afraid of getting shot. He'd faced hostile fire many times. Any onlookers should be safe behind him, near the courthouse door. This was where he'd take his stand. Satisfied with his preliminary plan, Mike headed home.

As he drove, Mike evaluated his choice of weapons. It would be poetic justice to shoot ABC with an AR-15, the same weapon that caused Caitlyn's death, but he knew carrying that large rifle would be too conspicuous. With the security expected that day, so would a holster. He needed a pistol he could hide in the pocket of his bomber jacket. His 9mm Beretta would be perfect. It was small but powerful enough to kill.

Later, when he walked into the kitchen from the garage, he was surprised to see Lisa taking a package from the refrigerator. "Hi," she said. "I thought I'd fix chicken parmesan for dinner."

If Lisa was cooking again, that meant maybe things could get back to normal for her. But not for him, so long as ABC still lived.

He kissed her cheek. "Sounds great, babe."

"Don't forget, the support group meets tonight."

"Right," he replied. *The fucking support group.*

They didn't help him at all, and he wasn't about to tell them what he was planning. He'd just keep quiet and let the others speak. Of course, everyone would be talking about the arraignment. He knew from their past meetings that at least two of the participants were in touch with the DA's office. Maybe they'd spill some helpful intelligence about the prosecutor's plans for getting ABC to the courthouse.

## Caitlyn

There was one good thing about being dead. She could be anywhere, anytime. Everything was up to her mind—she had no body. She was a collection of energy without a name or gender that wandered where it needed to go. Time was only a doorway. She moved as quickly as it took to flip her hair or drop a pencil. But she didn't have control. She drifted in and out, like when she was alive and in a dreamless sleep.

She wanted to find everyone, or just one, who might threaten those she loved. Her father, closed like a room without a door, was going places for no reason. This made no sense to Caitlyn. He was like fire. Her mother was like fog.

And Sofia, she was lost. She was making friends with Lily. Was she in danger? Caitlyn saw Lily now; she moved down the hallway to the biology lab with the splintered door. She walked alone. She glowed green. Color radiated from the top of her head, down her arms, and dripped from her fingertips. Her chest glowed yellow.

If she approached Lily, could she find out what she knew, why she was different from everyone that day? Even though she had no body, Caitlyn willed herself back into the lab. Lily looked into the room. Caitlyn concentrated on the body she no longer possessed. She wanted to be seen and heard. She focused her mind on the clothes—the denim skirt, the flowered shirt she wore the day the bones in her leg were shattered. She drew on the energy in the room, the buzz of the lights. The fear of that day, that still lingered.

*I almost died here.*

Lily jolted.

*She sees me!* Lily was breaking, on edge. Her glowing colors weighed her down. *Are you the one who let him in?* A voice came from the hallway, and Lily backed away.

Caitlyn moved through the biology lab and then was somewhere else. Below her sat the shooter on his prison cell cot. He was alone. He leaned over and collapsed to the floor, drew his knees up to his chest, and rocked; his body oozed ink. He cried black tears. Snot bubbled from his nostrils.

*You killed me. You killed so many people. Why?*

Caitlyn moved close to his eye, fragmented green and blue. *You had a choice to do something with your life. Instead, you ended ours. You shattered what was precious. I don't need to see you again. When you die, you'll be a piece of wire, the sharp edge of a knife.* He looked up, directly into her eyes. Did he see her? His body jerked. He dry heaved; his forehead rubbed against the cement floor.

She could do nothing for this person. But she could do something for the living. Caitlyn moved from the prison to her mom's side as she pushed a grocery cart in a store far from her house to shop alone. Here, no one would recognize the mother of the last person to die in the Rockwell High School shooting. Mom read the ingredients on the side of the can. She stopped reading and tossed it in the cart.

"What's the point," she muttered.

Her mother's frustration spread like a cold wave up and down the aisle. Caitlyn somehow was able to stir her mother's hair; like a whisper. Her mother paused and fingered the edges of her bangs. She must have known Caitlyn was there.

Caitlyn moved on to find Sofy. She had to tell her what she knew about Lily. That she was the girl in the hall. The one who was a different color.

## Sofia

Mr. Johnson, the science teacher she hadn't seen since the shooting, sat down next to Sofia in the support group. "How are you feeling about your friend?" he asked.

Sofia looked at him and turned her face away. She twirled a lock of pink hair with her index finger. The dark spiraled with the pink.

"Sofia will speak up in her own time," Debby said.

The circle intimidated her, everyone facing the center, with nowhere to hide. Thankfully, Lily had managed to sit next to her. Sofia had brought along the fabric Caitlyn's father got out of her locker. Somehow, she thought she'd be able to work on more of the embroidery in the group. They had been going for an environmentally friendly look— a long, sleeveless dress with a white skirt that flowed gently to the ankles and seemed to breathe on its own. The fabric was Caitlyn's choice.

She pulled the fabric out of her backpack and showed it to Lily. "We were going to applique insects on the skirt," she whispered. "The fitted bodice is supposed to be sheer voile."

"Insects?" Lily grinned. "That's interesting. No one else will have that."

Sofia nodded. "That's what we thought."

"I love it." Lily touched the voile. "It's so soft."

*It's perfect,* Caitlyn said.

*Glad you're here, Cat.*

*You need to be careful with her.*

"What?" Sofia put her hand over her mouth. She'd almost talked to Caitlyn out loud.

"Girls, Sofia, Lily, do you want to speak to the group?" Debby asked.

The adults stared. Their expressions of pity or sorrow or concern made Sofia sweat. She folded the pieces of fabric, trying to make them as small as she could before she shoved them into her backpack. The girls looked at each other, neither saying a word.

"We're in this together, sharing our experiences. Is there something you want to show the group?" Debby asked as she scribbled a note on her clipboard without looking at it.

Sofia glanced at Mrs. Moran, hoping for support. "No, not really."

Mrs. Moran blinked her eyes and smiled.

"Well, that was awkward," Lily whispered when Keisha started to talk.

Sofia dug out a little notebook from her pack that she used to write notes to Cat and scribbled, *do you still want to help me make the dress?*

"Yes," whispered Lily.

Sofia settled back in her chair, thumbing the pages of her notebook. She wanted to be home cutting a pattern, pushing fabric through her sewing machine. Maybe Lily could be a friend. Not like Caitlyn, but still a friend.

### Keisha

Keisha didn't think much of these support group meetings, but she was burning with questions about the accomplice. Nobody in this stupid group was even talking about it. As far as she could tell, this weekly meeting was a stupendous waste of time. Instead of making her feel better, she became more frustrated and angrier. Her jaw hurt from holding in all the things she wanted to say.

When she couldn't stand another second, she blurted, "What about the elephant in the room? We're all talking about our feelings as if it's over. It's not over. The accomplice is still out there. She could come into school and blow the rest of us away. Why aren't we talking about that? Why aren't we figuring out who it is?"

All of them turned to look at her, their faces stunned, like she'd thrown a grenade into the room. The therapist sat up straighter and composed her face. "You must be feeling anger and fear, is that right, Keisha?"

"Oh, for God's sake, don't mirror my feelings back to me. I know what I feel." In fact, she was close to tears, but she wasn't going to let them know that. She glared at Lily and Sofia. Why didn't they feel the way she did? "I don't want to be analyzed. I want us to solve the problem."

"And the problem as you see it is that there's still an unknown accomplice in your school who might harm you?"

"Yes." Keisha sighed. Debby had used her calmest voice, the voice that made Keisha want to shriek. "What I don't understand is why everyone doesn't worry about that. Why doesn't everyone want to do something about it?"

She looked directly at Lily, who seemed more likely to be someone who could do something about it. Lily was smart. Their class rankings were identical. Lily was quiet, like someone who was observing everything. If she had an ally in this group, it should be Lily, even if the girl went a little crazy now and then. Screaming at the debate prep was a bit much, but they were all over that, weren't they? Lily clenched her hands and looked away as if Keisha had committed some social faux pas by looking at her. *Well then, maybe not.*

Keisha turned to stare at Mr. Wilkins. "You saw something. Right? What about that, Mr. Wilkins? The girl in the hall? What did she look like?" She was pleading now, as desperate as if this were her last chance before someone tossed her off a cliff.

Mr. Wilkins lowered his chin and considered his knees. "I told you, I saw someone, but I'm not sure who it was."

Everyone stared at him. He tilted his head and looked at Keisha. His eyes flicked to Lily and then back to Keisha.

"I can say, this whole thing hurts me in ways I never thought I could be hurt." He shook his head and looked away.

"What difference does it make who the accomplice is," Charmaine blurted out. "My husband is still dead. Knowing who's responsible for that doesn't change anything."

Keisha rocked back in her seat, as stunned as if Alex's wife had thrown a rock at her head. Why would Mrs. Robinson be angry at her?

## Charmaine

Charmaine woke up with a start on Saturday morning and rushed to the bathroom to throw up. *I shouldn't have eaten Mama D's leftover mac and cheese last night.* She had often teased Alex about his unshakable faith in the powers of refrigeration, and now here she was, eating leftovers that had been around too long. *I've got to start taking better care of myself. I'm a nurse. I know better.*

She heard her phone ringing. Only one person called her this early on a Saturday morning. "Hi, Mom," she answered.

Tina got right to the point. "Dad and I are coming over to take you to lunch. We'll be there around 11:30. Think about where you want to go."

There was no use telling her mother her stomach was upset. Once Tina Parham made up her mind, that was it.

Charmaine usually went for a run on weekend mornings, but she didn't feel up to it today. She took a long hot shower instead and ate a piece of toast to calm her stomach.

Her folks arrived right on time, as usual. "You look peaked," Tina said. "Are you feeling all right?" She put her hand on Charmaine's forehead to feel for a temperature.

"I'm fine." Charmaine brushed her mom's hand away.

Her father ignored their conversation, focusing on more important matters. "Where should we go eat?"

Charmaine didn't care. She didn't care about much since Alex died.

They settled on Panera. Charmaine didn't think she was hungry, but she ate heartily when her soup and half sandwich arrived.

"It's good to see your appetite's coming back," Mom said.

"Didn't have much to eat today. I had a touch of food poisoning and got sick this morning."

Her mother gave her the quizzical look Charmaine hadn't seen since her teenage years— the wrinkled eyebrow stare of parental skepticism Charmaine and her friends had dubbed the hairy eyeball.

After they finished eating, Charmaine said, "I think I'll get a cookie. I'm still hungry."

"Come with me to the ladies' room first." Her mother led her through the crowded restaurant and cornered her outside the ladies' room door. She grabbed her daughter's hand and leaned in until their faces almost touched. "Charmaine, when was your last period?"

"What?" That was the last question Charmaine expected to hear. She stepped back. *Is Mom going crazy?* The question confused her. "I don't know," she stammered. "I haven't been keeping track lately. Other things on my mind, you know."

"I know the signs, same as with me. You're throwing up in the morning, and now you're eating like a linebacker. I think you're pregnant."

Charmaine stared at the triumphant look on her mother's face. For a moment, she couldn't move. Her fingers tingled, and warmth spread through her body. She felt something she hadn't felt since Alex died. Happiness. She grasped Alex's wedding ring, which she had begun wearing on a chain around her neck. "Oh, my God, do you really think so?"

"Yes." Mom's smile radiated confidence. "Check your calendar when you get home. You'll see."

Mom reached for Charmaine and pulled her in for a hug. The heavy scent of her favorite perfume made Charmaine want to throw up again. She freed herself from Mom's grip. *What if Mom is wrong?* She didn't want to get her hopes up. "Don't tell anyone, not even Dad, until I know for sure."

After her parents dropped her off at home, Charmaine checked her calendar. Over seven weeks since her last period. Her heart pounded as she hurried to the drugstore for a home pregnancy test. Back at the townhouse, she sat on the toilet and anxiously awaited the results, although she already knew the answer in her heart. She watched as the plus sign appeared.

She jumped up, threw her hands up in the air, and screamed. "Yes, yes." *Alex isn't gone completely. A part of him is still with me. A baby. We're going to have a baby. I don't care if it's a boy or a girl.*

She danced out into her bedroom and lay down. She gazed at her abdomen, still no baby bump showing, but she patted her stomach anyway. "I'll keep you safe, little one. I don't want you to grow up in a world where crazy people can get their hands on automatic weapons."

That girl Keisha was right. Maybe the victims' families and friends needed to do something about gun control. It's what Alex would have wanted.

## Lily

Lily's knee shook beneath the table as she took her parents' hands and bowed her head. Her mother rushed through the familiar words.

"Dear Lord, bless this food to the nourishment of our bodies and us to thy service. In Christ's name, we pray, Amen."

The Jeong family ate their dinner in near silence. This was normal. Ted needed time to decompress after a long day at work. He couldn't be interrupted by news of the long days his family may have endured until his stomach was full and his needs were met. Lily sipped her soup, patiently waiting until he set down his spoon and wiped his mouth.

"I won't be home after school tomorrow," she announced.

"Rehearsal?" her mother asked.

Lily hesitated, then spit out the words. "No, I'm going to a girl's house to help her with a project."

Stephanie placed her fingertips on the edge of the table. "What girl? What project?"

"Her name's Sofia. She's been going to the group meetings, too. Her best friend died. They were going to make a dress together. For a TV show."

Her mother shook her head. "Maybe it's not good to be around someone so sad."

Perhaps she was right, but Lily was drawn to Sofia, to her sad eyes and the pink lock of hair she sometimes twisted around her finger as if it were a conduit to her dead friend. Plus, in all of her grief, Sofia was kind to her. Lily could talk to her. They had even laughed together. Lily hadn't thought it would be possible to laugh again.

"She needs my help," Lily said. "And I think it is good for me to be around someone who's sad. Because I'm sad, too."

Silence returned to the table. Everyone's eyes dropped to their food as if Lily's words had never been spoken. As if no one cared that she just said she was sad. She wanted to bang her utensils against the table. Did this mean she could go or not? She was almost eighteen; she didn't need approval to go to a girl's house.

Just as Lily was about to excuse herself, her father said softly, "You should go."

***

The next day when the man opened the door, Lily's mouth dropped. He wasn't in his blue uniform, but she recognized his face. Hernandez, J. Did she have the wrong house? This had to be a mistake.

"You're Lily?" He smiled as if remembering her, too. "I'm Sofia's dad. Come in."

She stood frozen on the stoop in disbelief. Sofia's father was a cop? This couldn't be happening. She lowered her head and stepped inside.

"How's your hand?" he asked.

"Better."

"Hi, Lily." Sofia stood halfway out of a doorway at the top of the stairs. She waved Lily toward her. "Up here."

The room was not neat and organized like Lily's—more like the victim of a full-blown hurricane. In the wreckage of clothes, shoes, magazines, and bolts of fabric, Lily's eyes immediately found the small Polaroid photographs of Sofia and Caitlyn. They were tucked in the mirror, held up by tiny clothespins on a string, taped to the closet door. The framed photo on the nightstand looked like it was taken at a party. Sofia was wearing a blue and white gown and flowers in her hair. Caitlyn's short dress, spiked heels, and makeup made her look much older than fifteen. Lily struggled to swallow the fact that she would be fifteen forever.

"Sorry about the mess." Sofia pushed a pile of clothes to the side with her foot. "I haven't cleaned since . . ." Her eyes fell to a painted rock on the nightstand. She picked it up and tossed it from hand to hand. The motion seemed to infuse her with some energy. "Okay, truth bomb, I never clean my room. Caitlyn called me her chaos queen."

"Don't worry," Lily said. "Cleaning is way overrated."

"Exactly."

Inept at small talk, Lily used the silence that followed to examine the photos around the room. In one, the two girls were in bathing suits, ice cream dripping down their chins. Lily could almost hear their laughter. She pointed to it and said, "You must have been friends for a long time."

"Only since middle school. But it seems like forever. She was like a sister."

"I have a sister. We're nowhere near that close. I've never been that close to anyone. I can't imagine what it's been like to lose her."

Sofia sat on the edge of the bed and cradled the rock in her palm. "I lost my mom five years ago. I thought that'd be the worst thing that would ever happen to me. At least then I had Caitlyn."

Lily took a step to sit beside her but stopped. "You have other friends, though, right? Are they helping?"

"Friends, yeah, but I'm not as close to any of them as I was to Cat. I never needed anyone else. Besides, it seems everyone lost someone. Even if they didn't, that day changed everyone. No one is the same. No one will ever be the same again." Sofia's fingers closed around the rock. She squeezed it then released it with a long exhale. She dropped it on the mattress and hopped up from the bed. "But let's not talk about that. That isn't why you came."

Sofia moved to the headless sewing form in the center of the room. Several swaths of fabric spun around the bodice.

"As you can see, I haven't gotten very far with the actual sewing. I have some sketches." Sofia dug a sketch pad out of the rubble. "Like I told you, we were going to make a dress with insects—beetles and caterpillars on it. But that doesn't feel right anymore. Not without Cat. I still want it to be a piece of art. Any suggestions?"

Lily took the sketch pad. She was no expert—the art she practiced was self-taught and completely different—but as she flipped through the pages, she instinctively recognized the problem. The drawings showed great talent, but scattered thoughts interrupted the quick pencil strokes. Shadows of grief weighted the flowing skirts. None of the drawn models had a face.

"They're great," Lily said. "But maybe . . . maybe there's a lack of focus." She hesitated, worried how her suggestion would be received. "Maybe instead of a blank model, pretend it's your friend. Make the dress you were going to make with Caitlyn but make it *for* Caitlyn."

"Cat . . ." Sofia looked away from Lily. She stared at nothing for a long time, nodding once and smiling as if in conversation. When she turned back, her eyes had a soft, dreamy sheen. "Yes," she said. "I'll make the dress for Caitlyn."

Sofia began to yank pins out of the sewing form. Lily helped, following her around the headless, armless figure, matching the girl's frantic energy. Their circles made Lily dizzy, but in a good way, like when she sneaked a glass of champagne at her father's promotion party. Next, they pulled at the fabric, throwing it up over their heads as they went, laughing for no apparent reason. A stretch of white voile shrouded Lily's vision. When she swatted it away, a figure flashed in her periphery. Not Sofia—a blonde girl with a grim expression and a stripe of pink hair.

Lily's breath halted. She stumbled back against the dresser. There was no one there. Just Sofia and all the photographs of the same blonde girl.

Sofia spun to a stop. Still laughing, she asked, "Are you okay?"

Lily struggled to inhale. No, she thought, I'm not okay. *I just saw your dead best friend. She doesn't want me here. She doesn't want me near you. She knows I killed her.* Lily's knees buckled, and she dropped to the floor.

Sofia rushed to her side. "Are you okay?"

After finally forcing air to her lungs, Lily nodded. "Just got dizzy."

"Sofia!" Joe's voice rose up the stairs of the small house. "Come here quick! Come see this!"

The two girls exchanged quizzical glances. Sofia helped Lily to her feet. They hurried downstairs to the living room, where Joe stood in front of the television. There was breaking news.

*At this time, the FBI is only calling this girl, a student at Rockwell High School, a person of interest in the school shooting that occurred three weeks ago. As we all know, the ABC Killer, as he's called—we don't want to give notoriety to these mass shooters—was captured the day of the shooting, but there has been an ongoing investigation into the possibility of an accomplice. Someone let this boy into the school that morning. Our sources have not confirmed that investigators believe this girl to be that accomplice, but we do know that she had a relationship with the shooter. Investigators also believe this person of interest may have knowledge of the shooter's motive. As CNN has reported, investigators have not connected the ABC Killer to any known hate or terrorist group—*

The girl's yearbook image filled half the screen. Dark hair like Lily's. Dark eyes like Lily. Mixed race with a predominance of Asian. But it was not Lily. Once again, she could not breathe. She tried to remember if her finger had stopped on the picture of this girl's face when she was sandwiched between Special Agents Warren and Radson. What relationship did this girl have with Aaron? Was he seeing someone else this whole time?

"So, it was a girl," Joe said. "Do either of you know her?"

"I don't," Sofia said.

Lily felt her body list. Just as she thought she would topple over, Sofia's hand wrapped tightly around hers and kept her from falling.

**Beowolf @RockwellHighNews**
Skipping classes to go to the ABC arraignment today. Chemistry and French aren't as important as looking this mother fucker in the eyes. He didn't have the guts to show us his eyes the day he shot our friends & teachers. Will he today? #perpwalk #justice #RockwellStrong

# CHAPTER TWELVE

## Joe

Joe was off suspension, back in uniform, and assigned to keep the peace at the county courthouse for ABC's appearance. He adjusted his belt, settled his cap, and took his position on the top step. The chief had told them to expect trouble.

"Those kids are troublemakers," the chief said at the seven-a.m. meeting. "They'll be there. They might stir up the crowd. Your job is to prevent violence."

Joe's resentment simmered. The kids weren't the problem. The shooter was the problem. The system was the problem. If ABC hadn't terrorized his daughter's school, no one would be out in front of the courthouse today. The killer's accomplice was walking around free while his daughter grew thin and pale because her friend was murdered in cold blood—that was the problem. And now the police were supposed to protect the murderer. Nothing made sense anymore.

He tried to screw his head on right. Chen was here also, calm as a cucumber, standing opposite him only twenty feet away. Five more officers patrolled the area. Joe watched kids from the high school assemble quietly with their signs. They broke his heart with their silent courage. Clearly, it cost them something to stand there as witnesses to this travesty. It cost him something, too. Joe steeled himself for the first sight of ABC and reminded himself of his oath. *I will treat all individuals with dignity and respect . . .*

## Lily

Lily walked out of the school with the other hundred or so protesters, but when they turned right toward the parking lot for the drive to the courthouse, she turned left. It was just under three miles to her house. Her legs were short but fast. She'd make it home in plenty of time to see the planned spectacle on television. It was Tuesday—her mother's church book club would keep her away until noon. No one would be home. She could scream all she wanted.

Helicopters once again thundered above the trees. Lily peered through the last of the fall colors and counted three. She imagined the scene downtown. News vans with their mini-satellites. Reporters jostling for position. Keisha and her army of outraged poster carriers, though many were just there to skip class. Aaron was going to plead guilty. There would be no trial, no other chance for the vultures to converge.

Unless they came for her.

Or Miranda Keyes. The other girl.

Lily's feet kicked up a sheet of fallen leaves. *Miranda*. The name stuck in her throat. Her name was leaked soon after the story broke. They were still calling her a person of interest. Her teary parents had given a statement on television: "While our daughter went out with Aaron on a few occasions, she had absolutely nothing to do with the shooting at Rockwell High. We met this young man. Nothing in his demeanor hinted that he would be capable of such a heinous act. Our daughter is devastated . . ."

How many other girls did Aaron Blake Crofton devastate? Was she the only one stupid enough to fall for his fake plan?

She remembered him ranting as she cried in his dark basement hours after the debate. "These fucking kids and their fucking entitlement. Who are they to laugh? They don't know what real pain is. They don't know suffering. They need to know what pain is. I mean . . . how can they go about their lives, on their phones like fucking zombies when kids their age are starving, or being sold into slavery, when priests are raping little boys, when rich fucks are getting richer off the misery—"

"Stop it! Just shut up!"

Aaron gripped both her upper arms and brought his face down to hers. "They need to know what pain is. They need to suffer, too, like us."

She had seen him this way before, the way his moods could gnarl and twist like roots into the dark earth. She used to punish herself for having dark thoughts. Until she met him. His thoughts were much darker and sadder and somehow, magnificent.

"What are you going to do, shoot up the school?" She said it as a joke to calm him down. But his blue eyes were far away. The darkness had consumed him. And this time, he pulled her down with him. Three bombs, he said. All she had to do was open the door. He would take care of the rest. No one would get hurt. Their fear would be their suffering. She believed him. Or did she know his real plan? Deep down, did she know it all along?

As soon as Lily made it home, she turned on the television. She sat on the sofa and pushed both forearms against her nervous stomach. What would it be like to see Aaron on live television walking into the courthouse? Lily bet his hair had grown. Maybe he'd have a beard. As the news anchors ramped up their excitement, she became almost giddy. Just a little bit longer until a judge would send Aaron away forever.

## Mike

*Caitlyn twirled around to show off the new black watch plaid dress she was wearing for the first day of kindergarten. Her fine blonde hair brushed against Mike's face as he kissed her goodbye.*

*Have a good time in school today, he said.*

*Suddenly Caitlyn's joyful expression changed to a pout. I don't want to go to school, Daddy. I'm scared. Please don't make me go to school.*

Mike awoke in a sweat. These disturbing dreams of Caitlyn's childhood were becoming more frequent. At first, in the days following the funeral, he recalled his daughter only as a fifteen-year-old, as if he expected to come home and find her still there, tapping on her phone or hunched over the sewing machine with her best friend, Sofia. But lately, memories flooded back, the tiny infant who wrapped her fist around his thumb, the lopsided birthday cake she made him when she was just in second grade, and all those soccer practices and games where he cheered her on. His sons always called him "Dad," but to Caitlyn, he was "Daddy," and she was daddy's girl.

Maybe these memories were his way of acknowledging that Caitlyn now existed only in the past. Her present and her future died with her, thanks to ABC. Today he would make things right. Today was the day to carry out his plan.

ABC was to be arraigned at 9:30 that morning. Mike had already told Ernie he was taking the day off to go to the courthouse. His boss was understanding, or maybe he just wanted to avoid Mike's grief. "Do whatever you have to do, Mike," Ernie had said. "I've got your back." He didn't tell Lisa, though, and didn't worry about seeing her at the courthouse. He knew his wife had no desire to confront ABC. She had stopped watching TV because she couldn't even look at the murderer's photo on the news. He showered and dressed, drank his coffee, and kissed Lisa like he did every other morning before leaving for the office. But this time, he hid a loaded 9mm Beretta pistol in the pocket of his bomber jacket as he drove to the county seat.

He parked a few blocks away and walked to the courthouse. Several parking spaces in front of the plaza were cordoned off. *This is where the police will park and then walk ABC through the plaza to the courthouse door, just like I thought. So far, so good.*

Although ABC's perp walk wasn't scheduled for another hour, news crews were already setting up their gear, and a small crowd was beginning to gather. He recognized a few people from the support group, people like him who had lost their loved ones in the school shooting, and they exchanged waves and nods. Joe Hernandez and four other officers stood guard near the courthouse door. Keisha, the girl from the support group, was here with a gang of high schoolers carrying signs with the names of ABC's victims. That boy Eric was holding up the one with Caitlyn's name. *She'd like that. She was right about him.*

More onlookers were crowding near the courthouse door, making it harder to get a shot in that direction. Mike turned back toward the street. ABC would be an easier target when he was walking from the police car through the plaza. He could get off a good shot before ABC even reached the clock tower.

He scanned the plaza again. Others had joined him there to await ABC's arrival. Two policemen were chatting with the anchorwoman from the evening news and not paying much attention to anyone else. He figured more police would arrive with the prisoner. He stationed himself beside the clock tower and waited.

He wasn't nervous. On the contrary, he was experiencing a familiar war zone composure, relaxed and energized at the same time, keyed up but somehow calm, just like in Iraq when his troops battled Saddam's goons. He hadn't felt any qualms about killing then, and he didn't now. It was something he had to do.

He'd never told Caitlyn about the war. She was just a toddler when he was deployed. When he arrived back home, Lisa had been standing on the tarmac as he walked off the plane. The boys nearly tackled him—they had grown so tall. He leaned in to kiss the beautiful blonde-headed child in his wife's arms, and Caitlyn's eyes had filled with suspicion. She turned her face away from him.

"She doesn't know you," Lisa said. "Give her time."

Caitlyn quickly took to him all over again. The bond between them was instinctual, biological, and never to be broken, not even by death.

**Keisha**

They held their posters high. Each was painted black with white letters that spelled out the names of the dead. Fifteen signs to mark the fifteen people who died at the end of ABC's gun. Fifteen names over and over so that bastard would never forget. He had to face them today. The dead were his jury for the trial he wouldn't have.

Keisha held the one that said, "Alex Robinson." One of her team handed her the poster, and her heart quaked. She didn't need any reminders of her responsibility to the man who protected her from a madman with a gun.

Half of the senior class had arrived at the courthouse before the news crews, before the crowd, and formed a gauntlet on the stairs up which ABC would have to walk to get into the building. The turnout was gratifying. The day they learned he would plead guilty at his arraignment and avoid a trial, she had taken the petition to the principal. Six hundred kids had signed it.

"We want to go to the courthouse and stage a peaceful protest to let the shooter know he didn't annihilate us, that we're still living, still doing what we need to do."

Dr. Thompson was her usual calm self. She was someone Keisha emulated when she needed to keep her fiercer emotions in check. "Being there could put you all in danger, not only physically but emotionally."

"We're willing to take that risk to let ABC know we're not afraid of him."

"You might need a permit to assemble in a public place like that."

"Help us get the permit, then. You owe us that."

Dr. Thompson blanched. "I'll have to clear this with the Board," she said.

"Go ahead," Keisha said. "I'll wait." She sat in the chair opposite the principal, crossed her legs, and watched her make the call, and then another, and another. She admired the woman's persistence. It was another important lesson.

After an hour, the principal said, "You're set. You have permission." She walked around her desk and put her hand on Keisha's shoulder. "And my blessing. Be careful."

Sorrow, regret, guilt were all weapons that could be used to her advantage, Keisha learned. She tucked the information away.

Television crews arrived and set up. Cameras scanned them. Print reporters and news photographers got in their quickie two-sentence interviews. Keisha and her schoolmates were color for today's story. She didn't care. She was doing what she thought was right, standing up for the dead. Making sure they weren't forgotten. That was her job today. That was all she wanted to accomplish.

**Aaron**

I can't see out of the back of this van, but I hear the noise. The chants and jeers. All for me. This wasn't the plan, but this is better. If that asshat hadn't smashed me with a bucket in the hall, I'd already be free. But I wouldn't have this stage. I'll be on every screen in America. Live and in-person—and not the nice kid photo. The media won't admit it, but they're hard for me. They're probably wet wondering what I'll do. The ABC Killer—that's fucked up. When will they learn they're part of the problem?

The guard sitting across from me won't stop staring. "It'll be over soon," he says.

Like I want it to be over.

He folds his arms across his fat chest and sighs. He knows how ridiculous this all is. I heard him pressing to bring me in the back way. Not in this day and age, buddy. You gotta throw meat to the lions. I wonder what today's hashtag is.

#ABCguilty?

#fuckyouall

I tried. I tried to stop it, to bleed the poison out of me, but nothing worked. The noise kept getting louder. The burning inside wouldn't go away. Jet fuel pumped through my veins. I couldn't fly into a skyscraper. I had to do something.

I wonder if she's out there. No, she's too weak to come. They keep asking who let me in the building. As if I'd ever tell them. No one helped me. This was my show. Mine alone.

The guard slips his phone out of his back pocket. He pretends to be reading something, but I see him aim the phone at me.

"Print it out and bring it to me in prison," I say. "I'll autograph it for you."

"Shut the fuck up."

"Sell it. The New York Times will probably give you fifty-grand."

His eyes narrow at me. His face reddens with either embarrassment or hate, I can't tell. He probably doesn't know he's part of the problem, too.

Brakes grind beneath my feet. The van jerks to a stop. The doors swing open, and sunlight blinds me for a second. Just like stage lights. The crowd roars. Time for the big show.

**Mike**

Mike heard the sirens from blocks away and gripped the pistol still hidden in his pocket. The jail paddy wagon, flanked by two county police cars, pulled into the reserved parking spaces. The cops emerged first. ABC was the last to exit the police van.

*He's just a kid, a dumb kid. This is who killed my Caitlyn?* Skinny and gaunt, ABC didn't look threatening at all. Curly blond hair tumbling over his forehead gave him an angelic look, but his eyes surveyed the scene like a predator on the prowl. He wore the jail's orange jumpsuit, his hands cuffed in front, attached to leg irons, which would make it difficult for him to escape Mike's bullet.

The kid began his slow shuffling walk across the plaza with a cop on either side. Mike stepped behind the clock tower where the cops wouldn't see him and leaned against it. He hadn't been able to protect Caitlyn before, but he could make up for that now. He'd have a straight shot directly at ABC.

## Aaron

I shuffle, even though there's plenty of slack in my ankle chains. Shuffling is what people expect prisoners to do. Gotta give the audience what they want. Guards walk next to me, behind me. One has his clammy hand wrapped around my arm. He's leading me as if I can't see the path I have to take—the one lined with savages.

Gun nuts are here. And protesters with their clever posters. Both sides are fucked. What I did had nothing to do with either side. I'm just fuel for their cause. That's okay. They all have to live in this shit-filled world. For the rest of my days, I'll get three squares and won't have to deal with any of it. Hypocrisy, hate, greed, corruption, poverty, perversion . . . yeah, good luck and fuck you all.

People push in on us. Sound bends in my ears. Everything is garbled. For a second, I can't feel the sidewalk. Faces and cameras blur. I wonder if this is a dream. The crowd spews their volcanic bile at me.

Do they hate me enough?

## Mike

Mike pulled his pistol out, and as he started to raise it, he felt a breeze blowing in his face and heard Caitlyn's voice say, *Don't, Daddy. Don't do it.*

He shook his head. He never thought he'd hear her voice again. *What is happening?* He raised the gun, this time taking aim at ABC, but again his daughter's voice pleaded, *No, Daddy.*

Then he saw her face in the crowd, not in his mind, but right there, between him and ABC. Her big blue eyes, the silly streak of pink hair, and the determined half-smile he remembered. His vision blurred. "Caitlyn," he whispered as he slumped against the clock tower. When he looked up, he saw the moment had passed. ABC was already out of range. He had missed his chance at revenge.

## Joe

Joe watched the monster shuffle toward the steps, almost like he was doing a little dance for the media to show he didn't give a damn, as if he were above it all and knew something no one else did. A wave of fury surged through Joe again.

He tried to tamp down his rage, but right in front of his eyes, ABC lifted his cuffed hands as far as they could go attached to the chain from his ankles, cocked his thumb, and aimed his pointer finger right at the girl standing next to Joe—Keisha Washington, the one he helped out of the school the day of the shooting, the one who had been leading the protests.

ABC's finger twitched, and he leered at Keisha. *You're next*, the shooter was saying.

*That pig, that arrogant, stupid, self-satisfied pig. He's like every bully who ever punched or kicked me, every creep who ever stole my lunch or burned my homework.*

Outrage rippled through the crowd in front of the courthouse. Joe could see the way anger moved across their shoulders, seeped into their faces. The crowd was chanting, "Our Lives Matter. No More Guns." He wasn't the only one who hated this bastard.

ABC's lawyers and the police assigned as the shooter's bodyguards were on the fifth step. Two more steps to go, and then he was right there.

## Keisha

*The way he taunts us all, the way he walks, how he looks at us. At me.* Keisha shook with rage. Her arms vibrated so hard her poster rattled. She was right next to Officer Hernandez, Sofia's father, but she didn't feel safe. Just seeing ABC's face again brought everything back—Mr. Robinson shot, falling, bleeding. The sounds. The smells. She was going to faint.

Keisha lowered her head to stop the dizziness and saw Officer Hernandez touch his gun. She watched him pull it out of the holster. She couldn't breathe. His arm went up. Her eyes followed the barrel of the gun. He was pointing it at ABC. His finger was on the trigger.

"No!" She tried to yell, but the sound came out only as a whisper. "No! This isn't the way."

The crowd was pressing forward toward the killer. She watched Joe squeezing the trigger. Everything was happening in slow motion. She had to do something.

Keisha dropped her poster and grabbed his arm.

## Joe

He could hear a clamor behind him, all around him, but he couldn't understand any words. He was beyond words. His world was a swirl of wrath and revenge. One second, two, and now . . .

Someone grabbed his arm. Joe glanced over his shoulder. Keisha. He shook her off and aimed. He shot. ABC fell, groaning. A weight lifted off Joe; he was at peace, finally.

The crowd gasped. People screamed. Joe didn't want them to be afraid, particularly the kids. They'd had enough fear. He re-holstered his gun and put his hands in the air. Swarmed by his brothers in arms, Joe was handcuffed and hustled away to a holding cell inside the courthouse.

"Please," he said to Chen, "you need to call my parents. They need to get to Sofia."

He had done what he had to do. Some of them would think he was a hero. Sofia would understand someday.

## Aaron

A wave of bodies. I'm on the ground. A boot on my calf. My back smashed against concrete. I can't breathe.

Shouting, voices, screams. It all jumbles together; makes no sense. Now my shoulder is on fire. It's burning, burning, the jet fuel ignited. Jesus fuck, it burns. Someone make it stop. I gasp. A strange noise, like an animal—no, that noise is me, yelling at the burning pain. I still can't breathe. I struggle for words.

"Get off me!"

The face of the guard from the van almost touches mine. His voice in my ear: "Don't move."

I feel something wet on my shoulder. *Blood?*

Holy fuck, someone shot me. Here, in this crowd. No, this has to be a dream. But oh God, it burns. I'm fucking crying. But I'm laughing, too. Someone shot me. Is this what it feels like? Is this how it ends?

How fucking poetic.

## Keisha

Keisha lay on the courthouse steps. Dozens of legs and feet swarmed around her. *God, I must have fainted. What is wrong with me?* Then she remembered. She was knocked over. Hit on the chin by an elbow to her face. Hit by Sofia's father. None of this made any sense. Dragging herself to her knees, she sat back on her heels. Her head spun.

*There's a body over there. Someone is screaming. He's screaming. Aaron, he's been shot. There's blood.* Every time her eyes focused on one element in front of her, her brain sent another message, trying to connect the dots. *Aaron's been shot and . . . and Sofia's father shot him.* She couldn't put it together. The dots wouldn't line up. She remembered now; she tried to stop him, remembered being elbowed away, being knocked down by the crowd of people surging forward. She covered her face with her hands and rocked. That didn't stop the screaming in her head.

A cordon of navy-blue bodies formed around ABC, and another gathered around Sofia's father. The ambulance rolled right up into the plaza. A man barked orders in a loud voice. Over a bullhorn, a man was yelling, "Clear the steps, leave the area." Over and over as if once wasn't enough. People jostled against her. Someone helped her to her feet.

Keisha looked around her. Their signs were abandoned all over the steps and plaza. Classmates dropped them as they fled. She closed her eyes. The names of the dead had been trampled by people running from yet another man with a gun. Would it never stop?

**Intheknow @WRWL-TV**
BREAKING: The Rockwell High School assailant was shot by a county police officer while entering the courthouse. He was taken to Tri-County Hospital. Extent of injuries unknown. The officer was arrested. Details to follow.

# CHAPTER THIRTEEN

## Charmaine

News of the shooting of Aaron Blake Crofton spread quickly through the Tri-County Hospital ER. Sensing all eyes on her, Charmaine sat frozen at the nurses' station, staring straight ahead as if in a trance. Questions raced through her mind: *Who did this? Why? When will this violence end?*

The man who killed her husband was coming to her emergency room. She was a trained medical professional, expected to care for the wounded. Could she bring herself to treat him or maybe even save his life? He deserved to die for what he'd done. What would Alex have wanted her to do?

*I can't do it. I won't.*

Ambulance sirens wailed, followed by the tramping of EMTs rushing through the ER. A young man with curly blond hair moaned on the gurney. Blood-soaked gauze covered his shoulder. *He'll live. This kid who shot Alex will survive.* He moaned again. *I'm glad he's suffering.*

Dr. McGann approached. Charmaine got up and went to him. "I can't . . ." she began. He put his hand on her shoulder and said, "Why don't you take a break now, Charmaine? We've got this."

Grateful, she mumbled a thank you and fled to the nurses' locker room. She felt nauseous, and not just from morning sickness, as she pondered her decision not to help a wounded patient. Before Alex's death, she could never have imagined refusing to treat a patient. She was a nurse. It was her job. She was coming to realize that it wasn't just her life and her future that changed when Alex died. She had changed as well.

## Keisha

She held a sob in her throat and made her way to where her car was parked, a block from the courthouse. Her legs felt made of stone. The five classmates she'd brought with her stood waiting. Their faces were blank with shock; they hugged and whispered to each other. She walked into their arms.

The first text from her father was simple: *Are you OK?*

That was easy to answer: *Yes. Going home.*

Her mother's text was more detailed: *I saw what happened on television. Are you hurt? Do you need me to come home?*

Her mother still hadn't abandoned full sentences. Keisha typed: *No, Mom. I'm ok. I'll be home whenever you get there.*

Keisha asked Steve to drive her car. She wasn't in any shape to make the simple judgments driving required, like go when the light was green and stop when it was red, much less execute left turns at four-way intersections in traffic. While he drove, the babble in the car increased in decibels as her friends processed their shock. She answered texts from the principal, teachers, and classmates who didn't come to the protest.

It was exhausting, keeping them all updated. *If they really wanted to know, they should have been there.* Keisha checked Twitter, almost an automatic reflex.

@onemanarmy had tagged her in a post: GOT WHAT YOU DESERVED BITCH.

Her heart clutched. She blocked him and turned off her phone. After a momentary panic about being out of touch, she felt strangely relieved. She wasn't responsible for the world. She could turn it off. *I'm just a kid. I want to be a kid. That's all.*

Her friends came home with her. They normally hung out at her house after school anyway. Mikaela turned on the television in the family room to watch the coverage of the courthouse fiasco, as the news reader was calling it. Some pundit was blabbering about how the police had just made the ABC shooter a martyr. Steve put a bag of popcorn in the microwave. He knew where the bowls were. Another friend asked everyone what they were drinking and tossed soft drinks across the room from the refrigerator.

Keisha retreated upstairs to her bathroom, just to get her breath back, to try to find normal before everyone demanded something else from her. All her lofty plans for the future evaporated as she examined her reflection in the mirror over the sink. *Who am I? Where did I get this crazy idea that I'm supposed to do something important?*

She was tired, tired of trying. Tired of being the best. Tired of winning stuff. Tired of thinking about winning. What was it really that she had won, anyway? It was all meaningless. Nothing changed. It was as if her mind had tried to expand beyond her body and control everything, fix it, improve it. *What a joke. I have no power. That's what I learned today. I have no power to fix anything. I'm a loser just like everyone else, like Aaron, like that accomplice.*

Everything her parents had always told her about being special, about being someone who would do great things— that was all bullshit they told her to get her to do what they wanted. *I'm not going to do anything. I'm nobody.* She pulled open the top middle drawer in the bathroom vanity and found a pair of scissors. Keisha undid her ponytail, and holding up each braid, she cut her hair as close to her scalp as she could until nothing was left but a fringe of black fuzz. Her head felt lighter. She shook her head and glared at the new Keisha Washington in the mirror. *Yes. That's who I am.* Relishing the idea of her mother's restrained shock when she found the braids, Keisha tossed them in the trash can.

She walked slowly down the stairs listening to her friends' chatter, threw herself on the gray linen sofa, and closed her eyes. They all stared at her, but no one commented on her hair. *They'd better not.* Someone else could call the plays from now on. She was done quarterbacking. She just needed to be free from all of this.

### Mike

"What are you doing home so early?" Lisa asked. When Mike didn't answer, she studied him more closely. "What's wrong?"

Mike brushed his forehead with his shirt sleeve. He was sweating profusely, even though it was a cool autumn day. He sank into a chair and leaned forward, his head in his hands.

"You're scaring me," Lisa said. "What happened?" She plopped down on a chair across from him.

Mike looked up and confessed. "I didn't go to work this morning. I went to the courthouse instead to see the ABC killer get arraigned." Her disapproving frown didn't escape him. Did she suspect why he had really gone to the courthouse? After twenty-five years of marriage, she was probably on to him. He hurried on. "Someone shot the kid before he could enter the courthouse. I'm not sure, but I think it was Joe Hernandez, Sofia's father."

"Oh, my God. Is the boy dead? Is Joe all right?"

"I don't know."

He didn't tell her he got the hell out of there as fast as he could because he didn't want to be caught at the scene with a pistol in his pocket. He'd sat in his car for a good ten minutes, shaking. *What's wrong with me? I didn't really hear Caitlyn, let alone see her. I don't know what that was. I must be crazy to think I could assassinate that kid. A kid!*

His shame would never permit him to admit to Lisa what he had been planning or that their beloved daughter, whose body lay in a grave but whose spirit lived on in his heart, had saved him from becoming a murderer himself.

"Poor Sofia." Lisa got up to make coffee. "She'll need our help."

Mike wasn't thinking about Sofia just then. "Christ, Lisa, I saw the killer in person. He's just a kid. How the hell could anyone give a fucked-up kid like that an AR-15?"

Lisa slammed the coffee can down on the counter so hard it startled him. "So someone has to shoot him in retaliation? And the answer is more violence, more shooting, more killing?" She was shouting, but for once, tears weren't running down her cheeks. Instead, her face reddened with anger. "Is that what you think?"

Mike hung his head. He didn't know how to answer his wife. No laws would have stopped Joe Hernandez, a cop with a gun. While he still firmly believed in the Second Amendment, picturing any crazy kid with an AR-15 scared him.

"Our daughter is dead, Mike." Sobs caught in Lisa's throat. "We can't let this go on. We've got to do something about gun violence."

He had come so close to committing murder. He owed this to Lisa for what he had almost done, which would have ruined her life as well as his. He stood up and took her in his arms.

"I promise. I'll make sure of it. You can count on me."

## Lily

She watched the scene over and over, half in horror, half euphoric. Aaron's gesture, the *pop*, screams, and chaos as bodies flew in all directions. Every channel whipped up special graphics and music for their breaking news: *Shooting at Courthouse*. The screen split between professional and shaky cell phone footage. Talking heads dissected every second, just like the Zapruder film. But so far, none could answer the question that burned through Lily:

*Is he dead?*

A sea of blue had whisked him away. There was no word on his condition. The uncertainty crawled over her skin. Jittery, she stood, sat, paced the room. The ugly desire to wish another human being dead diffused through her veins like toxins. Was this how he felt that day? If he were dead, he could never speak her name. If he were dead, it could all be over.

When a field reporter mentioned the ongoing investigation into a possible accomplice, Lily stopped cold. A new question tore through her head: If someone were so desperate to see Aaron Blake Crofton dead that they would shoot him in a public space in broad daylight with the world watching, what would they do to her, the one who opened the door?

Lily spun away from the television. She grabbed her backpack and ran upstairs, where she dumped the contents on her bed: A.P. stats textbook, *Pride and Prejudice*, binders, pencils, and the ear-splitting whistle she'd stolen from the P.E. teacher that morning. Next, she gathered essentials. As she refilled the backpack with three clean shirts, jeans, and a week's worth of underwear, she plotted her move. She'd take a bus to New Jersey, to the church where her family went on a retreat when she was ten. She'd tell them she was lost. Or abused, raped—any sad story would do. They'd take her in, and in two months, she'd be eighteen. She'd go to New York and disappear.

Of course, she'd need money. The bank on her dresser held seven hundred and twenty-three dollars—money she'd earned tutoring stupid football players who didn't know the difference between variables and constants in algebra. How far would seven hundred dollars get her? She'd have to get a job. She'd tutor, wait tables, sell her art. Sell her body if she had to. It didn't matter. Aaron had tainted her forever.

*All you have to do is open the door.*

In the bathroom, Lily shoved toiletries and her retainer into the backpack. The television still blared downstairs. She stopped in the doorway of Violet's room. A trail of clothes ran from the closet to the bed. The purple comforter was tossed open as if she'd sprung from the bed to escape a fire. Lily scooped up all of the clothes, tossed them in the hamper, and then smoothed the comforter back into place. She sat Milo the sock monkey—the one she'd given Violet for her third birthday—squarely on the pillow and rushed back downstairs. She went straight to the front door. When she yanked it open, she met her mother's shocked face.

"Lily?" Stephanie gasped. One hand fell flat on her chest.

"Mother, what happened to book club?"

"Don't ask me about book club. Why aren't you in school?"

"There was another shooting . . . At the courthouse." Lily back stepped toward the television. "Everyone was hysterical. The principal said we could go home if—" A new face filled the screen. Lily blinked in disbelief.

*We can now confirm the identity of the person who fired one shot at the Rockwell County Courthouse today . . .*

Lily's body shook. Sofia's father? Sofia—who lost her mother and her best friend, who just wants to make a dress, whose life was already wrecked. Sofia was going to stay home today to work on the dress. Please God, Lily thought, please don't let her be watching this.

"I know him," Lily cried. "I know him. I have to go."

She sprinted to the door. Her mother came right on her heels.

"Where are you going?" Stephanie yelled, tugging at Lily's backpack.

"That's Sofia's father. She's my friend. I have to go to her."

Lily reached the door and pushed her mother away.

"No! Wait!"

Stephanie ran down the front walk and latched on to Lily's arm. Lily tried to wrestle away from her, but the grip was too tight.

"Lily, STOP!" Stephanie grabbed Lily's other arm and held her firmly. She waited until Lily stopped squirming, then met her daughter's eyes and said, "I will drive you."

## Sofia

Sofia pulled her buds out and rubbed her ears. She had been wearing them all morning as she worked. Scraps of fabric littered the floor, lethal pins stuck out from the carpet. Papi had given her a day off from school so she could finish the dress. The audition was coming up fast.

Sofia plunged onto her bed, laid there a second, then rolled over and scrutinized the dress she and Caitlyn had planned long ago. It looked like something an ancient vestal virgin would wear. She had only been able to embroider three insects onto the skirt. They crawled up the right side. Every time she pulled her needle through the fabric, she thought of Caitlyn and had to close her eyes. Less is more, Caitlyn had always told her. Wait until Lily saw it; she would be so impressed.

The doorbell rang. Did Papi forget his keys? Why was he at the front door and not the kitchen door? Sofia went down the carpeted stairs in her socks. She looked at the clock. It was only eleven. He shouldn't be home so early. The doorbell rang again. A scratching key sound made Sofia shiver. She peered through the side window. Her grandparents stood on the front porch under the portico, looking the way they had when her mother died.

## Lily

Stephanie drove in silence through tidy twenty-first-century neighborhoods. The afternoon sunlight made everything appear in high definition—stop signs, blades of grass, cracks in the pavement. *The worst things always happened on the most beautiful days.* It was cold when Lily stepped out of the car. She thought of the last time she was here, that flash of Caitlyn reminding her of what she had done. Would Mr. Robinson visit her next? Or the girl with no face?

Lily crossed her arms over her stomach and sped up the short walkway to Sofia's front door. She could hear the doorbell ringing inside the house, the way it echoed sadly off the walls. She knew at once that Sofia was gone.

Despite this certainty, Lily pressed the button again and again. She remembered her father on the trip to that church in New Jersey. A coworker had suggested a restaurant along the way, but the place was closed when they drove up to it. Deserted, actually, with windswept trash collecting outside the door and a layer of grime darkening the façade. Yet, Ted Jeong had circled the place, peering in every window and yanking every door. His disappointment consumed all of the air in the car, and Lily nearly suffocated by the time they reached the church. She never wanted to disappoint him.

"I don't think she's home," Stephanie said.

Her mother stood a few feet behind Lily on the walkway. She held her hands in small fists in front of her as if she were afraid of how Lily might react. One hand relaxed, and she held it out. "We should go."

Lily walked back to the car, wondering where Sofia was. Maybe she was with family or friends, or maybe she went to the police station to see her father. Maybe she'd never see her again. When she opened the car door, Lily spotted her backpack. She would go home and unpack. Because why should she be allowed to escape?

On the way home, her mother turned on the radio just in time for the top-of-the-hour news: Aaron Blake Crofton was in stable condition.

**Sofia**

When her grandparents came to pick her up, Sofia had asked where her father was. Abuela started to say, "Tu padre . . ." but instead, she placed her crooked fingers over her mouth to stifle a sob. Tears welled up in her eyes.

Abuelo placed his hand on Sofia's shoulder. "You must be strong, my girl. Tu padre has been taken to jail. He shot that boy on his way to the courthouse."

"What? Oh, my god, did he kill him?"

"No." Abuelo slumped against the door frame. "Go pack some pjs."

Sofia swayed and held onto a chair back. "I don't understand. What am I supposed to do now? What about my audition? What about school?"

"We will come back tomorrow and get your things," Abuelo said as if he were not standing before a grandchild nearly as tall as he was, whose head was aching from her period. "We don't want you to be alone." He held her hand the ten steps to the car as if he were afraid she would run away.

"Why can't I talk to Papi? Why can't I see him?"

Abuelo shook his head and didn't answer. When they were in the car, her grandmother turned around in her seat to face Sofia. "He has trouble, *mi alma.* He has to deal with it." Her face was full of sorrow. "We'll talk to him as soon as we can."

Nobody talked at supper, and neither she nor her grandmother could eat anything. They kept the TV on the news channel, hoping to hear something more about their son, but the newscaster only repeated his name and that he'd shot ABC. No one but them seemed to care what happened to Officer Hernandez after that.

Sofia was glad when it was time to go to bed. Abuela's sleeping porch was still as damp as it had been when she was young. She'd slept there with Cat before, tossing pillows at each other, talking about a boy, or food, or what they wanted to do the next day. Now her breasts and ribs pushed against the lumpy mattress, and her feet bumped the bottom bar of the cot.

The old quilt smelled like lavender. Sofia pulled it away from her face. It made her sick. She could hear Abuela outside the sleeping porch door shuffling in her old shoes. She sang a song as she turned out the lights. It was a song Sofia knew well from when she was tucked into bed as a child, the covers smelling like Tide, her grandmother's spicy scented hands pulling the sheets up to her cheeks. Now the song sounded different, sad, and childish.

Moonlight coming through the slats of the sleeping porch windows made bright stripes on Sofia's bed covers. It was cold out here, even with the space heater. She could not get to sleep. Her father, in a dark cell, was probably not asleep either. Was he lonely? Sofia turned her back to the door, pulled out her phone, and found Lily's number. Lily had told her it was a landline. Her parents wouldn't let her use her cell phone after seven.

"Is Lily there?" Sofia asked when a man answered the phone.

"Who is calling at this time of night?"

Sofia looked at the time. It was only 9:06.

"This is Sofia, Sofia Hernandez."

He sucked in air and breathed out a response. "Hernandez? Was it your father who was arrested today?"

The corners of Sofia's eyes burned. She should hang up, but she wanted to speak to Lily, the only person she could talk to since Cat died.

"Hello?" said a woman.

"Yes, hello. This is Sofia Hernandez. Please, may I speak to Lily? I'm sorry for calling so late. I won't talk long."

"Yes, I'll get her. I'm sorry for today, for what has happened to you." Lily's mother put the receiver down.

"Thank you," Sofia said to the dead air. She pressed her cheek against the pillow in the dark and waited. She could hear Lily's parents droning in the background in another language.

"Hi." Lily's voice was soft.

Sofia turned over to face the window. "I guess you heard what happened today with my father?"

"Yes, my parents know, too."

"Are your parents over your shoulder?"

"Yep."

Sofia felt sorry for Lily, having helicopter parents. But at least she had parents. "I'm at my grandparents, in that neighborhood behind the mall. I wanted you to know where I was."

"Okay." Lily was so quiet.

"I'm almost finished with the dress. But I don't want to do the audition anymore. I don't think I'm even going back to school." Sofia choked. "I don't . . . I don't know what's going to happen. I'm scared, Lily."

"I can ask my Mother if she'll drop me off at the hospital early, before the next group meeting. Do you want to talk then? Are you still going?"

The support group meeting was the last place Sofia wanted to go. All those people looking at her, thinking they knew something about her, about her father, not understanding. "I don't know."

"Let's meet before we have to go in."

Maybe that would be good, someone to talk to. "I'll ask my grandparents to take me." Sofia could hear Lily's parents talking, a hiss from the father. "Bye."

"Bye."

Sofia touched the red icon and dropped her phone. It lit up the quilt backing decorated with little ducks and umbrellas, and then it was dark.

*Cat, I'm scared. I'm worried about my dad.*

*I helped my father today.*

*You did?*

*Yes. He finally saw me.*

*Oh, my God, Caitlyn, can you help mine?*

Abuela came into the room to say goodnight, and Cat's voice faded.

Sofia yanked the covers over her head. She woke up much later, curled against the world.

**Beowolf @RockwellHighNews**

The hard part now is seeing the empty seats. Someone used to sit there, raise their hand with the wrong answer, grind through a test, make plans for the weekend. Laugh. Curse. Yawn. Breathe. Now it's just empty air. Why that seat and not mine?

# CHAPTER FOURTEEN

**Keisha**

Two days after the courthouse shooting, Keisha's mother walked into her bedroom at six a.m. and pulled off her covers.

"Get up. You're going with me today."

Keisha rubbed the sleep out of her eyes. "Going where?"

"To work."

"Why?"

"I want you to meet someone. Get dressed." Her mother walked out, closing the door behind her. From the hall, she yelled, "Ten minutes."

Keisha knew when her mother was serious. She was serious now. Since the arraignment disaster, no one had bothered her. She could sleep, eat, wander the house, talk on the phone, whatever she wanted. Her parents didn't ask any questions or demand answers. Today was obviously different. Keisha washed her face, brushed her teeth, and threw on a t-shirt and jeans. She didn't even check her hair. There was nothing to check. At least this way, it was clear to anyone she was who she was, nothing added, no pretense. She wasn't trying to be anyone. She was just being.

Her mother called from downstairs, "Let's go."

Keisha walked down the stairs expecting to be told to change, but her mother said nothing. She just held open the door to the garage. Keisha slipped on her sneakers and followed her mother to the car. Halfway to the hospital, she asked, "Who do you want me to meet?"

"A patient of mine."

"Why this patient? You've never done this before."

"You never needed it before."

Keisha turned her head and looked out her window. It was safer that way. She had never seen this particular look on her mother's face, a combination of determination and sorrow. There would be a lesson to learn, an example of fortitude or empathy. She steeled herself against all of that. She didn't want to learn anything else. She was done.

They stopped in her mother's office first, and Keisha re-membered being there when she was young and impressionable. She played under the desk while her mother had a consultation with another doctor, and they both used words she didn't understand. Her mother was smart—that's what Keisha took away from that day—and people respected her, looked up to her. Keisha had wanted to be like her mother. *Today, not so much.*

"Come on," her mother said and briefly put her arm around Keisha.

Keisha shrugged off her hand and stepped away beyond her reach.

"Okay, have it your way. We're going to room 201."

At the doorway to 201, they stopped. The girl in the bed was asleep. She had no hair, no eyebrows, no eyelashes. She was as pale as the sheets. Her eyelids were pink. Her tiny fingers twitched on the blanket.

"God, Mom, what's wrong with her?"

"She has end-stage cancer. She's going home today."

Keisha flung herself against the wall in the corridor. Her arm hit a food cart, and she flinched. "Is that why you brought me here—to meet someone who's worse off than me?"

"No. Pull yourself together. You are not the center of the universe. The world does not revolve around you. Go in there and wait for her to wake up. Stop thinking only about yourself and be a decent human being. That's your whole job today." Her mother turned on her heel and walked away.

Keisha sighed. She could see what her mother was up to. It wouldn't kill her, and it would get her mother off her back. She looked briefly at the chart in the door holder, saw the girl's name was Marissa. Walking into the room, she pulled the visitor's chair close to the bed and waited for the child to wake. By her size, Marissa couldn't be more than nine years old. Everywhere in the room were drawings, stuffed animals, flowers, and balloons. People loved her. A wave of something Keisha had no name for passed through her. She closed her eyes.

"Oh, wow, I love your hair!"

Keisha opened her eyes. Marissa was grinning at her. It was the last thing she expected. She ran her hand over her head and smiled back at the girl. "Yeah, well, it's new anyway."

Marissa beamed. "I've been watching you on TV. I wanted to meet you. I told your mom. I can't believe you came."

Keisha had never seen a smile like that or been its object. Her skin tingled. She reached out and squeezed Marissa's hand. "Why did you want to meet me?"

"*Pfft*. Why? You're my hero. You've been standing up to the bad guys and telling it like it is. You make me feel proud."

Keisha shook her head. "I don't think I'm a hero. I'm afraid like everyone else."

"Well, that's the whole thing, isn't it? To do stuff that scares you even when you're afraid. That's what courage is. Right? People doing things that they're afraid to do. My mom says that."

Keisha closed her eyes, shook her head, and grinned at Marissa. "I think *you* are *my* hero."

When her mother came to retrieve her, Keisha was reading out loud from the third chapter of *A Secret Garden*. She waited for the girls to embrace and say goodbye. From the doorway, Keisha turned back to wave again.

Marissa blew her a kiss.

On the drive home, Keisha broke the silence with her mother. "How do you do this day after day, Mom? How do you deal with the grief, with the failure?"

Akeelah kept her eyes on the road. "I cry. Sometimes I go out to my car and scream. I remember them." She glanced at Keisha. "I go to therapy and rail against fate and biology. There's no quick fix. You learn to live with it and keep going."

By the time they got home, Keisha understood she had to pull herself together and find her way through this mess. Another support group meeting was coming up. *This time, I'll press them. This time, we'll figure out who the accomplice is and make our school safe again.*

## Lily

At just past one-thirty in the morning, Lily finished securing the dried flowers to the canvas. They cascaded, pink and white, around a face made of buttons, a late slip, earrings, hair ties, shoelaces, and straws. One shoulder curved with yellow police tape. The neck was shadowed with a scrap of fabric found on the floor of Sofia's bedroom. Shards of glass formed the chin and jawline. Lily brushed a finger over the glass. The piece was almost complete. She only needed to finish the eyes. The eyes would be the most challenging. The eyes would give her girl life.

The staircase creaked behind Lily. Her head spun over her shoulder in a panic.

A voice croaked, "What are you doing?"

Violet stood on the third step from the bottom. One tangled crease of hair jutted out of the side of her head.

"Nothing." Lily tried to turn the canvas, but Violet's leap off the staircase startled her so completely she couldn't move.

"You're doing art again! After Dad forbid it!"

"*Shssh!*"

Violet tugged at the canvas. Lily struggled to keep it from her sister, but Violet had strength from a second wind, and Lily was too exhausted to fight. Violet freed the canvas and jumped a few steps away to study it.

"Tell Dad," Lily spat. "I don't care anymore. He can kill me if he wants. I don't care." Her sister remained quiet, her back turned. Words poured from Lily. "I had to do it. I don't know why. I couldn't sleep. I kept seeing a face . . . and then no face. The girl who had no face. So, are you going to tell Dad? Say something!"

Violet slowly lowered the canvas and met Lily's eyes. She looked to be in shock.

Lily repeated, "Say something."

"It's amazing."

The sincerity in Violet's voice made Lily cry. The two sisters embraced in a way they had never done before. Lily could not let go. Words formed in her head—words she was desperate yet terrified to confess. Three words. Three syllables. Seven letters. *It was me.* Seven letters that would end her life. But what life did she have anyway? Before the words could crawl from a place deep inside her, Lily heard footfalls overhead. Then her father's voice:

"Lily? Violet?"

His tone spliced the girls apart. Violet pushed the canvas at Lily and whispered, "Quick. Hide it."

"What's going on down there?"

Violet yelled up the staircase, "Nothing! We're coming, Appa!" As she spewed excuses about hearing noises and another alien dream, Lily carefully slid the canvas behind the hot water heater. She hurried back up the stairs and found both her parents in the kitchen.

"Get back to bed," Ted said like he was instructing his staff. "You'll be too tired to get any schoolwork done tomorrow."

As the family trudged back toward the staircase, Stephanie touched Lily's arm. "You've been crying," she said.

Lily brought both hands up to her cheeks. She didn't have the energy to lie, so she stood there mute.

Stephanie looked as tired as Lily felt. She said, "Tomorrow, I'll take you to the group session."

With her hands still on her cheeks, Lily nodded and climbed the stairs. She'd promised Sofia she'd meet her before the meeting to talk. Something stirred in her as if those three words she almost said to Violet were a dragon waking from a deep sleep.

## Sofia

Dry leaves littered the bench under the tree at the hospital. Age had cracked its wood slats. Sofia remembered when she sat there five years ago with Papi, the tree much smaller, while her mother slept in her bed in the room above them. Papi called it The Hope Tree. Mama came home the next day, better, but not well. She was never well again. Now, Papi was gone too. From one minute to the next, Sofia couldn't decide if she was angry or worried or sad.

Sofia pulled her sleeve over her palm and swept at the dead leaves to make a place for two to sit. The bench was a little damp, but she sat anyway, watching for Lily. Her new friend wasn't late. She was early. Abuelo hadn't trusted that he would remember the way to the hospital, so they left his house in plenty of time. His old blue Falcon had creaked along until he pulled up at the curb in front of the hospital.

"Here we are, my girl. Are you sure you don't want me to go in with you tonight?"

"Yes." Even though Abuelo was being sweet, Sofia wanted to get out of the car. He was trying too hard. She could see his pain and felt queasy. Although Abuelo had stopped smoking cigars long ago, she could still smell the aroma in the car.

"Thank you, Abuelo. I'll look for you right here when it's over."

"Okay. Your grandmother will make more beetles on your dress while you're here. Don't worry about it. I love you, *muchacha*," Abuelo said, his eyes liquid.

Sofia shivered in her coat, slammed the clunky door, and watched as Abuelo drove away. Blue smoke curled from the exhaust.

She sat on the bench and waited. Lily moved along the walk in a dark sweater and jeans. She waved. Her hair shimmered in the lamplight. Would Lily understand how awful she felt? Lily's shoulders curled in against the cold. Sofia saw a numbness in her new friend, a rawness of pain, but Lily had her parents, her familiar home.

"Hey." Lily sat down.

They shuffled their feet and crossed their ankles. Sofia stared at her knees.

"I really miss my father," Sofia blurted. "It's not the same at Abuela's. I feel like an orphan." She looked up at Lily's face, but she couldn't read her expression. "We've been through so much. We'll never be the same."

"No, we won't." Lily leaned forward and put her head in her hands.

"What is it?" Sofia asked.

Lily sprang back up, curled her hands into fists, and jammed them in her coat pockets. "I can't talk about it. Not here."

"But you said we would talk."

Lily pointed to Caitlyn's mother, hurrying toward them. "Oh."

"Are you girls okay?" Lisa Moran called out. "Why aren't you inside?"

Lily pulled off her glasses and wiped her eyes with the backs of her hands.

"Come on, girls, it's cold out here," Mrs. Moran said, "let's go into the meeting."

Sofia rose from the bench, her jaw clenched, confusion making her legs weak. She watched as Lily stood as still as a statue and then adjusted her glasses on her nose. Caitlyn's voice sounded in her head like a warning.

*Sofy, Lily is the crying girl from the hallway.*

*You already told me that.*

*She's dangerous.*

*Cat, I don't know what you mean.*

*She's the one who let him in.*

Sofia followed everyone into the hallway toward the meeting room, her mind reeling from the thought Cat had planted there.

## Charmaine

Even though she was still feeling a bit queasy, Charmaine didn't want to miss the support group. In some odd way, she didn't quite understand, knowing she wasn't the only one struggling with the loss of a loved one, and the fear of the future, gave her comfort. Now she had another reason to attend. Ever since she learned she was pregnant, she wanted the world to be a safer place for her and Alex's baby. Perhaps she should become an activist for gun control like Keisha. She sensed other survivors were feeling the same.

Lisa Moran waved her over as she entered the meeting room. She liked the Morans. They leaned on her because she had treated their daughter in the emergency room, she realized, and that made her feel worthwhile.

"We saved you a seat. How have you been?"

Charmaine hadn't told anyone except her mother about her pregnancy. She wanted to wait until her second trimester when she would be on safer ground. "Good days and bad days," she answered. "They brought Aaron Blake

Crofton to my emergency room, but fortunately, I didn't have to tend to him."

Lisa's eyes wrinkled with genuine concern. "Oh, how awful for you."

Charmaine didn't want to dwell on the shooter. "How about you two?"

"Hanging in there," Mike replied. Charmaine smiled at him. Even if he didn't show any emotion, her nurse's intuition told her he was hurting.

Lisa shrugged. "A little better, I think. I hear you've been in touch with my son, Connor."

Charmaine nodded. "Facebook friends."

"I probably shouldn't tell you this," Lisa said, "but Connor asked me to look out for you."

"Really?" She laughed. "That's funny because he asked me to do the same for you."

Lisa and Mike joined in the laughter.

"That's my boy," Mike said.

Charmaine thought for a moment. "I can understand his concern for you. You're his mother. But he hardly knows me."

Lisa put her arm around Charmaine and hugged her. "You must have made quite an impression."

Charmaine didn't know what to think about that before Lisa changed the subject. "You heard about Joe Hernandez?" For a moment, Mike looked away as if this were a subject he didn't want them to talk about.

"It's awful," Charmaine said. "I know him. He's the cop who came to the hospital to tell me Alex had been killed. He seemed like such a good guy, even insisting on driving me home."

"His daughter Sofia is here tonight," Lisa said. "I feel so bad for her."

"I feel bad for all of us," Charmaine said. She had been too preoccupied with school, then her job and her marriage, too busy to become involved in any cause. But everything was different now. Not only was the love of her life killed, but she was also carrying his baby. She promised herself her child would not experience the violence that deprived him or her of a father.

## Lily

The girls sat quietly side by side in the circle as the conference room filled. Lily attempted to compose herself even though the dragon stirred in her chest. Her eyes hurt. Just get through this meeting, she told herself. Get through it, go home and sleep. Sleep forever.

Lily glanced at Sofia, who sat with her arms held together, her eyes far away. "Have you seen your father?"

"No. Abuela keeps saying there's all these legal reasons, but I get this awful feeling he doesn't want to see me."

"Why wouldn't he want to see you?"

"Maybe he's ashamed." Sofia combed her fingers through her fading pink lock of hair. Her voice strained. "I just want to know why he did this to me; I've been through so much. What was he thinking?"

Lily turned sideways in her seat and faced Sofia. "He wasn't thinking. He couldn't have been. If he were, he would have known he was making a mistake. He would have understood the consequences. He would have realized how many people he was hurting. How many lives he was destroying."

Her voice carried on, but the words seemed to come from somewhere far off. "No, he couldn't have been thinking. Not at that moment. He must have had too much pain . . . too much. How could he think rationally with all of that pain? But I'm sure he's sorry now. His regret is . . . it feels like being burned alive."

Sofia's expression changed. Confusion filled her soft brown eyes. I said too much, Lily thought. She flicked her eyes away from Sofia and turned to face the front of the room. When the counselor started the meeting, Lily sat upright and gripped her seat. *Too much.*

"I'm so glad the young people are here this evening," Debby began.

Lily scanned the faces in the room. It was not as crowded as the first meetings. The only young people were herself, Sofia, and Keisha. Of course, Keisha is here, Lily thought. She was everywhere, at all times—a hologram that traversed dimensions. She'd cut off all her beautiful braids.

Some sort of statement, Lily assumed. It would get her more attention. As if she needed more.

The usuals were also in attendance: Caitlyn's parents, as grim as ever, Mr. Robinson's wife, her thumb making circles on the chair arm, and Mr. Wilkins, who seemed to grieve the most despite having no relationship to any of the deceased. The custodian liked to say, "They were all my kids." Lily wondered if any of them ever said hello to him in the hallway or thanked him for cleaning up the wasted food they dumped in the trash. Tonight, he sat with both elbows on his thighs, his hands clasped like he was praying.

Debby inhaled a long breath before her next words: "We all know the ABC Killer was shot earlier this week. Does anyone want to talk about that?"

The suddenness of the counselor's question sent a tremor through the room. She had wasted no time bringing it up. Why should she? It was certainly what everyone wanted to talk about. Aaron would be so happy about that.

Keisha spoke first. "I was *right there*." She stared straight ahead as if she were watching the scene. She made a gun gesture with her right hand. "He pointed his finger at me. He wanted to shoot me. Again. His eyes . . . the hate in his eyes cut right through me. He hates me. I don't understand why he hates me."

Lily chewed the words poised on her lips. She wanted to say, he doesn't hate you. Hate would require feelings. Aaron has no feelings.

"And then I saw Mr. Hernandez reach for his gun," Keisha continued. "I didn't understand what was happening. I tried to stop him, which is pretty screwed up. I should want Aaron Blake Crofton—yes, I'm saying his name— dead. I should want him dead. But in my mind, all I heard was, no, this isn't the way."

Debby leaned forward. "After everything you've been through, of course, you wouldn't want to see anyone else shot."

Keisha gave a slight nod to the counselor's words. The room went silent again. Lily glanced at Sofia, wondering what she would say about her father. Her expression hadn't lost the confusion it had since their conversation on the bench ended. What was she thinking?

Mike Moran shifted in his seat, crossed his arms over his chest. "I was there, too. I saw him. I didn't know what it would be like to see him in person—the person who killed my daughter. But when I looked at him, I thought, he's just a dumb kid."

Charmaine Robinson's head shot up. "A dumb kid who killed fifteen people!" Her mouth clamped shut. This was an unusual outburst from her in these meetings. She took a breath. Her hands shook as she continued to speak. "He came into my emergency room, and I couldn't do it . . . I couldn't take care of him. And I'm a nurse. I didn't see a dumb kid on that gurney. I saw the animal who killed my husband."

At once, everyone muttered condolences and sympathies to Charmaine. Mrs. Moran offered a tissue. Other people spoke about the effects the shooting had on them. Wounds that hadn't begun to heal were reopened. Even the soft-spoken words exploded in Lily's head. When the room quieted again, the counselor fixed her attention on Sofia.

"Sofia, do you want to say anything about your father?"

At first, Sofia remained silent and motionless, like she'd left her body in the middle of the meeting. She looked completely inside her head, consumed by some mathematical equation. Lily's mouth dried. She had said too much earlier. How could she take back those words?

Mrs. Moran reached out, even though she was several chairs away. "Sofia, sweetheart, are you okay?"

Sofia shook herself, like someone waking from a bad dream. She gave Mrs. Moran a weak smile and looked down at the floor.

"We haven't heard from you, Lily," Debby said. "Would you like to talk?"

No, Lily thought. She'd already talked too much and sent her friend into a near-catatonic state. Her fingers curled into fists as if she could shrink herself until she became a blip and disappeared. It didn't work. All eyes in the room were on her. Wasn't that what she always wanted? All eyes on her. Recognition. Acceptance. It's what started this endless nightmare. She was sick of it. Sick and tired and frustrated. Before she could stop them, words shot out of her.

"Mrs. Robinson is right. Aaron is a monster. More than anyone knows. I wish Mr. Hernandez had killed him."

The words didn't seem to come from her lips. Her voice echoed in her head. Lily heard other voices too, but the room fell silent when Sofia stood and turned toward Lily. Sofia stared at her. The confusion had left her eyes, replaced by something like shock or horror. Her voice was just above a whisper.

"It was you, wasn't it?"

The words wrapped around Lily's neck. She couldn't breathe.

"I—I don't know what you mean."

Concern creased Debby's face. "What are you girls talking about?"

Lily's eyes darted about the room, looking for help, for escape. Her heart kicked beneath her sweater. She met Mr. Wilkins' eyes. He finally unclasped his hands like his prayer had been answered. He knew. Lily stood, but the floor fell out beneath her.

"Nothing." She stammered, then caught her foot on the chair leg. "I don't know what she means. I have to go." She bolted for the door, but Keisha took three long strides and blocked her.

"What does Sofia mean? What does she think you did?"

"Move, I have to go—"

"Was it you I saw in the hallway?" Mr. Wilkins stood. "Were you the one who let him into my school?"

Debby stood and held her arms out. "Everyone, just take a breath. Just stay calm."

Lily's whole body shook. She squeezed her fists again, trying to disappear. Instead, she felt herself growing and growing until she was the size of the room, until her head broke through the ceiling and her elbows knocked down the walls. She couldn't hide. Couldn't slip away. No one would miss seeing her now. She shook her head. "I didn't know . . . I didn't know what he was going to do. He said he just wanted to make some noise. To scare people . . ."

Keisha gasped. She grabbed Lily's forearm. "You?" Her head shook in disbelief. "You're the one who let him into the school? You're the one that caused this?"

"I didn't—I swear, if I knew what he was going to do—"

"You knew him?" Keisha's fingers dug into Lily's arm. She tried to break away, but Keisha's grip only tightened. "You were with him?"

"Don't look at me like that! You never looked at me. In all these years of school, you never saw me, never tried to be my friend. You don't know what it's like. Everyone knows you. Everyone loves you. You don't know what it feels like to be invisible. He was the only one who looked at me, the only one who paid any attention to me. But he lied. He lied to me!"

Keisha shook her. "He lied to *you*? That's all you have to say? Samantha is dead because he lied. Mr. Robinson is dead because he lied. Caitlyn. Dead. Ryan. Dead—"

"Stop it!"

Lily yanked her arm free from Keisha. She threw both hands over her ears as if she could block out the names of the people who were dead because of her. Everyone glared in stunned silence.

Tears streaked Sofia's face. She whispered, "How could you?"

"I didn't know," Lily cried. "I swear I didn't know."

Lily doubled over with her arms crossed over her stomach. When Keisha grabbed both her shoulders, Lily spun away from her and ran out the door.

**Mike**

Mike pushed back his chair, jumped up, and chased Lily. He had sat silently throughout Lily's confession, trying to absorb the fact that this slight, innocent-looking girl was an accessory to murder. *Caitlyn is dead, but Lily is alive.* Was it really all about a boy who paid attention to her, that fucked-up kid he almost killed? He hadn't been able to shoot ABC, but at least he could capture his accomplice.

Lily had turned left outside the conference room and was fleeing down a corridor as long as a football field that led to the exit. He couldn't let her escape. His adrenaline pumped as he raced to catch her. *She's just a few yards ahead.*

Suddenly an office door opened into the hallway, and a woman in a business suit stepped in front of him. "What's going on?" she asked.

"Call security!"

Mike zigzagged around her, but during this interruption, Lily sprinted ahead. He couldn't let her escape. All his military training had prepared him to capture the enemy, even if she was younger and faster. She was running for her life, but so was he, and for Lisa's life, too.

His heart pounded and sweat erupted on his scalp. About a dozen yards from the exit, he came close enough to reach for her long hair. She eluded his grasp, and he fell forward. Regaining his balance, he pushed himself into a higher gear and leaped toward her.

"Stop!"

**Lily**

Her legs pumped. Through her tears, she focused on the door at the end of the corridor, a world away, the red letters of the exit sign trumpeting her escape. Garbled sounds screamed past her ears—a ringing phone, the beep of an elevator, a baby's cries.

*Exit . . . exit.*

Commotion erupted behind her. Her eyes shot over her shoulder. Mike Moran, the bereaved father, the one who wanted to kill the shooter *and* his accomplice. Rage burned in his eyes. He ran after her looking as if he would tear her apart limb by limb. *He wants to kill me.* This is the fear, she thought. This is what they felt, all of them, that day.

*Exit . . .*

She nearly collided with a woman who came out of an office. Lily careened to her left, hit the wall, then sprinted again toward the red letters. A hand grazed her shoulder, grasped for her hair. She dodged again, and he hit the floor. Finally, she reached the door. Her fingers wrapped around the push bar. Her breath stopped. *This is the fear they felt.*

She went back to that moment. That decision. That one act that caused all of this pain. What would happen if she opened this door? The pain would follow her. It would haunt her and everyone else. The pain would be endless.

Her hands fell to her sides. She breathed, a huge gulping breath as if she'd just burst through the surface of the ocean.

"Stop!"

He grabbed both her shoulders. The pain from his grip seared through her. It burned away her panic and left her with an odd sense of calm.

"You're not going anywhere."

He spun her around and slammed her back against the wall. That pain washed away any desire to open the door. She looked directly into his eyes at the horror of a father who will never see his daughter again. She waited for his fingers to wrap around her throat, even tilted her head back, an invitation, but he just glared at her. She thought for a second to offer *I'm sorry* but knew her words would mean nothing to him. Her body felt liquid in his grip. When his fingers loosened slightly, she dropped to the floor.

But she did not run.

The others from the support group surrounded them. Mr. Wilkins, Keisha, Debby, Mr. Robinson's wife—her face a mix of pity, rage, and relief. Sofia pushed herself through the crowd of people. And right beside her, just for an instant, Caitlyn Moran, her translucent expression one of approval and peace.

Lily braced herself when Sofia stood above her, but Sofia stretched out a hand. The act surprised Lily; she hesitated. Sofia pulled Lily to her feet, drew her arm back, and slapped her hard on the cheek.

That sting brought the most relief.

Sofia swiped away tears. "You killed her . . . my best friend ever. My father's in jail. Why did you pretend to be my friend? I trusted you, and you lied. Why?"

Lily ignored the other faces staring at her, the two security guards squeezing through the crowd, and focused on Sofia's hard eyes.

"Because . . ." Lily's body slackened, but she took a breath and straightened. "Because I needed you. I needed someone. You laughed with me. You were sweet. You showed me that I could have a friend . . . that I could matter. I can't—I can't ask you to forgive me."

The sound of sirens grew louder outside—not the wail of ambulances but police cars. Her time was running out. She looked at the other faces. "I can't ask any of you to forgive me. I don't deserve it. And there are no words that could ever make up for what I did. I just want . . . I don't know . . . I can't imagine how you feel."

She turned her eyes back to Sofia's. There was no forgiveness in them. They were empty now, shut down. I broke her, Lily thought. *She is broken like me.*

Mike explained what was happening to the security guards. Other onlookers stopped, and the crowd around Lily grew. Keisha, her arms folded, shook her head and walked away. A few moments later, the police arrived. Lily said nothing when they led her away. Her body shook with fear of what was to come. Her parents, her sister . . . what would they think? But still, Lily was relieved.

The worst part was over.

**Intheknow @WRWL-TV**

"I don't want prayers. I don't want thoughts. Will this bring closure? There is no closure to burying your child." —Lisa Moran, mother of a student who died in the Rockwell High shooting, after accomplice Lily Jeong was arrested by Rockwell Township police.

# CHAPTER FIFTEEN

## Joe

Joe slumped in the metal chair next to the table bolted into the floor. Sitting opposite him was the defense attorney provided by the police officers' union. He almost smiled at how strange the scene was. He was in jail, in the windowless interview room. He shouldn't be the defendant, the one charged with a crime. At least he wasn't shackled.

He shook his head. The lawyer was talking and talking. He knew he should trust her; the union was paying top dollar for her. But he didn't understand half of what the woman said—she sounded like she was chewing rocks. He couldn't pay attention to what she was saying, couldn't think of anything but Sofia alone without him.

Every once in a while, a word or phrase the attorney said beat around in his brain like wet laundry in the dryer: "diminished capacity," or "mental disease or defect," or "temporary insanity," and something about a trained response to a perceived threat.

Joe knew he wasn't crazy. He'd been over the incident in his mind again and again. Maybe he didn't plan it—it wasn't premeditated—but it wasn't accidental, either. He could see what happened in slow motion: he pulled his weapon, slipped off the safety, aimed the gun, and squeezed the trigger. Anyone who was there that day knew it, too. A hundred witnesses at least, saw him shoot ABC on purpose with intent to kill, not maim. He missed the kill shot by inches because Keisha Washington distracted him. Maybe he should thank her, but he didn't feel grateful.

He drew circles on the table with his finger. Emilia would have hated this. She would have been ashamed for him. Emilia would have understood what made him do it, though, and maybe she would have forgiven him. Sitting there, hearing the lawyer drone on and on, he realized again that he could have hit an innocent civilian in the crowd. That would have been far worse. He would have regretted that.

"Look, the kid's going to live," his lawyer said. "Worst case, you might have to plead to assault with a deadly. But that's really the worst case. Everyone saw the shooter aim at the crowd. In the heat of the moment, you responded to the perceived threat. We've got one trump card: the county prosecutor wants to be lenient."

Joe's life as he knew it was over. He'd never be a police officer again anywhere, and he might not be able to find any kind of job that paid as well. But he'd done what all the cops wanted to do: shoot that little bastard when he taunted the crowd on the courthouse steps. Every trained impulse in his body required it.

When this whole mess started, he'd just wanted to protect his daughter, everyone's daughter, from that miserable scum. But his fear had grown until he felt the threat was everywhere, that it was imminent, that at any moment someone could shoot his girl dead and he would be left alone with no one to love. The lawyer could say whatever she had to say. The world could think whatever it wanted to think.

A memory of the sneer on ABC's face rose up in his mind, the way he pointed his finger at Keisha. *I would shoot him again.* He didn't tell his lawyer that.

The department was doing its best to protect him. They were keeping him in a private cell in the local lockup, well away from the regular prison population, just to make sure no one knifed him with a sharpened plastic spoon on the way to the shower or in line for a meal. He got his one hour of fresh air a day with the yard all to himself, his meals were brought to his cell on a tray, and he stood in the shower ten minutes alone with a guard barring entry.

The loneliness was killing him. He was talking to himself. All his life, there had always been someone with him, his parents, his Emilia, his Sofia. At the thought of his daughter again, his composure crumbled, and he put his hands over his face.

"Mr. Hernandez, do you understand what I'm telling you? It's all good news. If you want to plead not guilty and go to trial, given the local fury at the shooter, you might even get off. At the very least, we'll get a hung jury, and the prosecutor won't retry."

Joe looked up at her, his face empty. "My girl, my Sofia. She must be so confused. Does she hate me? Could you tell her something for me? Would you tell her I love her more than anything in the world?"

The lawyer nodded. "Of course. I'll call her right after we're done here. Now, I'd like to know how you want to plead."

"Whatever you want. I'll do whatever you want. You tell me. Whatever gets me home the quickest so I can be with my girl. I'll mow lawns and weed gardens for the rest of my life like my father. You don't have to get me reinstated in the force. Please, just do whatever you have to do to get me back with my daughter."

The lawyer pushed a document across the table to him. "I'll do my best for you, Mr. Hernandez. Sign here," she pointed on the paper, "and here."

## Keisha

Ms. Arnold's office was as different from Alex Robinson's as was possible in a space exactly the size and shape of her previous adviser's. Keisha stood in the doorway, trying to control the shaking that started in her stomach and spread across her body.

*The gun, the weight of his body, the blood.* Would she ever be rid of this memory?

She wanted to flee. The last thing she wanted was to stand in this room and talk to this stranger about her future. Her eyes focused on Ms. Arnold's diploma. A master's degree, framed in gold, hung on the wall. *It must mean a lot to her. Maybe I shouldn't take people's accomplishments for granted.*

Keisha shifted her backpack and looked over at the woman sitting calmly behind the desk, waiting for her to say what she wanted, to stake a claim on her future. What could she tell her? Before the killings, she'd always had a goal, but all her goals went up in smoke when Aaron Crofton stormed through her school with an assault weapon.

Keisha looked down at her shoes, simple black ballet slippers that had been lying on the floor near her bedroom door. She'd put them on because they were handy, not because they completed some look she was going after. She was done with looks, with dressing for success.

"Okay," Keisha said, "I don't expect to be president of the country anymore." She looked up at Ms. Arnold and half-smiled. "I can't even change the laws to prevent people from shooting kids in school. But I have to start somewhere. I have to move forward to tamp down the screaming in my head."

Ms. Arnold leaned forward and tilted her head.

"I was going to apply to colleges for early admission, but all this . . ." Keisha waved her arm in the air. *That crazy girl opened a door, and people I love got killed, and that's all I can think about.* "Stuff happened, and now I'm late preparing my applications. Too late for early admission, anyway."

Ms. Arnold tapped the top of her black and gold pen on a pad and said nothing.

Keisha sucked in her breath. *Who gives a damn about this shit?* "Anyway, I'm going to just apply to the state university, get my requirements out of the way, and then transfer to Columbia after two years. What do you think?"

Ms. Arnold glanced at her computer screen. "I think with your grades, test scores, and level of participation in school and the community, you can pretty much do whatever you want to do."

Keisha sighed. The woman was not going to be any help. "I have to write my essay. I don't know what to write about." Actually, she wasn't sure what she wanted from Arnold. Maybe she was just on automatic, checking the box. Maybe she was hoping by some magic, Mr. Robinson would be sitting there behind the desk.

"Write about your experience, the experience we all just had." Ms. Arnold pulled two tissues from the box on her desk. "Write from your heart." She offered them to Keisha.

Keisha felt her cheeks. They were wet. "Oh." She took the proffered tissues. "I miss my friends; I miss the way we were before all this happened."

Ms. Arnold nodded. "Me, too."

"It feels wrong to just move on with my life, like I'm abandoning them."

Another nod. She might as well be talking to a bobble-head doll.

Keisha sighed, blotted her face, and blew her nose. "Okay, I got it. I don't get over this. I just keep moving, like a shark, if I want to survive."

She didn't bother to look at Ms. Arnold. She knew what she'd see. "Thanks," she said and headed out into the corridor.

## Lily

The Rockwell County Juvenile Detention Center was not too unlike high school: endless hallways, cinder block walls, classrooms, and a cafeteria that served awful food. Here, though, the seats were attached to the tables, and the tables were attached to the floor. The environment sent a clear message: You're not going anywhere. There was also a gymnasium, library, and rec room where the girls could watch television for an hour a day. They always watched the same shows: *Wheel of Fortune* and *Jeopardy.* Due to all of the media coverage of her arrest, Lily came into the center a pseudo-celebrity, but her *Jeopardy* skills really cemented her status.

*"What is Mississippi?"*

*"Who is Abigail Adams?"*

*"What is halogen?"*

She was still teased, threatened, and assaulted. But the physical pain of every arm twist, every shove, pinch, or slap was like a sledgehammer breaking through the heavy door of the cell she had been trapped in. The wood was beginning to splinter, letting in air and even pinpricks of light. On day four, a girl twice her size with scars running up both arms like ladder rungs pinned Lily to the shower wall and asked, "What does school shooter cock taste like?"

Naked and shaking, Lily looked the girl in the eyes and blurted the first word that came to mind: "Mustard."

The girl—Heather, in for stealing her mother's boy-friend's car, DUI, and reckless endangerment (her eight-year-old half-sister was in the car)—stared at Lily for six long seconds before bursting into laughter. After that, most girls left Lily alone.

Nights were hard. Lily, who'd only been to one sleepover in her life, usually lay awake listening to the sounds of the other girls' heavy breathing, the creaking metal bedsprings, and bodies jerking their way through nightmares. When Lily's eyes adjusted to the dark, she studied the perforations in the ceiling tiles. The holes became stars, galaxies, the Milky Way. She became a part of it, hovering endlessly in space, a speck, far away from this place, from Rockwell, from her future, her family, and all of the families who grieved because she opened a door. In the mornings, Lily returned to earth and lawyers and court dates, girls with scars and girls without mothers, guards with batons and thick black boots that seemed bigger than her head, and the smell of bacon grease. She missed the smell of ginger.

In the afternoons, after classes where Lily caught up on sleep because she was far ahead of the center's curriculum, she read her mail. Piles of mail that had already been opened and copied. There was so much of it that she enlisted Heather to help her read through it, even though Lily could read three letters by the time Heather got through one. Lily's face and her story had blasted across every news outlet. She had interview requests from *Dateline* and *60 Minutes*, Anderson Cooper, and Oprah. Oprah! She heard her parents were on the *Today* show, but it aired during a mandatory room inspection, so she didn't get to see it. People who saw it wrote her letters. Some quoted Revelations. *The two of them were thrown alive into the fiery lake of burning sulfur.* Others pledged undying love or offered marriage. A few asked for very explicit sexual favors (how did those get read and still passed along?). Young outcast, misunderstood girls wrote with compassion. Many just sent their thoughts and prayers.

The lawyer that her father hired had been in to see Lily every day. Anthony V. Ciccuto, Esq., J.D. He spoke slowly to Lily as if she didn't understand English. He'd also been on every news outlet, on multiple occasions, sometimes speaking right outside the detention center. *"Lily Jeong is a brilliant student, a talented violinist, she's a devout Christian, and she was an outsider who was abused and manipulated by a sociopath."*

Anthony V. Ciccuto's face was meant for television—square jaw, dark eyes, perfect white teeth. He had a warrior's demeanor, and Lily felt strangely protected in his presence. Still, she wondered by the shine of his watch and thread of his suit how much he was costing her parents. Surely, they couldn't afford him. Why didn't they just let her use a public defender? She would find out today.

Her parents were coming for their first visit.

*\*\*\**

The Contact Visitation Area had square tables, each with three chairs, because only two visitors were allowed at a visit. Guards monitored the visits both inside the room and through the surrounding windows. Lily read the visitation policies carefully. Her parents had to arrive forty-five minutes ahead of the thirty-minute visit to be registered, patted down, and scanned. They had to show two forms of I.D. They could not bring anything into the room. *Within safety limits, authorized visitors may have opportunities for physical contact.*

As Lily sat in the hard seat waiting for them, she burned with the shame they must have been enduring. She laid her hands on the table and spread her fingers into stars. Finally, there they were, looking small and old and broken. Without a purse to clutch, Stephanie held tight to her elbows. Ted took very small steps with a light hold on his wife's sleeve. Lily couldn't read his face. It was as if all emotion had been stolen from him. Lily expected rage or disappointment or at least fear, but he was nothing. Was it because she was now nothing to him?

Mr. Ciccuto had negotiated permission for hugs and light cheek kisses, but Lily's parents did neither. They sat in the two empty seats, avoiding the eyes of the guards and the other visitors. Girls pointed Lily out to their parents. There was a collective smugness about the room. Because yes, unknowingly letting a school shooter into the building was a far worse crime than any of their daughters had committed. Stephanie's eyes were moist. She chewed her lips before bristling, "Are you getting enough to eat? How is the food? Is your bed comfortable? Are you sleeping?"

"Mother, the food should not be good, and the beds should not be comfortable."

Stephanie's eyes dipped. She held onto the edge of the table like she might fall over if she didn't.

"How's Violet?" Lily asked.

"Scared," her mother said without looking up. "Now, she is the one waking in the middle of the night."

Lily's face flushed at these words. Violet. Sharp, sarcastic, never one to flinch. Violet afraid of her dreams. No. Violet will be okay. She had always been the strong one. Lily turned to her father and said, "I want you to fire Mr. Ciccuto."

"What? Why?" Ted sprang forward in his seat. The guard stopped his pacing and watched them. "He says he will make sure they try you as a juvenile. He says he can get the conspiracy and accessory charges dropped, that you were under duress and suffering PTSD when you confessed at that meeting, he can create enough doubt that no jury will convict you. He has great hope—"

"There shouldn't be hope!" Lily's voice cracked. She squeezed the metal seat with both hands until it hurt. "Those fifteen families don't have hope. And you can't afford him!"

Ted took a composing breath. His body tightened except for the muscles around his lips, which rippled as if they were holding back a flood of words. "We will pay," he said calmly. "We will pay whatever it takes."

Lily looked at him dumbfounded. "Why?"

His hand moved slightly. For a second, Lily thought he might take hers, but he looked sideways at the guard and clasped both his hands together. He said, "Because you're our daughter. There are people who don't have a daughter anymore."

Stephanie shifted in the hard seat. She kept blinking rapidly as if she were trying desperately not to cry. There were no tissues. She pushed one fist into her stomach. "I wish you would have told us."

"Me, too," Lily whispered.

Ted met Lily's eyes. His face contorted in a strange way that she had never seen before. "I wish . . . I wish I hadn't failed you."

Lily's mouth opened slightly. These were not the words she expected. She expected words that would reprimand

and shame her. She expected her parents to breathe disappointment like fire from a dragon's mouth. She knew she
had caused them pain, but it was a completely different
kind of pain than she imagined. She felt it all the way to
her bones.

"You didn't fail me, Appa. You wanted to protect me.
Maybe you just wanted to protect me too much."

Her father pulled in his lips. His shoulders twitched. Ted
Jeong would not cry. Not here in this bright room with
guards and juvenile delinquents and their parents with tat-
toos and cheap clothes. Maybe he would cry later on the
drive home or alone in the backyard while he filled the bird
feeders. He had regrets, too, Lily realized. Actions and consequences wrapped all around them like tangled roots. How
would they ever break free?

Stephanie lifted her face. She couldn't hold her tears in
any longer. "Why, Lily?"

The answer was so simple and so ridiculous that Lily
could only shrug. "Because he said he loved me. And I believed him."

Their table quieted. Other families finished their visits
and said their goodbyes. The guard gave them a five-minute
warning. Lily thought of the face in her basement, behind
the water heater, alone and unfinished. She said to her
mother, "Will you ask Violet to finish it for me?"

"Finish what?"

"She'll know." Lily looked from her mother to her father.
Fright and uncertainty filled their expressions. Lily
stretched her hands, palms up, toward her parents and
said, "We should pray for hope."

After a moment of hesitation and a glance at the guard,
her mother, then her father took her hands in theirs. Their
cold yet familiar skin triggered a flash in Lily's mind: A walk
through the snow, the sun high and bright, the world glis-
tening white around them. Her parents, one on each side,
lifted and swung her over a snowdrift. They laughed. Lily
felt happy and loved.

Stephanie and Ted also clasped hands, just as they did
at the dinner table. The family formed a small, solid trian-
gle. They bowed their heads and prayed.

## Charmaine

Charmaine surveyed the audience gathered in the hospital auditorium and nodded at the columnist from the local newspaper who had publicized this meeting. She recognized a few of the people in attendance, Lori and Dr. McGann from work, Keisha and others from the support group, high school students and teachers, even some of her neighbors. Connor Moran, home on leave from Germany, sat in the front row next to his parents. He saluted her with a smile, and she smiled back. Lisa leaned across Mike to say something to her son. But most of the people in the audience didn't know her. She'd have to tell them her story.

Her legs shook as she approached the podium, one hand unconsciously on her belly. Although not experienced in public speaking, she knew she could do this. She had to.

After the loss of her husband, after all the other deaths and injuries at the high school, after Officer Hernandez's desperate actions, she had thought this long trough of mourning had come to its end. But when she heard Lily admit to her part in the massacre, something snapped in her. The accomplice had been right there in the support group where they were most vulnerable. It was time to stop crying and start acting. Action was the best therapy for depression. Someone here had to start a group to oppose gun violence, and she had decided it might as well be her.

"Welcome to the first meeting of Rockwell Citizens United Against Gun Violence," she began. "I'm Charmaine Robinson, and my husband Alex was a guidance counselor who was killed in the high school shooting." Her voice broke, and she took a sip of water before continuing. "I'm an ER nurse at Tri-County Hospital. I was there the day of the shooting and also the day they brought ABC in."

The room was as silent as the snow falling outside. She paused and took courage from the earnest faces staring at her. "I just can't let this go on. That's why I and some of the other survivors decided to start this organization." She looked down at Mike, who flashed her the thumbs-up signal.

She paused again, considering once more if she should reveal her secret. "I'm pregnant with Alex's baby," she announced. Murmurs and gasps scattered through the crowd. Her voice rose. "I can't let our child grow up and face gun violence. I've never been an activist before or much involved in politics, but I have to do something about guns. We've all got to do something."

Connor rose from his seat and began to clap. Mike and Lisa stood up next, and then the entire room was on its feet, cheering in a standing ovation.

Charmaine smiled as she held back tears. It was a long road ahead, she knew, but they were off to a good start.

## Caitlyn

Sofia sat cross-legged on the clay dirt at the grave marked Caitlyn Moran. *Look up*, Caitlyn wanted to say, but there was nothing for Sofy to see but sky and mesmerizing clouds.

Caitlyn's thoughts moved erratically, without design.

*Being dead is being without a body. No tears, heart flutters, no words, or movements from here to there. Touch is gone, but I feel longing. Am I a ghost? My body was taken from me without my permission or desire. My eyes have no color; my hair is not pink. I don't need hugs or comforting, caresses, or kisses. I'm not human. My body melts in the ground below.*

"It's been a while since we talked," Sofia said to the gravestone.

*I'm up here, not down there.*

Sofia looked up. "Do you like the insect dress?"

*It's beautiful.*

"Your mom took me to the auditions. Did you see us? I didn't really feel you there."

*You didn't need me.*

"I got in. Can you believe it? I think they liked my tragic backstory more than the collection. I leave for New York in a week."

*That's amazing. You did it!*

"We did it. Your dad gave me a hug. He never did that before."

*I'm glad you have each other.*

"He'll always be your dad."

*We can share.*

"Will you go now, leave me?"

No response.

Sofia lay back on the grass. "Does this mean goodbye? Is it time?"

*Yes. But I want to tell you something. You're the best friend I ever had. I love you.*

She wanted to touch Sofia's cheek with her fingertips and smooth back her hair. Sofia closed her eyes.

"I love you, too. Forever."

Caitlyn moved, as quick as thought, to her father and mother, to Mr. Hernandez, and the girl who opened the door. She moved to the petals that fell from the white lily, the needle that pulled the thread, the bullet that pierced the bone. She moved to pails of soapy water that washed the floors of mucked-up hallways.

She followed the mops as they swirled over the tile squares of the schools, dipped, then rinsed as the bucket water turned grey and was poured down the sink. She followed the water as it flowed into the sewers and into the ground and rivers and out to sea. She moved through the clouds and toward the burning fury of the sun that would not harm her. She dispersed and spread into many particles, never to wrap her mind around anything anymore, only to just be.

The End

# ACKNOWLEDGEMENTS

Thank you to our beta readers Suzanne Hill Thackston, David Holloway, Pearl Luke, Lee Doty, Victoria Gladwish (who even counted how many pages each character got), and Katherine Cobb, for insight, guidance, and feedback that made us feel we were writing something meant to be read.

Thanks to the husbands who supported us through years of raucous collaboration and photo-bombed our virtual meetings.

Thanks to everyone at Sunbury, but especially Chris Fenwick, who gave us the encouragement we needed.

Thanks to Kira and Sarah, our go-to subject matter experts in all things thought, felt, experienced, and said between the ages of fourteen and eighteen.

To all the families who have lived this experience, our hearts go out to you.

.

# ABOUT THE AUTHORS

Lee Anne Post is the pen name for co-authors Catherine Baldau, Tara Bell, Ginny Fite, and K.P. Robbins. Stories by these award-winning authors have appeared in numerous journals and individually they have published nine novels. They have worked as reporters and editors, in politics and philanthropy, and in advertising and educational institutions. Having met in a writer's critique group for over five years, they were spurred by their collective grief and then admiration as they watched Parkland students deal with the aftermath of that shooting.

Pushcart nominated, **Ginny Fite** is the author of six traditionally published novels: *Cromwell's Folly; No Good Deed Left Undone; Lying, Cheating, and Occasionally Murder; No End of Bad; Blue Girl on a Night Dream Sea,* and *Possession.* Her collection of linked short stories, *Stronger in Heaven,* was shortlisted for the 2019 SFWP prize and a finalist for the 2020 Bakwin Prize. Her short stories have been published in numerous journals such as *The Delmarva Review, SFWP Quarterly,* and the *Anthology of Appalachian Writers.* A graduate of Rutgers University and Johns Hopkins University, her communications career included posts in journalism, higher education, government, and industry. She also studied at the School for Women Healers and the Maryland Poetry Therapy Institute. www.ginnyfite.com

**K.P. Robbins** creates strong female characters in her two traditionally published novels, *PMS: The Power & Money Sisters* and *The Stonehenge Scrolls*. Her short stories have been published on *WashingtonPost.com* and in the *Anthology of Appalachian Writers, Virginia Writers Centennial Anthology* and *Art Prize Anthology,* among others. A former Washington, D.C., advertising executive, she holds a degree in journalism from West Virginia University. www.kprobbinsbooks.com

www.catherinebaldau.com

**Catherine Baldau** is the Executive Director of the Harpers Ferry Park Association, where in her previous position as Publications Specialist, she edited several publications including the award-winning *Harpers Ferry Under Fire.* Her essays are published in the *Harpers Ferry Anthology* and *"To Emancipate the Mind and Soul,"* and her short fiction has appeared in *SNReview.* Her freelance writing has been featured in *Fluent Magazine* and other local publications. *Thoughts & Prayers* is her first novel.

**Tara Bell** writes of a tween who saves her family from a haunting in the Middle Grade novel *The Shell Ghost of San Cristobal*. For years, Tara was a contributing writer and editor for a local publication *The Good Shepherds, Good Town, Good News Paper*. She graduated from Shenandoah University in Winchester, Virginia, with a BS degree in Recreational Therapy. In the early '80s she was on the staff for the autistic unit at Grafton School in Virginia. For over fifteen years she has participated as a multimedia artist in The Over the Mountain Studio Tour in Jefferson County, West Virginia. She has been a long-time member of the Society of Children's Book Writers and Illustrators. www.tarabell.info

## Book Club Questions for THOUGHTS & PRAYERS

1. What did you feel at the moment Lily opened the door for ABC? Have you ever been in a situation where you knew something was wrong but did it anyway?

2. When Mr. Robinson saves her life, Keisha witnesses an extraordinary act of courage by a man she has just pegged as ordinary. How does this experience affect her?

3. Joe Hernandez has dedicated his life to two things, the law and his daughter. But when his world is shaken apart by a school shooting, he eventually sacrifices both of them for revenge. Was he right to shoot ABC?

4. Who was the character in THOUGHTS & PRAYERS you most identified with and why?

5. People who have experienced traumatic events like a school shooting sometimes have difficulty making decisions. They feel numb, lose their appetite, and have nightmares. The closer they were to witnessing a death, the stronger their reaction. How do the survivors in THOUGHTS & PRAYERS deal with their reactions?

6. Sofia says she wants to be bolder, perhaps be more daring, like her friend Caitlyn. By the end of the book, has she become more daring, bolder, and how?

7. Is Caitlyn really a "ghost?"

8.  Have you ever had a near-death experience? Is Caitlyn's experience similar to or different from yours?

9.  What role does social media play in shaping people's thoughts about a tragedy?

10.  After the death of his daughter, Mike wanted revenge. Do you think that changed? Why or why not?

11.  How did Charmaine's pregnancy motivate her to change her life?

12.  Do you agree with the authors' choice to focus on the survivors' experiences and not the shooter?

13.  Did the shooter's point of view appearance toward the end of the book change your thoughts about him?

14.  What do you think about Charmaine's initial resentment of Keisha?

15.  Lily and Keisha debate whether hard work or talent is more important to achieving success. How did their views on the debate stage differ from their lives? Did this change for either of them by the end of the book? What do you feel is more important in your life?

16.  Lily creates art collages from found (or stolen) objects. Why do you think she chooses this method? Why do you think it was important for her to finish the face collage?

17.  How did Mike's love for Lisa motivate his actions?

18.  Do you think Lily should go to prison for her actions? If so, what is a fair sentence? If not, why?

## CRISIS RESOURCES

THOUGHTS & PRAYERS is a work of fiction. All characters and events are fictional. If you or someone you know needs help, below are some resources to consider.

- Call 911

- https://www.samhsa.gov/disaster-preparedness

- CALL or TEXT 1-800-985-5990 (press 2 for Spanish)

- 1-800-662-HELP (4357) and TTY 1-800-487-4889 (Substance Abuse and Mental Health Services an agency of the US Department of Health and Human Services)

- For Deaf and Hard of Hearing ASL Callers: To connect directly to an agent in American Sign Language, call 1-800-985-5990 from your videophone. ASL Support is available 24/7.

- Text "TalkWithUs" to 66746 answered by a network of independently-operated crisis responders

- https://suicidepreventionlifeline.org/ National Suicide Prevention Lifeline: 1-800-273-TALK (8255) for English, 1-888-628-9454 for Spanish

- https://suicidepreventionlifeline.org/chat/ Lifeline Crisis Chat

- https://www.childhelp.org/hotline/ National Child Abuse Hotline: 1-800-4AChild (1-800-422-4453)

- https://findtreatment.samhsa.gov/ Treatment Services Locator Website

- https://data.cms.gov/Government/Map-Selected-Federally-Qualified-Health-Center-FQH/hqut-bhwm Interactive Map of Selected Federally Qualified Health Centers

- How To Contact The Crime stoppers Hotline: The phone number is 1-800-222-TIPS or 1-877-903-STOP
- Safe School Helpline https://schoolhelpline.com/
- Bullying Prevention: http://www.stopbullying.gov/
- Cyberbullying: http://www.education.com/topic/bullying/cyberbullying/

For more reading on the effects of school shootings

**What Happens to the Survivors?**
https://www.apa.org/monitor/2018/09/survivors
**Trauma, Violence, and School Shootings**
https://healthysafechildren.org/trauma-violence-and-school-shooting
**Coping with Mass Shootings**
https://www.apa.org/news/press/releases/2017/10/mass-shootings
**Managing your distress in the aftermath of a shooting**
https://www.apa.org/topics/gun-violence-crime/mass-shooting
**Restoring a Sense of Safety in the Aftermath of a Mass Shooting: Tips For Parents And Professionals**
https://www.cstsonline.org/resources/resource-master-list/restoring-a-sense-of-safety-in-the-aftermath-of-a-mass-shooting-tips-for-parents-and-professionals
**Caring for kids after a school shooting**
https://childmind.org/article/caring-for-kids-after-a-school-shooting/

Parenting a Child Who Has Experienced Trauma

Child Trauma Toolkit for Educators

Talking to Children about the Shooting

**Going Back to School After a Tragedy**

https://childmind.org/article/going-back-school-tragedy/

**Video, Echoes of Columbine**

https://www.fbi.gov/video-repository/echoes-of-colum-bine-2019a.mp4/view

*This is not a complete list of Crisis Resources. The information about providers and services contained on this list does not constitute an endorsement or recommendation by the authors or Sunbury Press, Inc. It is your responsibility to verify and investigate providers and services.*